Nickel

FALLEN LORDS M.C.

BOOK 1

WINTER TRAVERS

2

FALLEN LORDS MC '87

For questions or comments about this book, please contact the author at
wintertravers84@gmail.com

Table of Contents
Acknowledgements

Acknowledgements

For my readers who have been with me since the start with Loving Lo.
Nickel is for you.
Much Love!

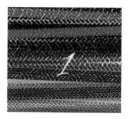

Karmen

I couldn't find a box big enough to fit him in.

Well, that makes me sound like a murderer or something. Nickel, the man in question, is still very much alive, I assure you. I should probably go back a little bit and explain.

My father went to prison when I was thirteen, and I can't remember my mother. She left before I could even have a memory of her. He always told me we were better off without her. Things were rough for us, but we always had each other. Well, I had my dad. My dad had me and beer. I can't remember a time I didn't smell hops on his breath.

I went to my first day of preschool and asked the teacher why her breath didn't smell like my dad. That ended up with my dad in the principal's office for an hour and me crying the whole way home while my dad yelled at me. That was the last time I ever mentioned my dad's drinking to anyone. I was a fast learner and caught on quick. One mess up, and I never made the same mistake again.

The night my dad went to prison, I was at home, like normal, while he was out at the bar three miles down the road. He regularly walked to the bar and stumbled home, but that night, there was a severe storm predicted to blow in, so he decided he would take the truck. That decision changed my life and made me see everything in a whole new light.

I was sprawled out on the living room floor, watching TV, when there was a loud pounding on the front door, and I figured it was my dad. It was normal for him to forget his keys and bang to get inside.

I opened the door to two police officers, with my grandma, Vivian, standing behind them. I only saw my grandma at Christmas. I knew the second I laid eyes on her, something was not right.

It seemed my father had decided to call it a night after drinking almost a twenty-four pack of beer and tried to drive home. In that three-mile drive to the house that had no turns or curves on it, my father had managed to hit a soccer mom in her minivan with her three children in the back. Only one child survived.

The police told me I had to go with my grandma until they figured something out. Meanwhile, she stood behind them, arms crossed over her chest, tapping her foot impatiently. After they were done, my grandma barged between the two police officers and started firing off orders about packing a bag and getting all my stuff ready to go. We weren't going to stay in the "hell hole" anymore.

While I was packing up my things, completely in shock, I heard my grandma down the hall, bitching and moaning about having to take care of me. I knew then and there that things were never going to be the same.

After she hauled me over to her trailer—that was not much better than the "hell hole" I used to live in—I begged to see my dad. Every day, she told me, and I quote, "I couldn't see the bastard yet."

Two weeks after I went to live with Vivian—she hated when I called her Grandma—I finally got to see my dad. After I was searched, I was led to a room with a glass wall and partitions separating small stools that faced the window. I was told to sit on the stool furthest to the left and wait. Vivian sat in the corner, pissed off that the guards said she had to be in there with me, even though I honestly didn't want her there.

It had taken ten minutes before my father walked through the door. He looked the same as the last time I had seen him, except for the orange jumpsuit he was wearing. He sat down on the other side of the glass and picked up the phone. He motioned his hand for me to do the same. I put the receiver to my ear and held my breath.

"Hey, baby." He always called me baby. I couldn't remember him ever using my real name unless he was serious, and serious didn't often happen with my dad.

"Hi, Daddy," I whispered.

"Everything going okay over at Vivian's?"

I nodded but didn't speak.

"I'm sorry, baby. I didn't plan for this to happen." My first thought was, what a stupid saying. Who the hell plans to drink twenty-four beers and then plow a family off the road? There's probably a very short list of people who plan for something like that.

"It's okay." What else was I supposed to say?

"I think I'm going to be in here for a while."

I nodded again, because it finally hit me. Seeing my father behind a thick glass wall in an orange jumpsuit was hammering it home, that life as I knew it was about to change. A tear I had been holding in streaked down my face and landed on the small ledge in front of me.

"Don't cry, baby." His eyes were on me, watching the tears I was so desperately trying to hold in finally run down my cheeks.

"I don't know what to do, Daddy," I wheezed out. My tears were coming fast and furious now. I was five seconds away from becoming an emotional, blubbering mess.

"You don't need to worry. Vivian is going to take care of you. I had the police call her as soon as they could," he said, trying to reassure me.

I was unable to talk. I tried wiping at the tears, but by the time I whisked them away, new ones were falling, taking their place.

"Karmen," he sternly said into the phone. I glanced up and found him staring at me. "Handel's don't cry, Karmen. Dry your tears. Nothing can be done now but to go on and make the best of the situation we are in."

I wiped my eyes again, willing the tears to stop. I reached into my pocket and pulled out the Kleenex Vivian had pressed into my hand as I walked to the door before. My father's words rang in my head. He always used to say, "We need to make the best of our situation." He would always tell me that when we would run out of money or had to find a new place to live.

"I don't know how to go on, Daddy. Vivian doesn't want me there," I hiccupped into the phone.

My dad shook his head and ran his fingers through his hair. "I don't know what to tell you, baby. We both have to do things we don't want to right now. I wish things could be different, but they can't."

"I know," I whispered. I didn't want my dad to worry about me when he was in prison. I'd have to keep my fears to myself about living with Vivian.

"Go on, I need to talk to your grandma now." I nodded my understanding. "I love you, Karmen. Please don't forget that."

"I love you too, Daddy," I whispered. I hung up the phone and quickly dashed out of the room before I started crying in front of him again.

After my grandma spoke to him, we went home, where she started making dinner and told me to sit at the kitchen table so we could have a talk.

"We need to get a few things straight, Karmen," she said, lighting a cigarette and blowing a puff of smoke in my direction. "Your father told me you said I didn't like you. Is that right?" she asked, staring me down.

I nodded my head yes because there was no point in lying.

"It's not that I don't like you, Karmen, it's just that I am well beyond the age of taking care of a teenager. I'm upset with your father, not you."

"Okay."

"I think we will get along just fine if we both just stay out of the other one's way. I know you are thirteen years old and more than capable of taking care of yourself. Lord knows you have been taking care of that sorry excuse for a father since you were old enough to talk."

I didn't argue with her because she was speaking the truth. I couldn't remember when my dad and I had switched roles. I had been taking care of him since I could remember.

"All right then, that's settled. Now, why don't you run to your room and work on your homework or whatever," she said, dismissing me with the wave of her hand, as she turned to the fridge.

I didn't need to be told twice. I slammed my door behind me and leaned against it and slid down.

After I wrapped my arms around my raised knees, I rested my chin on them. I was so angry and upset at my father, but I had no one to talk to about it. I closed my eyes and banged my head on the door.

"It's not fair," I said to my barren bedroom.

Vivian had only given me a mattress on the floor to sleep on and a three-drawer dresser.

I had boxes sitting in the corner of things I used to have in my room, but I didn't want to take them out of the boxes. Taking all my pictures and possessions out of the boxes made this real. As long as I lived out of those boxes, this was all just a bad dream.

I thought about how putting everything in boxes made things better and decided to start putting everything I didn't want to feel into a box. The first thing I put in my little boxes was my anger with my father.

Opening that box in my head and placing that anger inside and then slamming the lid on top helped. I didn't have to feel that anger anymore.

Every day, for the past twelve years, I filled my tiny little boxes. Sad because I was all alone? Put it in a box and don't think about it. An "A" on my math test and Vivian ordering me to go to my room when I tried to tell her? Put it in a box and don't think about it.

All through my teenage years, I had probably thousands of tiny boxes that I neatly put on a shelf and never thought about again. It even worked well into adulthood. Things always fit nicely into the boxes.

Everything except for Nickel. As much as I tried to shove his gorgeous smile in the box, I could never forget about it.

Almost a year ago, his grandmother was transferred to the nursing home I worked at as an RN. Every week, on Tuesday at nine o'clock, he would come in and visit her like clockwork.

I still remember the day he appeared in her room while I was checking her blood pressure. He waltzed in as if he owned the place, and I haven't been able to stop thinking about him since. His grandmother was one of my favorite patients. She was sweet but had a smart-ass streak to her.

Every Tuesday, he would hold up a bakery bag and insist on me staying and having a snack with them. He would track me down if he didn't see me in her room and ask me how my day was going.

He always had a leather vest on that had his name, Nickel, on it and a huge patch on the back that was the insignia of the Fallen Lords. All I knew about the Fallen Lords was that they were a motorcycle club, and they rode bikes everywhere they went. I was seriously oblivious to everything he was.

The only thing I wasn't oblivious to was his gorgeous smile and dark blue eyes. Whenever he was done talking to me, he always winked and smiled as he walked away. That wink and smile drove me crazy.

That man was everything I didn't want in my life, and that was the exact reason I needed to find a box big enough to fit him in. I needed to slam the lid down on him and never think of him again.

If only things were that easy.

****

Nickel

Tuesday. Also known as Blue Ball Day.

Every Tuesday, I would come and visit my grandma, and every Tuesday, I would leave with a raging hard-on from seeing Karmen. I tried to get her to talk to me every time I saw her. I was starting to get desperate.

I had recently started bringing her shit from the bakery in town to try to entice her to sit with me, but she never took the bait.

Today was no different. After she had coolly let me down, I had walked out the front doors, deciding I was done trying to get her to go out with me. I had never worked so hard for a chick in my life. I still had some pride left, and she wasn't going to strip me of that.

I pulled out a cigarette and lit it. As I was taking my first drag, my phone started ringing, and I dreaded answering it. I looked at the display and saw it was Pipe, my VP, calling.

"Yo," I said, putting the phone to my ear.

"We need you to do a run tonight. Brinks had some shit come up and can't make it."

"Fuck no. I got shit to do this evening. I told Maniac I would help him with the fireworks for Shake the Lake tonight," I spit out. I was so fucking sick of this bullshit. I seemed to be the only one who could fucking be counted on. You think I would get respect from these fuckers. Fuck no. Don't even get me started on not wanting to go on these fucking runs.

The Weston chapter of the Fallen Lords had recently voted on taking on muling for a notorious drug lord. The vote had gone through eight to four. Three other brothers and I were the only ones to vote against it.

Except, since the vote happened, I had been the one doing most of the runs and taking most of the risk. This shit was getting real old quick.

"You go now, you'll be back before fucking sundown."

"You know I'm not down with this shit, Pipe," I bit off. Pipe also voted against the muling, but with the vote going through, he had to be behind it now.

"I know, Nickel, but I got no one else to do it. You and Boink just need to drop a couple of things off and grab one thing, and you'll be done for the night. Promise."

"I better be back by fucking six, Pipe."

"You will be, Nickel." I ended the call and shoved the phone in my pocket. Gah, this was fucking bullshit! I paced the sidewalk, running my fingers through my hair, wondering how the hell shit had gone sideways so quickly in the club.

"Nickel!" I spun around and saw Karmen standing at the door of the nursing home.

"Yeah?"

"Um, I think you might have left your keys." She looked around nervously, a set of keys dangling from her fingertips. Even in hospital scrubs, this chick drove me crazy.

I patted down my pockets, searching for my keys but didn't feel them. They must have fallen out when I kissed Nan bye. "Yeah, babe, they're mine."

She glanced around again, deciding if it was safe to walk toward me. I should have been a gentleman and approached her, but I didn't. I wanted to see if she would make a move. She looked like a scared little lamb, and I was the big, bad wolf who wanted to make a meal of her.

"Um, is everything okay?" she asked, taking a step toward me. "I heard you yelling into the phone before and didn't want to interrupt you."

I shook my head and laughed. "Nothing a six-pack won't fix."

"Oh, well, here's your keys." She held them out to me from five feet away and waited for me to grab them.

"You got plans tonight?" I was done chasing this chick. It was time to get straight to the point.

"Um…"

"You say that a lot, babe."

"What?" she asked, confused.

"You say um a lot."

"Oh, I guess I never noticed." She stood there staring at me.

"Plans? You got any tonight?"

"Um." She realized she said um again, blushed red, and her eyes darted down. "No plans."

"You ever been to Shake the Lake?"

"Once, when I was seventeen. I didn't get to see the fireworks, though."

I reached out to grab my keys but grabbed her hand instead. "Come with me tonight," I pleaded, our eyes locking.

She tried to jerk her hand out of my grasp, but I tightened my grip. "I can't," she insisted.

"Sure, you can. You just told me you don't have plans."

"Um, I forgot that I have to go to…um…badminton practice," she stuttered.

"Badminton practice?"

I didn't think she could blush anymore, but her cheeks turned a dark shade of red, and she nodded yes. "I felt that I needed to broaden my horizons and figured that would be a good place to start."

"Well, how about you broaden your horizon with me tonight, and you can pick back up with your badminton practice next week." Her eyes darted to the left, and I knew she was scrambling to find an excuse not to go. "Please," I begged.

"Um, what time is it?" she asked hesitantly.

"Dusk. I need to help Maniac set things up, so you can either come with me and wait while I work or I can swing by after we're done, and we can watch the fireworks together." Holy shit, I think Karmen was actually going to say yes.

"I have to work in the morning, so I can't be out all night." She jerked her hand from mine and clasped both in front of her.

"I'll have you home in time to slip into bed with a full night's rest."

She just stared at me, her eyes uncertain. This was the moment of truth. Was Karmen going to give me the time of day?

****

Karmen

Crap. Crap, crap, crappity crap. I couldn't go out with Nickel. Except I couldn't think of a reason not to go. The best lie I could come up with was badminton, and he saw right through that. My brain was not functioning, and I had no idea what to say.

"One night, baby, that's all."

I swooned a bit when he called me *baby*. I had never been called anything but Karmen by anyone other than my dad. Nickel calling me baby made me weak in the knees, and I was sure I would say yes to anything as long as called me it again. "I don't get off work 'til seven."

"Dusk isn't until after nine. I can pick you up at eight." He shoved his keys in his pocket and looked down at me.

Eight. I could do eight. Maybe. I only lived five minutes away from work, so I would still have almost an hour to get ready. "I don't know."

He reached out and caressed my cheek. "Just say yes. It's easy."

"Yes," I breathed out, mesmerized by his touch and his piercing blue eyes.

His other arm snaked out, wrapping around my waist, and he pulled me flush against him. He leaned down, placing a kiss on my forehead. "You just made my day a whole lot better, baby."

I leaned into him, burying my face in his neck and inhaled his soothing scent. My brain was fogged, and all I knew was, I had never felt more at home than in Nickel's arms. "Glad to help," I whispered.

His body shook while he laughed at me. He placed one more kiss on my forehead and pulled away. "All right, you get back into work, or neither of us is going to get anything done today if I touch you any longer."

I stumbled out of his arms, catching my balance before I tumbled into a bush. "Um, okay. I'll see you at eight?" I still couldn't believe that I had just agreed to go on a date with Nickel tonight. I think I was losing my mind.

"Eight on the dot, baby." He grabbed his keys out of his pocket, twirled them around his finger, and winked at me. Tearing my eyes away when he walked over to his bike was impossible. I couldn't move from the spot I was in.

He swung his leg over the bike, cranked it up, revving the engine, and gave me a two finger wave right before he roared out of the parking lot.

"You did it, finally," I heard from behind me. I glanced over my shoulder and saw Nikki holding the door to the nursing home. She had a huge, smug smile plastered on her face.

I rolled my eyes at her and glanced one more time at where Nickel had been before I walked back in. "I don't know what you are talking about."

"Oh, please. It's about fucking time you cut that gorgeous hunk of man a break. He's been fawning over you for a year. I don't know any man who would put that much time into a woman who hasn't given him the time of day." Nikki held the door open for me, and we walked over to the front desk.

"That man is going to go on one date with me and then run for the hills when he sees how boring and unfun I am." I crossed my arms over my chest and leaned against the desk as Nikki walked around to the receptionist chair and plopped down.

"You don't give yourself enough credit, Karmen. What you see, is not what he sees."

"He must be looking in the wrong mirror because I'm boring and nothing like the girls he is used to."

"On that point, you're right. You're class, and those other girls are all trash. You aren't even in the same realm as those skanks from the club." And that was why Nikki was my best friend and had been since we were fourteen. She always told it to me straight.

"Oh, Nikki. What the hell have I done? Why did I say yes?" I buried my head in my arms and tried to figure out how to get out of this. Maybe when he showed up, I could say I was sick and couldn't go. Or maybe when I opened the door—

"Stop!" Nikki yelled, pulling me from my scheming to get out of my date. "You're going. I'm coming home with you and making sure you walk out with that man when he knocks on your door."

"What?" My head snapped up, my mouth hanging open. "You can't be serious. I can't have you there acting like my mom, watching me go out on a date. For all I know, you'll yell, 'Have her home by ten,' as we walk to his bike."

Nikki threw her head back laughing, almost falling out of her chair. "You know me too well."

"I do."

"I'll hide behind the curtains and promise not to yell anything besides 'Nice ass' when you walk out the door."

"I'm sure you don't need to tell him that, he probably already knows." I laughed, grabbing the chart I needed and walked down the hall.

"I wasn't talking about his ass," she called. I shook my head but kept walking. Nikki was crazy and would probably do it. "I'm coming home with you, Karmen. You are not backing out of this date!"

I raised my hand in the air, admitting defeat and ducked into the medicine closet. I tried to calm my breathing, realizing I was on the brink of hyperventilating. I rested against the shelving, the cold metal of the rack cooling my forehead. What the hell did I get myself into?

Let's review everything I knew about Nickel. 1. He was in a motorcycle club. 2. He had the sweetest grandma I have ever known.

That's it. Those two facts were the only things I knew about this man. Well, I also knew he was the sexiest man I have ever laid eyes on, but that was something you would know as soon as you saw him.

I closed my eyes and counted backward from ten. By the time I got to two, I knew what I needed to do.

I had to find a box to put Nickel in. All I needed to do was break down everything I felt and knew about this man and put it all away into tiny boxes, then I could toss them all away and never think about him again.

Just looking at Nickel, I knew he was everything that could and would disrupt the tiny, peaceful world I had built.

After I had graduated high school and escaped my grandma's house, I worked two jobs, went to school full-time, and got an apartment of my own. I still lived in that same tiny apartment because it was where I felt safe, and it always helped to remind me that I was independent and could do things on my own.

I worked my ass off for four years before I graduated and got a job at Acadia Nursing Home and finally had smooth sailing for the first time in my life.

Nickel was not about to walk into my life and mess everything up. All he was getting was one night. I'm sure he would see that I was not the woman he thought I was and that will be that. The only reason he had asked me out was because I was something unattainable to him. I was probably more of a challenge to him than someone he wanted to spend time with.

So, new game plan. Stop the freaking out, go out with Nickel, and then get back to my regularly scheduled life.

I grabbed the meds I needed and took a deep breath. Nickel wasn't going to get more than I was willing to give him.

****

Nickel

"This is complete bullshit. This isn't what I signed up for," Slayer said as we watched the drugs we had just dropped be loaded into a black SUV. Boink had bailed on me, and Slayer had been forced to ride along. Nobody wanted to do these fucking runs anymore.

"You ain't gotta tell me, brother. I voted against this shit." Slayer and I were sitting on our bikes, ready to head back to Weston. I had to meet Maniac in an hour and pick up Karmen in two and a half hours. I was tempted to skip helping Maniac and butt my way into Karmen's house and convince her to stay home with me.

"Things are changing, Nickel, and I don't like where things are headed."

I pulled out a cigarette and offered one to Slayer. He couldn't be more right. Once you get as deep as we were headed, there was no turning back. I had been having a nagging feeling lately that it was time to make some significant changes of my own. "I belong to the Fallen Lords, Slayer, but I don't think this chapter is the right fit for me anymore." I lit the cigarette and inhaled deeply.

"You thinking of transferring?"

I exhaled, a cloud of smoke billowing up into the sky. "I don't know if transferring is the answer, either. I've been thinking about asking Wrecker if I can start up a new chapter in Nittleton."

"No shit."

"Yeah, brother. I think the only way I'm going to be able to stay with the Fallen Lords is if I can spearhead my own chapter. I need this." I had been thinking about this before the vote. Now that we were officially muling drugs, I was ready to make my idea a reality.

"I know if I get Wrecker in my corner, I can take it to the mother chapter and get things lined up quickly. I need this, Slayer. I can't keep going the way things are right now."

"You get shit rolling; I'll be there, brother. It's about time someone breathed some fresh air into this club."

I couldn't have said it better myself. Now if I could convince Wrecker of the fact that it was time for a change, and I was just the guy to make those moves.

Karmen

"I swear to God, if you don't sit still, I am going to rip all your eyelashes out with the curler. Calm your tits, woman," Nikki scolded as she put the finishing touches on my makeup.

We arrived at my house forty-five minutes ago, and we had been going non-stop. I had jumped in the shower as Nikki ransacked my closet looking for something to wear tonight. I had no idea what she was going to find. I knew I had to dress differently this evening, but I also knew my closet was lacking. If I wasn't at work in my scrubs, I was curled up on my couch wearing yoga pants and reading.

"Sorry, it's just that he's going to be here any minute, and I'm going crazy."

"Just stop freaking out about it, and just go with whatever he wants to do. Did he say what you guys were going to do tonight?" Nikki gave me one last look, scanning the miracle job she had just done on my face.

"Um, we're just going to the fireworks. He didn't mention anything else." I glanced in the mirror as Nikki walked over to my closet, and I didn't recognize the person staring back at me. "Holy shit, that can't be me."

"Ha! Better believe that chick is you, babe. I've known all along what a babe you are under those scrubs every day."

"Please, I am anything but a babe."

"That's why I'm down with you going out with Nickel. I believe that man is just what you need to make you see just what you are. Your witch of a grandma needs to be shot for making you doubt yourself so much." Nikki pulled out my favorite pair of jeans, tossing them over her shoulder at me and continued looking for a shirt.

"You gonna bring my grandma back from the dead to shoot?"

"Phft, in a heartbeat. That woman was stone cold." Nikki threw her hands up in the air and turned around. "How the hell do you not have anything sexy to wear?"

"Because I have nowhere to go that requires sexy. I work. That's it."

"Well, thank God you at least have a pair of jeans that give you a shape that isn't baggy. Put those on, and I'll see what I can find that doesn't look like it's been washed fifty times."

I walked into the bathroom, leaving the door cracked so I could listen to Nikki's rambling. "I just bought a couple of new t-shirts the other day. They are in the top drawer of my dresser." I shimmied out of my scrub bottoms and worked the jeans up my legs. They were boot cut and fit me like a dream.

"Hmm, this will have to do. Thank God, you, at least, bought woman's cut t-shirts and not baggy men's." Nikki reached into the bathroom, the t-shirt hanging from her fingertips. I grabbed it and tossed it on the counter.

"Am I just leaving my hair down?" I glanced in the mirror, taking in my dark, chocolate brown hair.

"Hell yeah. I don't know how you have such soft, full, bouncy hair. If I didn't like you so much, I'd hate you for it."

"My hair is all I have going for me. Now out." I pushed the door shut and pulled off my top.

"I'm gonna look for shoes. You better have some good ones, or I'm calling it a wash and you a lost cause!" Nikki yelled.

I shook my head, laughing, and pulled the black V-neck t-shirt over my head. Nikki was going to be pleasantly surprised when she saw my unhealthy obsession with shoes. It was my guilty pleasure that I kept to myself. I smoothed my shirt down, thankful I had at least invested in some sexy bras and panties. Not that Nickel was going to see them. *I think.*

"Sweet mother of God, where have you been hiding all of these shoes?" Nikki exclaimed from my bedroom. I slipped out of the bathroom and saw Nikki in the middle of the floor with all my shoe boxes strewn around her.

"In my closet." I stood over her with my arms crossed over my chest.

"Oh, my God, none of these have ever been worn! What is wrong with you? This is a crime against the shoe gods!" Nikki cried, outraged.

"I like cute shoes, I just never have anywhere to wear them."

"Girl, these shoes are not cute. They. Are. Gorgeous." Nikki held up my favorite pair of purple sling backs and beamed up at me. "Can I please try these on? I will love you forever."

"Have at it. Just be careful on the rug in the living room, I always trip over it whenever I have them on." I reached to the left of her and picked up a pair of black flats.

"Are you kidding me?" Nikki said, kicking the boxes out of her way and then slipping on the purple shoes. "All of these shoes you have and you are going with the most grandma-looking ones." She curled her lip up in disgust as I grabbed my purse and slung it over my shoulder.

"We're going to the fireworks. I can't wear four-inch heels in the grass. I'd fall on my face, and then he would have to carry me everywhere."

"And that would be a problem because?" Nikki waved her hands in front of her and laughed.

"Because I don't need anyone to take care of me, that's why."

Nikki stood up, wobbling a bit and walked over to the full-size mirror I had rested against the wall. "One day, Karmen, you are going to need someone. I know you had a shitty childhood, and it taught you not to rely on anyone, but there are good people in this world who will help you and not ask for anything in return."

Nikki told me this all the time, but I didn't believe it. No matter the person, they are always looking to get something. "I think you are the only person I can say that is true about."

"That's because I'm awesome." Nikki winked at me and moved down the hall to the living room.

My one-bedroom apartment was small, but it was home. With a small kitchen, somewhat large living room, and one bathroom, it was perfect for me.

I adjusted my purse and looked in the mirror.

I was plain and ordinary and would more than likely fade into the background with Nickel. What he saw in me, I was blind to.

"Karmen! He's here!"

I gave myself one last glance in the mirror and slipped down the hall to Nikki. "Would you stop peering out the window like some psycho? I thought you said you were going to hide when he got here?"

I tried nudging Nikki out of the window, but she refused to move. "Shh, can we please just take a moment to recognize the smoking hotness that is Nickel Cunningham and thank his momma for bringing him into this world?"

I caught a glimpse of Nickel as he walked to the front door of my building and had to agree with Nikki. He was one fine specimen of a man. His jeans fit immaculately, tight in the thighs and widened out at the leg encasing his perfectness. He was wearing a light blue t-shirt with the Fallen Lords logo stretched across his back. His dark brown hair was windblown, and it begged for me to run my fingers through it.

"Sweet mercy, can that man be any sexier? I think I just came."

"Nikki!" I screeched, pushing her out of the window. "You're freaking crazy! Hide in the bathroom. I'm afraid to have you in the same room as him when he comes in. You might jump him."

Nikki moved down the hallway, turning halfway. "If anyone is going to jump that man, Karmen, it's going to be you." She sprinted the rest of the way back to the window and peeked out at Nickel again. "Oh, man. I need to check my panties."

I grabbed a throw pillow off the couch and tossed it at Nikki as she raced down the hall. "God dammit, Nikki. Your ass better stay in that bathroom until I leave."

"You won't hear a peep out of me," she promised, shutting the door.

I looked around my apartment, trying to find a place to hide when there was a knock on the door. Crap! I froze, staring at the door. He knocked again, but my feet felt like they were glued to the floor.

"Psst!" I turned my head to the hallway and saw Nikki sticking her head out. "Answer the door," she hissed at me.

"I can't!" I whispered back.

"Oh, my God, I'll—" Nikki started but stopped when another knock sounded.

"I know you're in there, Karmen. I can hear you talking to your girl," Nickel called through the door. Nikki waved her hands at me and ducked back into the bathroom, slamming the door shut behind her.

"Baby girl, open the door," he called again, his voice soothing and hypnotic.

My feet came unstuck from the floor, and I slowly walked to the door. My hand grabbed the knob, but I didn't twist it. I needed to get a grip. Nickel was just a man I was going on a date with. Something I had done tons of times before.

Okay, well, maybe not tons of times, more like five times. Or was it only four? Ugh, thinking about my almost non-existent dating life was not helping. I twisted the handle and stepped back, pulling the door open.

Holy shit. Nickel looked even better up close. "Hey," he said, winking at me. Oh my, I think I needed to check my panties like Nikki.

"Hi," I wheezed out.

"Good, you didn't wear heels," Nickel said, his gaze traveling up my body. I glanced down at my feet. I couldn't even remember putting my shoes on.

"Ugh, I didn't think heels would be good on grass."

"Right on, baby. You ready to go? I got Maniac holding a spot for us right now. The park filled up a lot faster than I thought it would."

"Um, yeah. I think I'm ready." I glanced around my living room, hoping a big hole would open and swallow me up. The bathroom door was cracked, and I knew it was taking all of Nikki's will power not to open the door and walk out here.

Nickel grabbed my hand, turning my body back toward him. "Come on, baby, if you don't have it right now, you don't need it." He pulled me out the door and slammed it shut behind us. "Keys?" he asked, holding his hand out.

I numbly dug through my purse and gave him the keys. He grabbed them and made quick work of locking the door and then dropping them into my bag I was still holding open. "I know your girl is in there, but you can never be too safe." He was still holding onto my hand, and he tugged me behind him down the stairs and out the door, never letting go.

"I've never been on a motorcycle," I said dumbly, watching Nickel grab a helmet and hold it out to me.

"First time for everything, baby. Stick with me, and I won't let anything happen to you. Just strap this on and climb on behind me."

I grabbed the helmet out of his hand and quickly put it on, buckling the chin strap. Nickel swung his leg over the seat gracefully, obviously have ridden thousands of times before. I scrambled on behind him, surprised I didn't kick him in the back or catapult myself off the other side.

"Just hold on tight," Nickel reached behind him and grabbed my arms, wrapping them around his waist, "and lean with me in the turns."

I clutched to him, confident I could hold on but doubtful about the leaning with him. I hoped I didn't make him crash. He started the engine, the bike coming to life underneath us, rumbling and vibrating me to my core.

He kicked up the kickstand, and I realized I was about to go for my first motorcycle ride. I was putting my life into the hands of this man who I barely knew anything about, and I was surprisingly calm about it. Don't get me wrong, I was terrified, but I figured the best person to go with the first time was probably someone who had ridden a motorcycle more than they have walked.

I squealed as he took off and buried my head in his back, not wanting to see. His body shook, and I knew he was laughing at me. We drove for five minutes before I finally opened my eyes and peeked over his shoulder. The familiar streets that I had turned down numerous times before were speeding by in a blur, and the wind was blowing my hair out behind me.

Nickel maneuvered turns and corners with ease, and by the time we made it to the park, I almost wished that we didn't have to stop. Almost.

"You get off first, baby," Nickel ordered. I awkwardly slid off, my legs feeling like Jell-O underneath me. Nickel reached out for me right before my legs gave out. "Easy," he chuckled, pulling my body close to him.

"I'm fine," I whispered, trying to push away from him.

"I know you are, baby. That's why I've been chasing you for a year." He winked at me and slid one arm around my waist. We started walking toward the huge crowd of people who were all over the park.

I was speechless and had no idea what to say. Had Nickel been chasing me for a year? I thought he was just kind to me because he was a nice guy. I mean, I knew he had a bad boy side to him, but I figured he was friendly because I was taking care of his grandma. "Um, is your friend going to watch the fireworks with us?"

"Nah, Maniac is gonna be lighting them off and blowing shit up. He lives for this shit." We snaked our way through the crowd, dodging large groups of people who were camped out on big blankets. "When did you say was the last time you came to the fireworks?"

"Um, I was seventeen. I think it was only the second year they organized Shake the Lake. There was maybe a quarter of the people there that are here now. This is insane," I mumbled. Nickel went left to go around a group of people, but one guy backed up into me, knocking my hand out of Nickel's, and I stumbled backward.

"Hey! Watch it!" a girl screeched at me as I stepped on their blanket.

I started to mumble an apology when I felt arms wrap around my waist from behind. "She got pushed. It wasn't her fault," Nickel thundered at the girl.

The girl who was ready to scratch my eyes out for stepping on her blanket seconds ago now looked up at Nickel with lust in her eyes, and I could tell I didn't even register with her anymore.

"It's okay. She can't help that she's clumsy," the girl said, brushing off the blanket I had stepped on. "There's plenty of room on my blanket if you want to sit with me. There're no other places to sit." She batted her eyes at him, and I swear to God, pouted her lips. This was almost comical.

"I think your boyfriend sitting next to you might have something to say about that." Nickel nodded his head at the guy who was sitting next to the girl. She didn't even look ashamed at the fact that she had just hit on another guy when her boyfriend was with her.

"He's just my date for the night," she stuttered, her eyes not leaving Nickel.

"Either way, I'm not interested." He pulled away from me, his hand trailing around my waist, and grabbed my hand, tugging me behind him once again. I glanced back at the girl who was pouting her lips and giving me the evil eye. I shrugged at her and continued following Nickel.

"We're just on the other side of the lake." I stuck close behind Nickel, careful not to get knocked into anyone, and we finally made it to the spot he had saved for us. There was a tall guy standing guard at the edge of the blanket; his arms were crossed over his chest as he talked to a short blonde who had tight shorts and a crop top on. Her breasts overflowed out of her top, and she was leaning on his arm, rubbing against him.

"This is us." Nickel pulled me close again, wrapping his arm around my waist. "Yo, Maniac," he called, getting his attention. Maniac and the girl turned to us, each of them looking me over. I got the sense of approval from Maniac, but the woman looked puzzled as her gaze bounced between Nickel and me.

"I gotta head back. You good, Nick?" Maniac asked, picking up a bag next to his feet.

"All right, brother." Nickel kneeled on the blanket and held his hand out for me to follow. I glanced at Maniac's retreating back with the blonde following him close behind.

I kneeled down next to Nickel. "Um, I'll sit over here." I crawled over to the other side of the large blanket, trying to put as much distance between us as possible.

"Did you eat dinner?" Nickel grabbed a small cooler from the corner of the blanket and flipped it. He pulled out two sandwiches, a container of something, and two beers. My stomach growled as he unwrapped a sandwich and ripped off a bite. "I'll take that as a no," he chuckled, handing me a sandwich.

I sat down and opened the package, inhaling half of it without actually tasting it. I hadn't eaten since eleven o'clock that morning, and it was going on seven-thirty. Hungry was an understatement at this point.

"So, how long have you worked at the nursing home?" Nickel popped open the top of one of the beers and handed it to me.

"Um, a little over four years. Thank you," I mumbled, grabbing the bottle from him.

"You like working there?"

Hmm, did I like working there? It was a job, but I could honestly say that I did enjoy being there every day. It felt like I was making a difference, no matter how small it was. "I do. I love getting to know all the patients and spending time with them. Some of them feel like grandparents to me."

"Do you have any? Grandparents, I mean."

"Um, no. I don't have any family. My father is in prison, and my grandma died over a year ago."

"What about your mom?"

"She left when I was barely one. She decided being single and childless was a better suit for her."

"I'm sorry, baby."

"It's okay. It's hard to miss something you never really had."

We sat in silence as we both ate. I could tell Nickel's eyes were trained on me, but I kept my eyes everywhere else but on him.

Nickel stretched out on the blanket, his elbows propping him up, and crossed his legs at the ankles. "How come you always avoid me whenever I visit my grandma?"

I folded my hands in my lap and stared down at them. "I don't avoid you. I know you are there to visit with your grandma, and I don't want to interrupt." That was the partial truth. The other half of the truth was I never knew what to say when he talked to me. I was a bubbling mess around him.

"I can tell you right now, Nan is only half of the reason I come once a week."

"Do I want to know what the other reason is?"

"It's you, Karmen. There's something about you that won't let me stay away."

"Were you drinking before you came to pick me up, Nickel? You're talking crazy right now. There is nothing about me that would make you want to stay."

"I think that's the ultimate turn on for me, baby. The fact that you have no idea how sexy you are and how much I want to take off all your clothes right now and have my way with you. The only way you could call me crazy is because you drive me crazy with your sweet, sexy innocence."

I ducked my head down, embarrassed by what he was saying. None of this made sense right now. "You're crazy," I mumbled.

"Just for you. Now scoot on over here and watch these fireworks with me." He patted the spot next to him, beckoning me to lay down there.

"I can see them just fine from here," I insisted. I looked up at the darkening sky. It would only be a matter of minutes before they started the fireworks. I squealed when Nickel grabbed both of my legs and yanked me over to him.

"I don't like to say things twice, baby. I want you in my arms while we watch the fireworks," he growled low before grabbing another blanket he had rolled up and laid down, shoving it under his head. "Lay your sweet ass down, before I make you."

His aggressiveness should have scared me, but I hesitantly laid down next to him and rested my head on his outstretched arm. "I'm gonna have to show you what you are, baby. You are so much more than what you think."

I glanced up at him; his head turned down to look at me. "I've seen the same thing my whole life, Nickel."

"And what's that you see?"

"Nobody. There's nothing to see."

He reached over, tilting my chin up. "You are the furthest thing from nothing, baby. Whoever told you that growing up was dead wrong."

"You don't even know me," I whispered.

"I've watched you for a year. I know more about you than most. I see the gentle way you talk to all the patients.

How you always check on my grandma when I'm there. Even if you don't come in the room, I see you walk by, making sure everything is okay. I know when you're upset, you run your fingers through your hair and twist the ends. When you're happy, you have a smile that lights up the room, making everyone else happy. I see you, Karmen. Everything you think is missing, is shining through. Bright like the sun." He leaned down, his lips a breath away. "You've become my sun this past year, and you didn't even know it."

"I...I..."

"Shh, baby. You don't need to say anything. Just let that sink in. Everything I said, you are going to start believing." He closed the gap between us, his lips brushing against mine.

I moaned under the light pressure of his touch. His lips were warm and soft while his body pressed against my side was hard and unyielding. His mouth claimed mine, taking what I wasn't even sure I was ready to give.

I reached up, threading my fingers through his hair and held on, not wanting to let go. He coaxed my lips open, sliding his tongue in.

"Whoa, sorry dude," I heard mumbled from above right before someone came crashing down on us.

"What the fuck?!" Nickel pushed the guy off us and pulled away from me. I sat up, patting down my hair, and tried to figure out what the hell I had been thinking ten seconds ago. What the hell made me make out like a teenager in the middle of a crowded field surrounded by people. Nickel was pissed off we had been interrupted, but it was exactly what I needed to bring me back to reality.

"What the fuck is wrong with you?" Nickel thundered, standing up.

The guy who had fallen on us scrambled backward like a crab trying to get away from Nickel. I glanced around and found everyone watching. Nickel grabbed him by the collar and hauled him to his feet. "I'm sorry, man! I didn't see y'all there, I swear!" He held his hands up in surrender, his eyes filled with fear.

"Next time, open your eyes when you're walking, asshole. You could have hurt someone." Nickel tightened his grip on the guy's shirt and shook him.

"I will...I will totally...I totally will," the man stuttered.

Nickel shook his head and pushed him away. He stumbled backward, almost falling onto someone else's blanket but righted himself before he fell. He scurried away, looking over his shoulder at Nickel the whole time, making sure he wasn't being chased.

"What the hell was that?" I whirled around, trying to see who was talking. A tall guy with a leather cut like the one I had seen Nickel wear before walked up to us with two guys following close behind. I tried to see their patches with their names on them, but I couldn't make any of them out.

"Some drunk ass fell on Karmen and me. I don't think he meant to do it, but maybe Clash could follow him for a bit."

"Clash, see what that hippie is up to." The guy turned towards me, and I saw his name was Wrecker. The man who I assumed was Clash sauntered off in the direction of the drunk guy, and I turned my attention back to Nickel.

"You sure it wasn't anything?" Wrecker asked.

Nickel ran his fingers through his hair and shook his head. "I'm sure. I could smell the booze on the guy's breath."

"All right," Wrecker inclined his head and stuck his hands in his pockets. "This place is fucking packed. You think we could sit with you?"

"You're fucking kidding me," Nickel cursed.

Wrecker held his hands up and chuckled. "Not trying to cock block, brother, just ain't got anywhere else to go."

"You mind, baby girl?" Nickel asked. All eyes turned to me, and I nervously patted down my hair, fidgeting.

"I don't mind."

"At least, your date has more manners than you." Wrecker slapped him on the head and sat on the other end of the blanket. Thankfully, Nickel had put down a big blanket because with three big guys and me, it was full.

Nickel wrapped his arm around me and pulled me close. "I'm sorry, baby. This isn't how I imagined this night to go," he whispered into my ear.

"It's okay," I quietly replied. I turned my head, looking up at him and smiled.

His lips descended on mine, and he stole a quick kiss. "I knew you were special." He kissed me one last time, his lips lingering. I could tell he wanted more and so did I. "You live with your girl?"

"Um, what?" I asked, dazed from his kiss.

"Your friend from work…you live with her? I heard her in your apartment before I knocked."

"Oh, Nikki, you mean. No, she just came over after work for a second," I lied.

"Good."

"Yo, you got any beer left?" the guy who Nickel hadn't introduced yet asked.

Nickel pulled away, his eyes not leaving mine. "Check the bottom of the cooler."

"Nice," he mumbled. I heard him dig through the cooler. "So, you gonna introduce us to your girl, or you just gonna be an ass?"

Nickel shook his head and laughed. He tore his eyes off me and looked at his friends. "I'm pretty sure Karmen doesn't need to know you two assholes."

"Hey, Slayer here resembles that remark," Wrecker laughed.

"Ha ha, yuk it up, dipshits." Slayer grabbed three beers out of the cooler and handed them out.

"That asshole with his hand in the cooler is Slayer." Slayer smirked at me and took a long pull off his beer. "And that guy sitting next to you is Wrecker. He's the president of the Fallen Lords."

Oh, crap. I was sitting next to the president of the club. I had no idea what to say or do. "Hey," I croaked out, lamely waving at them.

Wrecker threw his head back and laughed while Slayer smirked at me. "How the hell did you manage to get this sweet girl to agree to go out with you?"

"Wasn't fucking easy. It took me a year and about one hundred dollars in donuts," Nickel laughed, smiling down at me.

"You made him wait a year, darlin'?"

My face heated, and I buried my face into Nickel's chest. "She totally made him wait. Son of a bitch, I think I like this one," Wrecker laughed.

"Shut the fuck up and watch the fireworks," Nickel said, annoyed. "You okay, baby? I can tell these guys to leave, if you want."

I shook my head no, not wanting Nickel to have to choose between his friends and me. "I'm okay. I just didn't expect them to ask that."

"Yeah, these assholes don't have any manners. You'll get used to it." He brushed a quick kiss on my lips and laid back down on the edge of the blanket. He stretched his arm out again, and I put my head on it, curling into his body.

Wrecker and Slayer leaned back, drinking beer and talking.

A loud boom sounded, making me jump. "What the hell was that?"

"That would be Maniac. He always does a countdown. I bet he'll do one each minute until the fireworks start."

"He scared the crap out of me," I laughed, realizing I had thrown my leg over Nickel and was holding on tightly to him.

"I'll keep you safe, baby," Nickel promised.

I rested my head back on his arm and prayed to god I was ready for whatever came my way.

****

Nickel

The fireworks were close to being over, and all the *oohs* and *aahs* Karmen was making at each display were going straight to my dick. All I wanted to do was toss her on the back of my bike and head back to her house where I could have my way with her.

"Oh, look at that one!" She pointed up to the sky as the huge firework crackled off, leaving light trails in the sky.

I had never seen her so happy and carefree before. She had a grin permanently on her face the whole time, beaming up at the sky. When she wasn't pointing up, she would rest her hand on my stomach. Every time she moved her hand, it took all my willpower not to grab it and rest it back on me.

"Here comes the finale, baby."

She turned her head at me, her eyes huge, "You mean it's going to get better than this?"

"Hell yeah. You haven't seen one of Maniac's finales. You're going to love it."

She turned her attention back to the sky, amazed. I couldn't remember the last time I had seen someone so entranced by something so simple. Karmen had an innocence about her that scared the living shit out of me. I was so jaded and hardened from all the shit I had seen that watching Karmen made me stop and see things through her eyes.

"That was incredible! I had no idea you could make fireworks into shapes." She looked up at me, her eyes wide with excitement, and a grin spread across her face.

"Yeah, it's pretty fucking cool, baby. You ready to get out of here?"

"It's going to take forever to get out of here." She surveyed the park, watching everyone pack up their blankets and shit.

"Not on my bike, baby." I stood up, holding my hand out to her. She grabbed it, and I hoisted her up and kissed the top of her head. "Wait right here," I said, walking her over to the corner of the blanket.

"Leave the fucking blanket. We're going to wait for Maniac to get done. He's got Ginny with him tonight, and she's always got friends who are always up for a good time." Wrecker laid down on the blanket, sprawling out.

"Thanks, brother. There should be a couple of more beers in the cooler. I'll see y'all tomorrow."

I grabbed Karmen's hand and led her through the massive crowd that was slowly surging to the parking lot. She was glued to my back, not wanting to get crushed by the mass of people. We passed several brothers who were at the fireworks hanging out. I nodded at each of them, not wanting to stop for small talk. I saw them every day in the clubhouse. Right now, I was focused on getting out of here with Karmen.

We made it to the bike, and I quickly strapped the helmet on her head and straddled the bike. She scrambled on behind me and wrapped her arms tight around my waist. "Hold on, baby girl."

She rested her chin on my shoulder and kissed my neck. "I will," she whispered into my ear.

A tremor rocked through my body at her touch, and I cranked up the bike, revving the engine. That was the first time she had willingly touched me, and it drove me insane.

I maneuvered the bike through the cars that were at a standstill waiting to get on the road and pulled onto the street.

"Wow, I guess driving your bike tonight was a good idea," she laughed.

"I wouldn't breathe a sigh of relief yet; we still need to get around the long line of cars in front of us," I pointed out.

"Go down the next side street. We can take the back way to my house."

I spotted the next street up. "Hold on." I revved the engine, deciding there was more than enough room to squeeze in between the stopped cars. Karmen squealed, ducked her head in my back, and wrapped her arms around me tighter.

After we had maneuvered around the cars, we shot down the side street in the direction of her house.

"Man, even though it's over eighty degrees, it sure does get cold on your bike." She slid off the motorcycle, unhooked her helmet, and rubbed her arms.

I grabbed the helmet from her hand and hung it on the handle bars. "Sorry, baby. I should have told you to bring a sweatshirt." I swung my leg over the bike and leaned against it.

"Um, so I had a good time tonight. Minus the whole getting trampled on by that drunk guy. Your friends seem nice."

"They're more than friends, baby. They're my brothers. I'd do anything for them."

"Oh, well. It's nice that you have people like that in your life." Her eyes darted to the left, not wanting to make eye contact with me. I knew there was more to Karmen then what I had seen the past year. There was something beneath the surface that I didn't think anyone saw.

"You got anyone like that in your life, baby?" I pulled a cigarette out of the pack in my pocket and grabbed my lighter.

"Those will kill you," she said as I lit the end.

"So will fifty million other things." I smirked. I blew out a cloud of smoke away from her and stared her down. "You didn't answer my question."

"You don't always need people in your life."

"Seems pretty lonely. What about your girl? The one who works with you."

"Nikki? I've known her since I was fourteen. She's a friend."

"What about your family?"

"I don't have any family. I'm freezing, I'm going to head in." She turned around and moved to the front door.

What the hell just happened? "That's it? Not even a goodbye?" I called.

"I'm not saying goodbye. I'm just going in. I never said you couldn't come," she said over her shoulder with a smile spread across her lips.

Well, I'll be damned. She wasn't blowing me off after all. I grabbed the keys out of the ignition and followed Karmen through the door and up the stairs to her apartment.

"You want some coffee?" she asked, opening the door and tossing her purse and keys on the table next to the door.

"Sure," I said, shutting the door. I looked around her apartment, taking in the small touches that I could tell were glimpses into who Karmen was.

She slipped into the kitchen, kicking her shoes off on the way. I heard her putter around, grabbing mugs down and running the water.

"You can turn the TV or radio on if you want," she called.

I walked over to the radio and hit play on the CD player, wondering what kind of music she listened to. Bob Seger came pouring out of the speakers singing "Turn the Page."

"Baby, you listen to Seger?" I asked, amazed. I imagined she listened to some indie, whino band.

"Yeah, I like classic rock. Segar, Doobie Brothers, Tom Petty."

Huh, didn't expect that. "I didn't imagine someone your age to like that kind of music."

Her laughter bubbled out of the kitchen, "How old do you think I am?"

Oh shit. This could be a loaded question. "Twenty-three." Better to go lower than high.

"Nope. Close, though. I'm twenty-five." She walked out of the kitchen carrying a cup and handed it to me.

"You're not having some?" I asked, grabbing it from her.

"It's a Keurig. My cup is brewing right now." She sat down on the end of the couch and folded her legs underneath her. "I'm surprised you picked the radio instead of the TV."

"I don't watch a lot of TV. I'm always out doing something for the club, so I don't have time to get caught up in shows." I sat down on the other end of the couch and took a sip of my coffee. Strong and black. Just the way I liked it.

"Hmm," she hummed, folding her hands in her lap. I watched her nervously fidget, not knowing where to look. The carefree girl from the park had disappeared and shy, nervous Karmen was back.

"Why'd you run when I asked you about your family?" Probably not the best question to ask when she was pulling away from me, but I wanted to know.

"I didn't run; they're just not something I wish to talk about. My mom left when I was a baby; my dad isn't around, and my Grandma is dead."

"There's no one else?" she shook her head no and walked back to the kitchen.

I leaned back into the couch, going over what she had just said. So she had a family, but she didn't think they were family. I had to assume her dad must have done something bad for her to say she had no family. Maybe that was why she was so guarded. "I'm sorry, Karmen," I called.

"Nothing to be sorry for. I obviously didn't win the parent lotto," she laughed and reappeared in the living room. She sat back down on the couch and stared down at her coffee cup. God dammit. One second, Karmen was open and talking to me, and then the next, she shut down and wouldn't even look at me.

"Karmen," I called. Her eyes slowly lifted to look at me. "Why won't you look at me? What's going on in that head of yours?"

She set her cup down on the coffee table and looked me right in the eye. "Truth?" I nodded my head yes, wanting to know. "What the hell are you doing here?"

I reared back, shocked by her question. "You want me to leave?" I set my cup on the table next to hers and stood.

"No! That's not what I meant." She stood and rubbed her hands down her jeans. "I mean, I can't understand why you *want* to be here. Why…just why!" she said, throwing her hands up in the air. "It doesn't make any sense!"

I shook my head and ran my fingers through my hair. "Karmen, I don't know why you think it doesn't make sense. I like you. I'd like to think that the feeling is mutual."

"But what doesn't make sense is why you like me. I am nobody. I can count on one hand the number of dates I've been on in my entire life. FYI, that is counting tonight. I'm not skinny, and I'm not fat. I'm not pretty, and I'm not ugly. I'm just…just ME! I'm seriously starting to question your sanity."

I tilted my head back and looked up at the ceiling. "I can't believe this shit. Normally, it's the chick trying to convince me to go out with her, not this shit."

"How I feel is not shit!" she snapped back. She shoved her hands through her hair, causing it to stick up and fly all over the place.

"How you feel about this *is* shit. Close your eyes," I ordered.

"I'm not going to close my eyes." She crossed her arms over her chest and cocked her leg out.

"Do it."

"No, this isn't—"

"Do it, now!" I thundered. Her eyes snapped shut, and she bit her bottom lip. She stood there, her body slightly trembling and I'm sure terrified. "Do you want to know why I'm here?"

She nodded her head yes, not speaking. I walked around her, my eyes traveling up and down her body, and I grabbed her hand and pulled it behind her back. I tugged her to me, eliciting a gasp, and wrapped my other arm around her waist. "I'm here because I want you. You've driven me crazy the past year, and I can't take it anymore."

She gulped at my words and looked over her shoulder at me. "So it's just sex you want?"

I shook my head no and leaned down, my lips a breath away from her ear. "If all I wanted were sex, I'd have you bent over this couch already, taking what I wanted." Her body trembled, and I knew my words were making her want me. "You make me want more. More than I've ever had."

"I don't have a lot to give," she whispered.

"You have more inside you than you know. I can tell you use your past as an excuse to hide away. I'm not going to let you hide anymore."

"There are things about my past that you don't know. My dad killed someone. My mother knew right away she didn't want me, so she left."

"None of that matters to me. Your mom doesn't know what she's missing, and your father's past has nothing to do with you."

She leaned back, resting her head on my shoulder. "I want to hear you, Nickel, but I can't. I can't let go to trust."

"Just stop thinking, baby. Just feel." I trailed kisses down her neck as she tilted her head to the left, giving me permission I needed. "Feel my lips on your soft skin, baby."

She moaned, a tremor running through her body. "Tell me to stop now, or I won't be able to later."

She shook her head no and flattened her hand against my hip. "Please don't stop, not yet," she pleaded.

I spun her around and wrapped my arms around her. "Do you know what you're asking, baby? I keep going; I make you mine."

Her eyes clouded with lust, and she rested her arms on my shoulders, "I'm scared that I don't want you to stop. I shouldn't want this."

"Trust me, Karmen. I promise not to hurt you."

She leaned up on her tiptoes, stretching to meet my lips. "Don't stop, Nickel," she whispered.

I crashed my lips down on hers, finally taking what I had wanted for so long—her complete submission. She molded her body to mine, rocking her hips into me. I grabbed her ass, lifting her up, and she wrapped her legs around my waist as we devoured each other. I had never tasted a kiss so sweet before. I couldn't tell where Karmen began and where I ended. "Bedroom," I gasped, ripping my lips away.

She pointed over my shoulder down the hall, her head buried in my neck while she sucked on my ear. I moved in the direction she pointed, my fingers digging into her sweet ass, itching to touch all of her.

I kicked the door open, and Karmen reached over, flipping the light on. "Bed, now," she panted.

I stumbled over to the bed and tossed her down. She bounced on her back and scrambled to her knees, kneeling in front of me. "Last time for me to stop."

She put her hands on my fly, her fingertips gripping the zipper. "No stopping now, handsome."

She yanked the zipper down, and I held my breath. Holy shit.

****

Karmen

I don't know what the hell Nickel was doing to me, but I knew the last thing I wanted him to do was stop. I slid the zipper down, slowly exposing the cotton of his boxers. The button flicked open easily, and I tugged his jeans down.

He slowly hissed as his pants hit the floor, and I tugged on the waistband of boxers. He grabbed the hem of his t-shirt and tugged it over his head, tossing it on the floor. "Wait." He pulled my hands away and held them over my head. "Slow down, baby."

Holding my wrists with one hand, he reached down with the other and pulled up my shirt. "Keep your arms up." He pulled my shirt over my head and tossed it over his shoulder. His gaze devoured me, his nostrils flaring as his eyes raked over me. "So fucking perfect," he growled.

"Touch me, Nickel," I pleaded. He lunged at me, pushing me back onto the bed, his hands roaming, trying to touch me all at once. I delved my fingers into his short hair, holding on as he ravished my breasts.

"This needs to come off," he mumbled, his lips not leaving my skin.

I leaned forward, snaked my arms under me, and quickly undid the hooks. He ripped it off before I had a chance to lay back down. I arched my back as he teased my nipples—his tongue, and teeth, tugging and pulling, driving me insane. "Nickel," I gasped, when his rock hard cock dug into my leg.

"I need you, Karmen. Fuck me, I need you so much," he vowed. His hands quickly unbuttoned and unzipped my pants and tugged them down my legs. He pulled them off and slowly climbed back up my body, trailing kisses as he moved.

"This can't be real," I murmured, looking down at the gorgeous man who was kissing my body like his life depended on it.

"It's real, baby girl. Get used to it." He yanked my panties down, tossed them over his shoulder, and sat back on his heels. "Fuck," he moaned, his eyes roaming over me. He pulled his boxers off, balancing from knee to knee. "Your sweet body laid out before me...I don't know how long I'm going to last."

"There's always next time."

"Damn straight, baby. Now, spread those legs for me." I slowly opened my legs. My eyes shut as he trailed a finger up my leg, his destination clear.

"I wonder if these lips taste as sweet?" he wondered. I felt him move between my legs, a tremor running through my body at the light touch on my thighs. He parted the lips of my pussy, his finger zoning in on my clit, flicking it. "You're so wet for me, baby, and I've barely touched you."

I moaned as he circled my clit with his finger, almost giving me what I wanted, but keeping it out of reach. "Nickel, please," I begged.

"All mine," he whispered. I opened my eyes just in time to see him lower his head between my legs. His tongue flicked my clit, and I dug my hands into the bed, trying not to scream.

I could have sworn I heard him say "heaven" but was in such a fog of lust that the house could be on fire, and I wouldn't have noticed. He pumped a finger slowly into me as he sucked on my clit, a slow burn of passion beginning in the pit of my stomach. Nickel was building something inside me I had never felt before.

He continued the torturously slow assault. "So fucking tight," he growled.

"Faster," I pleaded, needing something more.

"You need to come, baby?"

"Yes, God yes."

"Not without my dick wrapped in your sweet pussy." He sucked my clit into his mouth, nipping it with his teeth. The sharp bite of pain made me buck my hips, begging for more.

"Mine," he growled, releasing my clit, flicking it with his finger.

He grabbed something from the end of the bed, ripping it open with his teeth. Thank God someone was thinking. He rolled the condom onto his dick, and that was the first time I looked at it.

It was huge. The condom stretched, forming to his cock, contouring to every bulging, throbbing vein. "Oh my," I mumbled as he stroked it.

Nickel burst out laughing, his dick bobbing up and down. I refocused my gaze on his face, realizing this man was even more handsome when he laughed. "I hope 'oh my' is a good thing."

"It is, I think." I blushed. He leaned down, caging me in with his arms.

"Well, why don't we find out?" He reached down, grabbed his dick, and stroked it again.

"Are we sure that will fit?" I wasn't a virgin, but I sure felt like one looking at Nickel.

"I'm pretty sure we were made for each other, baby. It just took us a little bit to find each other." He guided his cock into my tight hole, slowly pushing in. I bore down on my feet, spreading my legs further, trying to relax as he filled me.

"Fuck," he hissed when he was fully in. He looked up, his eyes connecting with mine. "Mine." He slowly drew out, and it felt like I was losing a part of myself with every inch. I reached up, threading my fingers through his hair, praying he wouldn't pull all the way out.

"You okay, baby?" he asked when just the tip was still in.

I nodded, unable to speak. He plunged back in, taking me by surprise, and I moaned loudly, pleasure overtaking my body. "Faster," I pleaded with each thrust of his hips. He leaned down, devouring my lips. I ran my hands over his body, trying to remember every plane and valley.

"Say my name," he ordered, driving even faster.

"Nickel," I whispered, tossing my head back, arching my back. I was on the brink of ecstasy, and it would be only a matter of seconds before I tipped over the edge.

"Louder," he growled, slamming into me. He leaned down, sucking my nipple into his mouth, and I moaned, loud. This man knew exactly what to do to drive me insane.

"Nickel!" I screamed as he nipped the side of my breast.

"You're mine, Karmen. I can't go back," he vowed. He reached down, sliding his hand in between us. He stroked my clit, rolling it between his fingers, and the slow burn he was building inside me detonated, stars exploding behind my eyes.

"Nickel," I yelled, sure the neighbors could hear everything.

He kept thrusting, sealing his lips with mine. I sucked on his bottom lip, biting it, and he groaned low in his throat before he exploded inside me. He buried his head in my neck, slowly thrusting in and out, his breathing labored and short. I wrapped my arms around him, not wanting to let go.

"I don't want to move," he mumbled. He pressed a kiss to my throat and looked up at me. "What the hell did you do to me, Karmen?"

"I'm asking myself the same question." I laughed.

He rolled off of me, pulling me into his side. "Round two, ten minutes," he promised.

"Hmm, I feel like one of those ring girls from wrestling are going to walk through the bedroom with a round two sign any second."

Nickel laughed, his eyes shining at me. "You're the only girl I want in this bedroom, baby."

"Good, although I'm pretty sure after round two, I might need a nap."

"Round two and then sleep." He winked at me, pressing a kiss to my forehead. "I'll be right back, baby." Nickel rolled out of bed and rummaged around on the floor.

"What are you doing?" I asked, leaning over the edge of the bed, watching him. The span of his shoulders was tattooed with the patch of the club, and his arms were covered in thick, black tribal tattoos.

"Looking for my boxers," he mumbled, grabbing his pants and tossing them over by the door.

"You were tossing everything around; I have no idea where they sailed off to," I laughed, looking around the room.

"Fuck it, I was trying to be a gentleman, but I can't find the fucking things." He stood up and stretched his arms over his head.

"Hmm, I'm okay with you not being a gentleman if this is the show I get." I propped my head on my hand as Nickel winked over his shoulder at me.

"Be right back, baby, round two in five minutes." He walked out the door, his perfect ass tempting me to follow.

I flopped back on the pillow and ran my fingers through my hair. Gah, what the hell just happened? I had finally let go and gone with my gut. Nickel could hurt me, but he could also make me the happiest I had ever been.

My phone dinged from the living room. I slipped out of bed, pulled Nickel's t-shirt over my head, and padded down the hall. I grabbed my phone and saw I had a new voicemail from a number I didn't know. I grabbed our abandoned cups of coffee and dumped them in the sink.

"Baby?" I heard Nickel call.

"Kitchen." Just as I was about to hit send to listen to the voicemail, the number called again.

"Who the hell is calling you so late?" Nickel asked, appearing in the kitchen. He had his boxers on, so he must have detoured to the bedroom before walking out here.

"I don't know." I swiped left to answer it. "Hello?" Nickel slid his arms around me.

"Hello, Karmen." My blood ran cold and the phone slipped from my fingertips.

Holy shit.

****

Nickel

Karmen's body tightened in my arms, and the phone fell to the floor. "Baby?" I spun her around and examined her pale face.

Her fingers shakily touched her lips, and she shook her head. "It can't be," she whispered.

"What? What can't be?"

"I don't know how he found me. My number isn't listed. I've moved since he last knew where I was. He's not supposed to find me," she rambled.

I brushed her hair out of her face. "Karmen, you need to tell me what the hell is going on, baby girl."

She shook her head and slipped through my arms, dropping to the floor. "I need to turn my phone off. I need to get a new number. This can't be happening." She crawled on the floor, scrambling to find her phone.

I spotted it under the kitchen table and nabbed it before Karmen's fingers grasped it. I scrolled through her call log and put her phone to my ear after connecting the call. "You have reached Winchester Prison after hours. To be connected to—" I hung up and shoved her phone in my pocket. "Who's calling you from the prison, Karmen?" I was ninety percent sure I knew who it was, unless Karmen knew more than one person in prison.

She sat back on her ass and looked up at me. "I made him promise he would never contact me. I did everything I could to disappear. I should have left town, but I couldn't leave the only place I've known." Her eyes were bloodshot from crying so hard, and her cheeks were stained with tears. The woman who I had shared the best sex of my life with was gone and was replaced with a terrified girl.

I scooped her up in my arms and carried her back to the bedroom. "We need to talk, baby girl."

She laid her head on my shoulder and sighed. "I'd rather just sleep."

I bumped the lights off with my elbow and laid her in the middle of the bed. "As soon as we talk, then you can sleep."

She rolled over on her side and bunched up the pillow under her head. "Once we talk, you're going to want to leave."

I fell into bed next to her and pulled the pillow out from under her head.

"Hey," she protested.

With the pillow folded in half under my head, I gathered her in my arms, and she rested her head on my shoulder. "Talk," I ordered.

A small grunt came from her mouth, but she didn't talk.

"Karmen, you can't freak out the way you did in the kitchen and not think that I'm going to ask questions. Tell me who was on the phone," I demanded.

"My father," she mumbled.

"Your father in prison."

A sigh escaped her lips, and she nodded against my shoulder. "Yes, we've already gone over my crappy childhood."

This shit was going to be like pulling teeth with her. "You're going to have to give me more."

"I told you he killed someone, right? Well, his luck ran out on driving drunk, and he managed to smash into a mother and three kids."

My arm flexed around her. "None of them made it?"

"Only one kid lived. His mom and siblings were gone in an instant because my father didn't want to walk home in the rain. Killing three people was better than getting a little wet." She sniffled and buried her face in my neck. "I haven't talked to him since I was eighteen. I tried to forget everything he had done, but I couldn't. I told him I never wanted to talk to him again. He was always good at making promises, but the man never kept one"

"So why is he calling you now?" I asked.

"He's probably up for parole and is looking for me to help him get released early."

"How long is he locked up for?"

"Thirty-five years. My hands sifted through hair. "Baby girl, that doesn't make sense." I had been around guys in and out of prison my whole life. Hell, I had done a stint in jail for six months when I had first joined the Fallen Lords. You didn't get to make phone calls after midnight to ask your kid to come to a parole hearing. They sent letters in the mail for that shit.

"I'm not going to help that man get out of prison, Nickel. He deserves to be there."

I pulled her up my side 'til we were face to face and looked her in the eye. "I'm not disagreeing with you. What

I'm saying is, he shouldn't be calling you after midnight when he's in prison. They have certain hours they can make calls at, and midnight is not one of them."

"Oh," she whispered. "Then how did he call me?"

"He must have pulled some strings, or he has someone in his pocket who was able to connect him to you after hours. He hasn't tried to make contact with you at all in four years?" Something wasn't adding up.

She shook her head. "No, I swear. And before that, it was three years."

I sat up, pulled her over my body to straddle my waist, and leaned against the headboard. "Then there must be something that he needs to tell you if he is calling you after visiting hours."

"But there isn't anything he needs to tell me. Even if he had managed to get paroled early, he knows that I don't want to talk to him. My dad messed up my life, and I know if I let him back in, he is just going to do the same thing again. I'm at least old enough this time to tell him no."

"So what are you going to do if he calls again?"

She scoffed and rested her hands on my shoulders. "Not answer."

I brushed her hair back from her face. "I don't think that is going to help this go away."

"Well, what is going to do the trick, then?"

"Let me help you. I'll find out what is going on with your dad, and you won't have to deal with him."

She cradled my cheek with her hand, and her eyes watered. "Why are you so nice to me?"

"It's not nice. It's called taking care of you."

"No one has ever done that before." Her voice was quiet, and her eyes were focused on me, but I could tell she was far away. "Even when I went to live with my grandma, she didn't want me. She said I was old enough to take care of myself. Hell," she laughed hollowly, "even my mom didn't want me. She left before I could even remember her."

My anger boiled knowing that Karmen had that in her life. "Right now, we're dealing with your dad. Later, we'll deal with what your messed up past has done to you."

"Hey," she protested, "I happen to think I've turned out pretty decent."

"More than decent, baby girl. But it's twisted the way you see things."

She laid her head on my shoulder and curled up next to me. "I'm sorry," fell from her lips.

What the hell did she have to be sorry for? Was it her fault she had a shit childhood with even shitter parents? Hell no. I ignored her unnecessary apology. She was fading fast on me. "I need to know his name."

She looked up at me, her cheeks tear-stained. "What, why?"

"So I can find out what is going on. Just give me his name." The phone call already told me what prison he was in, so his name was the last thing I needed.

"Fritz Handel. But what are you going to do, Nickel? I don't want you to get into trouble for me."

Karmen had no idea of the shit I was in with the Fallen Lords. Looking in on a deadbeat in prison was going to be a walk in the park. "Don't worry about me. Your father isn't going to hurt you or me." I brushed her hair from her face and pressed a kiss to her lips. "I just got you, I'm not going to let you go anytime soon."

She huffed and shook her head. "I think we might need to get your head checked."

A grin spread across my lips. "And why would you say that?"

"Because you are in bed with one of the most boring people you will ever know."

"Well, I know you're the most beautiful woman I've ever seen, and tonight was one of the best nights I've had in a hell of a long time."

She crawled into my lap and straddled my hips. "Oh my God, Nickel, I think we need to get you to the eye doctor immediately. I think you might be going blind." Her hands cradled my face, and she had a sly smile on her face.

I wrapped my arms around her waist and flipped her over, my body covering her. "Then it's a good thing you're a nurse. I guess I'm going to need some personal care."

Giggles bubbled from her lips as my hands ran over her body, and my lips blazed a trail of kisses up her neck. "Nickel, you're so corny," she gasped.

"You bring it out in me, Karmen. It's all your fault." It was all her fault. I would never act like this in front of the club. Hell, it was rare for me to even crack a smile when I was at the clubhouse anymore.

She wound her arms around my neck and pulled me closer. "I guess I can take the blame for that," she whispered against my lips. "Thank you for helping with my dad."

"You're gonna find out there isn't much I wouldn't do for you, baby girl."

Her eyes closed, and she sighed deeply.

I meant it when I had told her nothing was going to touch her. Starting tomorrow, I was going to find out what her dad wanted and do my best to keep her safe.

****

Karmen

"Shut up."

I shook my head and grabbed the next chart off of the cart.

"You didn't."

Honestly, I was in shock as much as she was, but I was also slightly offended that she was so surprised. "Pick your jaw up off the floor, Nikki, and try not to act like Nickel and me together is so crazy. You were the one who encouraged me to go out with him last night."

She grabbed my arm and spun me around to look at her. "No! That's not why I'm so shocked. I knew that man was head over heels in lust with you, I just didn't know if you were going to actually do anything about it or get caught up in your head like you normally do."

"Well, Nickel was good at keeping me from thinking." I didn't think about anything 'til he left, and the weight of everything that had happened last night and early in the morning had come crashing down on me.

Not only did I have to deal with the fact that my quiet little world was blown to smithereens by Nickel, but I was also now worried about why my dad was trying to call me.

"So, when are you going to see him again?" Nikki asked eagerly.

I sighed deeply and tried to push all thoughts of my dad out of my head. There wasn't much I could do about him while I was at work. Thankfully, I only worked a six-hour shift today, and it was already more than half over.

"Hello, earth to Karmen." Nikki waved her hand in my face. "When are you going to see him again?"

"Um, I think he said he had some stuff to take care of today and he would come over when he was done." Part of me hoped he would, but the other half of me wished he wouldn't.

You know those tiny little boxes where I put my problems? Well, for the past four hours, I had been trying to shove Nickel into one, and it just wasn't working. He pushed past every barrier and wall that I had built up around myself, and that was only after spending one night with him. I was terrified of what would happen when we spent more time together. He was liable to blow my whole world apart, and I wouldn't be able to put it back together.

"Stop."

I looked up from the floor and tilted my head. "Stop what?"

"Stop wrinkling your nose and trying to talk yourself out of being with Nickel." She grabbed the chart out of my hand and walked into the empty room that we were prepping for a new resident. "You are one of the smartest people I know, Karmen, but that always isn't good. You could talk yourself out of winning the lottery if you put your mind to it."

"Nickel and the lottery are complete opposites."

Nikki scoffed and dropped down onto the empty bed. "They are one in the same. Both things that are good for you and could change your life. Besides, I'm sure that man knows his way between the sheets."

My cheeks heated at her words, and I subtly fanned myself. She was not wrong about that. Nickel had made me feel things that I didn't think were possible last night, and I'm sure there was more he could show me. "I wouldn't kick him out of bed," I mumbled.

Nikki smiled slyly. "Just remember that whenever you start thinking of all the bullshit reasons to run." She wiggled her eyebrows and jumped up. "Maybe you could hook me up with one of his buddies."

I thought of the guys that I had met at Shake the Lake, and couldn't picture Nikki with any of them. Hell, I couldn't even picture myself with Nickel, but he seemed interested in me. "I only met some of them for a few minutes. I'm not sure any of them would work."

She scoffed and wrinkled her brow. "Did they have names like Meat and Death? I don't think I could handle introducing them to my grandma if that were the case. At least with Nickel's name, it's not horrible. Did he tell you what his real name was?"

I blinked slowly, not even realizing 'til now that Nickel wasn't even his name. At least, it might not be. I wasn't sure who would actually name their kid Nickel, but there had been weirder names that I had heard. "Um, I don't know his real name if he has one, and the guy's names were Slayer, Clash, and Wrecker." Or was it Wrench? I was horrible at remembering names, especially strange and different ones.

"Hm, I think I'll take Clash. Not sure if I could handle Slayer or Wrecker. Unless his name means he's crazy in bed, then I might be okay with it," she pondered.

I moved around the room, making sure everything was set up while Nikki rambled on about possible biker names she could manage dating.

"Yeah, I'm going to have to say that unless their name has some kick ass story behind it, I'm not going to be able to date a biker."

A laugh bubbled from my lips, and I grabbed her hand and pulled her out of the room. "I'll talk to Nickel about getting you just the right biker."

Nikki threw her arm over my shoulder, and we pushed the cart down the hall to the front desk. "And that is why we are best friends. You get a biker, I get a biker, everyone gets a biker!" she yelled.

"I want peaches," Marvin, one of the patients yelled from his room. "Screw a biker. Give me more peaches."

Nikki and I busted out laughing with shouts of promised extra peaches for dinner for Marvin.

"This job never gets old," Nikki mumbled.

"Ain't that the truth," I agreed.

"But honestly, no joke here. Enjoy that man, Karmen. You're going to regret it if you let him go." Nikki patted me on the shoulder and pushed the cart ahead of me.

I stopped in the middle of the hall and hung my head. I hoped to God I could shut my brain off and stop thinking of all of the things that could go wrong and just live in the moment. Hell, if I did it last night, I'm sure I could do it again.

Hopefully.

****

Nickel

"Where are you headed off to?"

I swung my leg over my bike and rested my hands on the handlebars. It was half past six, and I was itching to get over to Karmen's. She had gotten off of work over two hours ago, and I knew she was getting lost in her head again. I had texted her around noon, and she had only responded with one-word answers and hadn't answered the phone when I had called. She said she was swamped with work, but I knew she was too busy thinking of all of the ways we weren't going to work.

"Someone I need to see."

"Wouldn't happen to be the brunette I heard about, would it?" Pipe asked. He crossed his arms over his chest and leaned against the truck that was parked next to me.

"Does it matter?"

"Well, I was wondering if you wanted to have a little chat about shit that I've been hearing, but if you've got better things to do, I'll just keep listening to the rumors."

I bowed my head and knew I was going to be late getting to Karmen's. "And what rumors have you been hearing, Pipe?"

He pulled a cigarette out of his pocket and put it in the corner of his mouth. "There are a few rumors going around, but the one with you is that you're leaving."

Slayer had a big fucking mouth. "Who you hear that from?"

Pipe smirked and pulled his lighter out of his pocket. He cupped his hand around the cigarette and quickly lit the end. "You already know the answer to that," he mumbled on an exhale of smoke. "What I want to know is if there is any truth behind it?"

"You know I'm not happy around here. This is not what I signed up for all of those years ago." I had been a part of the Fallen Lords for over fifteen years, and lately, it had started feeling longer than that. "Putting my ass on the line for something I don't wanna do isn't my idea of brotherhood."

Pipe took a drag off his cig and ran his other hand through his hair. "You're not the only one feeling this way. Hell, Wrecker regrets the decision to let the muling in every day."

"Then why in the hell are we still doing it?" I asked, fed up. If the damn president of the club didn't want to do this shit anymore, then why in the hell were we?

"Because you can't just tell Jenkins you want out. This was pushed onto Wrecker from up above, Nickel. I know you think you know everything that went down, but you don't. Wrecker is feeling pressure from all around, not just from us."

While Wrecker was my president and who I reported to, he also had someone above him he had to answer to. The Fallen Lords had twelve different chapters in a five-state radius. The River Valley chapter was the mother chapter where everything started and where all of the orders came down from. Ninety percent of the time, each chapter had say of what went down, but there were times where they had to do what River Valley wanted. "Why the hell would River Valley push this shit onto us?"

Pipe shrugged. "Because that's what they wanted. You think if you branch off and open your own chapter that you aren't going to have to deal with that shit? River Valley has their fingers in each of these chapters. We're lucky that we are the furthest away from them that they forget about us sometimes."

I scowled and shook my head. "They sure didn't forget about us when it came to this muling shit."

"They didn't, but I've heard from other chapters that they are in much deeper than muling."

"That's bullshit."

"Yeah, it is, but where do you think the drugs are coming from? They need someone cooking them. And if you don't be careful and think before you open your mouth, you might get roped into being their next club to start cooking. I'm assuming you want to go further south in the state, and from where I'm standing, River Valley would see that as prime opportunity to expand their already torrid path."

Son of a bitch. Pipe was more than right, especially if what he was saying was the truth about the muling being pushed on us. "So, we just sit here like good little errand boys and more than likely take the fall? How the fuck are we going along with this?"

"Because right now, we don't have a choice, Nickel."

"Why don't we bring this shit up in a meeting and band together to get the hell out?"

Pipe looked around and tossed his cigarette on the pavement. "Because not everyone is who you think they are."

"Why do I feel like you're about to start spouting some shit about conspiracy theories, and how we're really not alone?"

Pipe rolled his eyes and crossed his arms over his chest. "I'd just be careful of who you open your mouth to, Nickel." He nodded and disappeared back into the clubhouse.

I hung my head and gripped the handlebars. Why the hell did shit have to be so fucking complicated? To find out that no one in Weston actually wanted the muling but had no way of getting out of it was a fucking kick to the nuts.

Everyone always had a choice, it was just figuring out if it was worth the loss to get what you want. For me, it was getting out of muling for the Weston chapter, but if I spearheaded my own chapter, I might find myself in even deeper shit.

"Fucking shit," I cursed.

All along, I thought I had the answer, but come to find out, I wasn't anymore ahead than I was when this shit all started.

I started my bike and revved the engine. I may be back to square one on getting out of Weston, but at least I had one thing going for me.

Karmen.

****

Karmen

White wine?

Wine cooler?

Bottle of Jack Daniels?

I needed to take the edge off of my nerves, and while I didn't actually drink often, alcohol seemed to be the answer to my problem.

Nickel had texted me ten minutes ago that he was on the way over, and I swear to God, I was even more nervous than I was last night.

Last night, I had figured Nickel would get bored of me after half an hour and drop me back at my place. Now I knew that wasn't going to happen, and I somehow had to figure out how to entertain a big ol' biker in my tiny apartment.

I poured a shot of the Jack and quickly tossed it back. It burned down my throat and warmed the pit of my stomach. Well, that just might do the trick.

Three shots later, I was leaning heavily against the door as I opened it to Nickel, and a hiccup escaped from my lips. I might have gone one shot too many. "Hey," I whispered, my free hand saluting him.

Yeah, I just saluted Nickel. Kill me now.

He pushed his way into my apartment, his arm circling my waist, and he pulled me to his side as he closed the door behind us. "Baby girl, did you start the party without me?" His face nuzzled my neck, and his lips brushed against my skin.

My arms instinctively wrapped around his neck, and I closed my eyes, breathing in his scent. "You smell good," I sighed. I needed to bottle him up and put him on my dresser. His scent, that is, although, I actually wouldn't be opposed to having Nickel in my room whenever I wanted him. "We should go to my room. It has a lock on the door." I was tipsy enough to turn the lock on my bedroom door and never let him out.

A wonky smile spread across my lips, and Nickel leaned back to look down at me. "My girl is half in the bag and goofy as shit."

Horny more than goofy, but I wasn't going to point that out. I had gone from nervous as hell to putty in this man hands. "I might have had a drink or four."

Nickel walked us over to the living room and pulled me down onto the couch with him. He grabbed my legs and swung them over his lap, and I leaned against the arm of the couch. "I confess, it was four."

Nickel smiled, and I thanked God I wasn't standing because I'm pretty sure I would have ended up on the floor. His eyes fell on the open bottle on the coffee table and the single shot glass. "I guess I'll just have to catch up to you."

"You can't get drunk just by staring at the bottle," I hiccupped. I leaned toward the bottle and almost fell out of Nickel's lap and onto the floor. His arms wrapped around me and pulled me back onto the couch.

"I'll get a drink in just a minute."

I sighed and leaned against the couch. Nickel looked as handsome as always, but he didn't look as relaxed as I felt. I reached up, brushing his temple with my fingertips. "How was your day?"

He leaned into my touch and closed his eyes. "Better now."

"Bad ass bikers have bad days?"

A smirk spread across his lips. "Yeah. I just found out something I thought was a good idea turned out to be a bad one."

I hummed and ran my fingers through his hair. "Then come up with a new one."

His eyes popped open, and the corners of them crinkled from the huge grin on his face. "If only it were that easy."

"Is there anything I can do to help?"

He shook his head. "Just keep doing what you're doing, baby girl."

"I'm tipsy and petting you, Nickel. How is this helping?"

He grabbed me around the waist, slid me onto his lap, turned my body towards him, and I straddled his waist. "You make me forget all the shit I don't want to deal with."

That sounded nice. I liked being able to do that for him. "You do the same for me," I whispered.

"So, we both give each other amnesia when we're together, huh?" His hands rested on my thighs, and I rested my arms on his shoulders.

"Hmm, more like you help make the world fade away. I forget how nervous I should be or how you are way out of my league."

He shook his head. "I think you got that backward. You are leaps and bounds out of my league, but I'm not gentleman enough to let you go. I'll take any and everything you're willing to give me." His hands traveled up my body, blazing a trail to my head where he delved his fingers into my hair. "You tipsy enough to kiss me?"

A sly smile spread across my lips. "I don't have to be tipsy to kiss you, just breathing. I can't seem to resist you anymore, Nickel."

"One less thing to worry about then," he whispered against my lips. "Now I just have to keep you."

His lips claimed mine, and this kiss was great. Nickel knew exactly what he was doing, and all I had to do was wrap my arms around him and hold the hell on. I pressed my body into him, needing to get more of him and well, everything. My fingers slid into his windblown hair, raking it between my fingers. "Nickel," I moaned as his lips traveled over my skin and down my neck.

Our bodies were entwined, and I didn't know where I ended and where Nickel started. I never wanted this feeling to end. I was free and careless when I was in Nickel's arms. I could feel and say whatever I wanted.

Nickel pulled my arms from his head, resting them at my sides, then delved his fingers into my hair all while his mouth possessed mine again. Did I mention the man could kiss? Holy freakin' hell.

I shivered against him and made a small noise in the back of my throat. Nickel's eyes darkened, and the atmosphere of the room shifted. My hands moved, exploring his back as the kiss became unbridled and hurried. He twisted, knocking me over onto the couch, and his body covered me. "It's amazing how I can miss something so much when it's only been hours since I last had you."

"You missed me?" I asked meekly.

"You're about to find out just how much I missed you."

****

Nickel

Her arms wound around my neck. I leaned back and stood up with her body wrapped around me. "Grab that bottle," I ordered. She leaned down and snatched the bottle of Jack off the coffee table. "We're gonna move this party to the bedroom."

I stalked to her bedroom, my legs eating up the short distance to her bed.

"It's only five-thirty, and we're already going to bed? I had your whole biker persona wrong," she giggled. "I think you're more of a senior citizen who should be driving a moped."

She managed to not spill a drop of the bottle of Jack when I tossed her on the bed and bounced around. "You're gonna pay for that," I growled. My hands grabbed the hem of my shirt and ripped it off over my head.

With a sassy grin, she pressed the bottle to her lips and took a sip. Her gaze traveled over my body, her eyes hooded with desire. "How do you do this to me?" she asked as she sat up, leaning on her elbows.

My fingers wrapped around the neck of the bottle and slid it from her grip. "Do what?"

"Make me act like, well…like I can't control myself."

I shook my head and set the bottle on her dresser. I didn't need the high of alcohol when Karmen was around. She was the only drug I needed. "You always need to be in control?"

Her teeth nibbled on her bottom lip. "I don't tend to do anything that would let me be out of control. Living with my father showed me just what being out of control can do."

Her fucking father. I still really had no clue about the guy besides what Karmen had told me. I hadn't been able to get any info today since I was running around doing bullshit for the club. "There's a right and wrong way to be out of control, baby girl. Your father seemed to have fallen down the wrong path." I placed one knee on the edge of the bed and grabbed her feet, spreading her legs.

"I'd have to agree with you on that one," she whispered.

"But if you wanna lose control, I'm just the man for you to do that with." I crawled onto the bed, sliding over her while raining kisses on up her body. "I don't mind at all taking all of the control."

"I bet you don't mind at all." Her breath hitched as I nudged up the hem of her shirt and then pulled it over her head. She fell back onto the bed, her hair fanning out around her while she covered her chest with her arms.

"Arms down," I ordered. She wasn't going to hide away from me.

She hesitantly lowered her arms to her sides and gripped the comforter in her hands. "Nickel, I just..." She sighed and closed her eyes.

"Stop thinking, Karmen. It's like the light dies inside you as soon as you start overthinking everything. Just fucking feel."

"You know," she sassed, "that's easy fo—"

I cut her off, knowing she was just going to throw some bullshit excuse at me, and honestly, I didn't want to hear it. All I wanted was to feel her lush body beneath me and forget the day. "Stop. The next word out of your mouth better be my name or you begging for more. That's it."

I grabbed her wrists and pinned her arms above her head. My left hand held her in place while my right glided down the soft skin of her arm and cradled her cheek. Her eyes were half-mast, but I could see the fight she was having inside her head to just let go. My lips descended, catching her mouth in mine. Her body relaxed, and a soft moan whooshed from her lips the second I touched her. My tongue slid over hers while my hand cradled her breast.

She arched her back, pressing herself into my hand. "Please," she gasped.

I didn't know why she fought this when she knew when we were together that it was better than anything. I pulled down the cup of her bra, and my thumb swept over her puckered nipple. "Yes, baby girl." Her body responded to every touch, begging for more. I slanted my mouth over hers and deepened the kiss. A moan glided from her lips into my mouth, straight to my dick.

Every hitched breath, moan, and small noise from her mouth drove me crazy. I was doing that to her. My touch was driving her crazy, and I planned to wring every last moan from her tonight.

She wrapped her legs around my waist and slid her arms over my shoulders. "Nickel," she breathed. Her fingers delved into my hair, gently tugging to keep my lips on hers.

My fingers quickly unbuttoned her shorts. My hand cupped her sweet pussy the second her zipper slid down, and the welcomed heat of her warm mound drove me insane.

I jack-knifed off the bed, toed off my boots, and stripped off my jeans along with my underwear. "Ten seconds to get all of your clothes off." I stroked my cock, watching her laid out before me with her shorts undone, shirt off, and a look on her face like I was the only man in the world. "Ten, nine…" By the time I got to five, she had snapped out of her daze and jumped off the bed, ripping off the rest of her clothes.

Her bra dropped to the floor when I growled "one," and she was naked before me.

"Now what?" she whispered.

I crooked my finger at her. "Come here, baby girl."

She shuffled in front of me, her arms at her side, and her bottom lip between her teeth. Was I ever going to get used to having Karmen this way? I prayed to God I never would because I never wanted to take her for granted. "This is going to be hard and fast, but it's going to be damn good."

Her body trembled at my words, and she sucked in a quick breath. "Okay."

I grabbed her around the waist, spun her around, and pushed her onto the bed. She moved to crawl up to the pillows, but my hands gripped her hips, stopping her. "Stay right here." I covered her back with my body, my dick nestling in between her lush ass cheeks. "Good girl," I whispered in her ear.

My hand snaked down in between us, and she spread her legs, letting me nestle in between them. "Put your knees on the bed, but stay on the edge," I ordered quietly.

As soon as she had both knees on the bed, my dick plunged into her wet, slick pussy, balls deep. "Nickel," she gasped.

Her tight pussy milked my dick with each thrust. "Fuck, you feel so good."

Each time my balls slapped against her, a whimper escaped her lips, driving me insane. "Feel it, baby. Fucking feel it," I growled.

"Please, Nickel please," she begged. Her head was tossed back, and her eyes were shut. I grabbed her hair in one hand while the other hand gripped her waist, holding her in place.

"Touch yourself, baby. Touch yourself and come around my dick."

She went down on her elbow, one arm holding her up, while the other sought out her clit. Now I wished like hell I had flipped her over, but seeing her lush ass as I sunk into her wet cunt was sending me to the brink.

"Fast, baby girl. I'm gonna come," I grunted.

Her hand grazed my dick, and I exploded inside her. Stars flashed before my eyes, and I collapsed on top of her, my hips involuntarily thrusting. "Oh, fuck yeah," I shouted as my balls emptied.

She yelled my name, her voice muffled by the blanket she had her face shoved into. She whimpered and whined, her pussy milking my dick dry. Both of our breathing was labored, and I brushed her hair out of her face.

Her face was turned towards me, and her eyes were shut, a content smile was on her lips. "Wow."

I couldn't even think of a word to describe what had just happened. Hell, I could barely think. My fingers trailed up and down her back, drawing lazy circles.

"Did you go mute?" she asked. Her beautiful green eyes were searching my face, concerned.

"Damn near." My voice was gravelly and hoarse.

She hummed under her breath and wiggled her arm out from under her. "I'm starving, but I'm pretty sure my legs are Jell-O right now."

I glanced at the clock on the nightstand. "Chinese or pizza?"

"Hmm, both?" she giggled.

I gathered her in my arms, rolled to my back, and draped her over me. "I worked you up that good, huh?"

She slid between my legs, her elbows on my chest, and her head resting in her hands. A slow smile spread across her lips as she looked down at me. "Or maybe I'm refueling for later?"

"Put on my shirt, find something to drink, and meet me on the couch."

She wrapped her arms around my neck and pouted her lips. "I'm surprised you want me to get dressed."

My lips pressed a kiss to the tip of her nose. "Delivery guy ain't gonna see what's mine, baby girl, and we both need to eat. That damn sure isn't going to happen if you're naked."

"Fine," she huffed as she moved out of my lap.

She shakily took a step and looked over her shoulder at me. "I blame you for my wobbliness."

I shrugged. "That's one thing I don't mind taking credit for." I snagged my pants off the floor and tossed my shirt to her.

She pulled it over her head and piled her hair on top of her head. "Nickel," she called.

"Yeah?"

"You can tell me why you had a bad day, you know that, right?"

That was the shit of all of this. I couldn't tell her what the hell was going on. No one knew club business unless they were a patched member of the club. "I know. Just not much to tell."

"Okay, but just remember, I'm a good listener." She disappeared out the door with a wink over her shoulder at me.

I fell back onto her bed with my phone in my hand and sighed deeply. Not only was she hot as hell and fan-fucking-tastic in bed, but she was also probably one of the best people I had met in my life.

I was going to go to Hell for corrupting Karmen and making her mine.

Sweet and innocent meets ruthless and wild.

Definitely going to Hell, but what a fun ride it was going to be.

****

Karmen

"Hit me."

"What? Why?"

Nikki sighed and laid down on the couch, resting her head in my lap. "Because it's Friday night, and we're both sitting in front of the TV watching lame movies from the 80s. Just hit me. It'll make this shit night complete."

I pushed her off my lap and grabbed the remote off of the coffee table. "We do this every Friday night. I don't know why you suddenly think this sucks." Well, last Friday night we hadn't. I had told Nickel that I normally hung out with Nikki, but he decided that he was coming over and I really didn't get a say in the matter.

Don't get me wrong, I loved spending time with him, but sometimes, the man's pushiness drove me a bit batty.

"Because you have a smoking hot boyfriend who you should be spending every waking minute with, and I should be out there finding my own Adonis." She flopped onto the floor and kicked her feet. "We are so pathetic," she whined.

"Speak for yourself. My body could use a break for one night," I mumbled. From what Nickel had told me before he had left, I was more than likely going to get a couple nights of rest before he came back.

Nikki sat up, leaning back on her elbows. "Oh, you poor thing. You're so worn out from getting too much good dick. Whatever will you do?"

"Have you always been this bitchy?" I asked, smirking.

"It's the condition I have."

I leaned forward and looked down at her. "And what condition is that?"

"Bitchiness due to Lack-A-Dick-Itis."

"Oh Jesus," I laughed. "You think you're gonna make it, or should I start planning your funeral?"

She fell back on the floor and tossed her arm over her face. "It's terminal. The only thing that's going to bring me back is a good dicking."

"A good dicking?" I sputtered. "Where the hell do you come up with these things?"

She tapped her finger on her head. "It's all up here," she giggled. "So, how has the first week been being with your motorcycle god?"

I managed to step over Nikki and walk into the kitchen. "It's been different," I mumbled.

"Yeah, I'd definitely say going from not having sex for months to getting it on the daily is a difference. I mean everything else."

"Well, there hasn't really been much of anything else. We talk, but mostly it's about me." I grabbed a bottle of cheap wine from the fridge and filled a glass half-full. "Did you want some wine?" Nikki had already had half of the bottle and probably wasn't done yet.

She scrambled off the floor and nabbed her glass from the coffee table. "Fill me up," she muttered, holding the glass out to me. "So, what you're saying is, you're boinking like bunny rabbits."

That was a pretty accurate description. "Yeah." I filled her glass and screwed the cover back on the bottle. "What the hell am I doing?" How did I end up in a relationship where all we did was have sex? Nickel and I did talk, but ninety percent of what we talked about was me, and the other ten percent was trying to figure out what we were going to eat.

"Getting a good dicking." Nikki clinked her glass against mine and shuffled back into the living room. "Oh, and you're living life without thinking."

I huffed and grabbed a brick of cheese from the fridge. "When did thinking become such a bad thing?" I swiped a sleeve of crackers from the pantry and a small cutting board and knife from the counter.

Nikki watched me drop everything on the coffee table in front of her and looked up at me. "Where's the sausage?"

"Jesus," I muttered. "Where it always is."

"You're the best," she called as I grabbed the log of summer gauged from the fridge and dropped it next to the cheese. "You're cutting."

"Sure thing, boss."

I plopped down on the couch next to her and hit play on the next movie. "So, are you going to explain to me why not only you, but also Nickel, keep telling me to stop thinking all of the time?"

Nikki rolled her eyes and grabbed the knife off of the cutting board. "There isn't anything wrong with thinking in general. It's more you obsessing and stressing out over things that you need to just let be and let God."

"What the heck does that mean? Let God?"

Nikki laughed and started slicing the cheese and sausage. "It means sometimes, you just need to let things go and let the universe and God handle them."

I grabbed the blanket from the back of the couch and draped it over my legs. "I don't know what I want, so how the hell am I supposed to believe that the universe knows what's best for me?"

"Because you gotta have faith, girl." Nikki finished slicing a pile of cheese and sausage and sat back on the couch with the cutting board. "You knew all along that Nickel had a thing for you, and you ran. Even though you ran, he still managed to catch up to you. Just think of all of that time you wasted running when you could have been in his bed every night." She wiggled her eyebrows and shoved a piece of cheese into her mouth.

I sighed and leaned my head back. "Nikki, this is way too hard. I can't shut my brain off. Well, that's not exactly true. When Nickel is around, he manages to completely snucker me, and I can't think at all."

She held out the cutting board to me. "And that is a good thing, Karmen."

"It is until he leaves and then everything I normally would have worried about comes rushing back to me, and I swear to God, it's almost impossible for me not to have a panic attack every morning when he leaves." I grabbed a handful of cheese and sausage and reached for the sleeve of crackers.

"Really?"

"Yes, really. I had a shit time growing up, Nikki. I honestly just want to live a quiet life in my tiny little apartment with a boring job that no one bothers me at." I rolled my head to look at her. "Putting everything in a box then snapping the lid down on it helps me cope with, well, life."

"Boxes? Huh?"

Crap. Now I was going to have to explain the weird and bizarre way I dealt with life. I had never told Nikki about my tiny boxes before. Even I knew the words coming out of my mouth were going to sound crazy. "It's just a way for me to move on from things. My father was a drunk who killed three people. Instead of letting it destroy me, I shoved every thought about it into a box in my mind, put the lid on it, and shoved it away on a shelf."

Nikki slowly blinked. "You do know that doesn't work, right? That even if you don't think about it, it's going to come back to haunt you until you take care of it."

I had made my peace with my father. He was a man I didn't want in my life even if he was my father. Although he was coming back to haunt me, that had nothing to do with the box I had put him in. "It's been working for years for me."

Nikki tapped a finger against the side of my head. "How many boxes you got in there?" She curled her lip and quirked her eyebrow. "Am I in one of them?"

I knocked her hand away. "No, you ass. Why would I put you in a box?"

She grabbed the crackers from me and shook her head at me. "You got a weird coping mechanism, girl. Although, it does explain a lot about you."

"Hey," I protested, "what is that supposed to mean?"

"It means it explains why you are so quiet and reserved."

"Exactly, and that is why I can't be with Nickel because he is anything but quiet and reserved. The man says exactly what he wants, whenever he wants, and doesn't care what anyone thinks about him. He's part of a motorcycle club with loud, boisterous guys that are exactly like him and here is the kicker, Nikki...I know absolutely nothing about the man other than I know he can do amazing things with his tongue."

Nikki fanned herself with her hand. "I knew that man would know how to use that tongue piercing."

My jaw dropped. "How do you know he has a tongue piercing?" He totally did, but it wasn't anything that I had shared with Nikki. And he knew how to use it, FYI.

Nikki chuckled and shook her head. "You do live in your own little world, don't you, Karmen. If you had talked to the man for more than five seconds and actually looked him in the face, you would have seen right away that he had one."

I crossed my arms over my chest. "Whatever." She was right. I hardly ever looked people in the face when they talked to me. It helped to make the conversation short, and people couldn't judge me if they didn't look me in the eye.

Nikki patted my leg. "Okay, that's enough for tonight. I can tell you're ready to permanently retreat into your shell."

I sighed and turned up the volume on the TV. "It's just not easy for me, Nikki. You can walk up to anyone and start talking to them. It took me almost four months to actually talk to you."

Nikki laughed. "Yes, it did take you that long. I seriously thought you were a bitch when I first met you."

"Hey, I was fourteen! You can't think someone is a bitch at fourteen. I barely knew who I was."

She shrugged and kicked her feet up on the coffee table. "You should just be thankful that I stuck around to find out that you weren't a bitch. Hell, girl. You made Nickel wait a year before you gave him the time of day. That man deserves a medal and blowjobs for life."

I leaned over and rested my head on Nikki's shoulder. "You are completely insane, but I don't know what I would do without you."

She patted my head and laughed. "Damn straight. Just like I wouldn't know what to do without you. I mean, who would reel me in and let me know when I've got a crazy idea?"

"You do get a lot of them," I joked.

"Or who would set me up with one of their hot biker boyfriend's hot biker friends?"

"I wouldn't get your hopes up too high on that one. From the way things are looking, it doesn't seem that Nickel is going to let me out of the bedroom."

Nikki scoffed and leaned back into the couch. "You say that like it's a bad thing."

It wasn't a bad thing, but it made me wonder if there would ever be more.

****

Nickel

"Drink."

"I'm good."

"I said drink, mother fucker." Slayer pushed a bottle of Jack across the table toward me. "This isn't the time to be sober."

That was the damn truth.

An easy run to the River Valley had turned into a complete shit show that I was getting fucked over on. I grabbed the bottle of Jack and drank. "Explain to me how the fuck this is happening again, and why I'm the one who is being screwed over?"

Pipe shook his head and leaned back in his chair. "It wasn't my idea, brother. Jenkins picked you, and there isn't a damn thing you or I can do about it."

"Why the hell can't he pick a guy who doesn't have an ol' lady. Do you know how much this fucks up my life right now? She's always running scared, and now I'm going to have some chick living with me. You really think any chick would be okay with that?"

"Jenkins didn't know you had an ol' lady, but honestly, I don't think he would have given a fuck. He picked you to take care of his sister, and that's what the hell you are going to do."

And that, right there, summed up how fucked my life was right now. I wasn't making any of the decisions, and I just had to deal with it.

Pipe and I were sitting in the common room of the River Valley Fallen Lords surrounded by the assholes who had made my life a living hell. "You think they could have sprung this shit on me sooner?" Pipe and I were planning on leaving early the next morning to get back to Weston before noon.

"They waited because they knew that you were going to shit a brick when you found out. None of us want a chick weighing us down that isn't connected to us. Hell, you're one of the rare few that have an ol' lady in Weston."

"And for that, I get shit on by River Valley."

Pipe looked around. "You might want to keep your disdain for Jenkins and his cronies to a minimum until we leave."

I leaned forward and stabbed my finger into the table. "This fucking club shouldn't even have the goddamn last say in anything anymore since Skeeter died. He was the last of the original five, and you and I both damn well know that as soon as they shoveled the last pile of dirt on his coffin that Jenkins took over and fucked up this club more than any of us can fix now."

"I fucking repeat, you might want to leave this shit until we get the fuck out of River Valley."

"Tell me you don't fucking agree with me," I hissed.

Pipe set his bottle of beer on the table and glared at me. "I hear you, and I fucking agree with you, Nickel. But now is not the fucking time to be talking about this. Take it back to Weston where you'll find most fucking agree."

I sat back in my chair and sighed. This was all fucking bullshit. Nothing was going the way I needed it to right now.

I was about to have some chick I didn't even fucking know live with me, the club I used to love was falling apart at the seams, and I hit a fucking brick wall when trying to find out what the hell was going on with Karmen's dad. "You got any connections at Winchester Prison?"

Pipe quirked his eyebrow. "What the hell you got going on now?"

"It's not me, exactly, it's for Karmen."

Pipe laughed. "I thought you were dating some shy, quiet nurse. What the hell does she need an in for at Winchester?"

"She is shy and quiet, it's her family that isn't. Her dad killed a couple people drunk driving a few years back and is in prison."

Pipe whistled low. "Jesus."

I nodded. Jesus was right. We may live crazy and wild in the club, but we knew drinking or smoking and then deciding to drive was fucking stupid. Unfortunately, some people didn't get that memo before they learned it too late. "Yeah. I haven't even met the guy, and my view of him is far from perfect. The first night I was with Karmen, he called after fucking midnight."

"You just said he was in prison. How in the hell did he manage to get a call out at that hour?"

"That was my first thought, too. He called, and she freaked the fuck out. She cut ties with the asshole years ago, and apparently, he only calls when he's about to get paroled."

"That's an asshole move."

I dipped my head in agreement and took a sip of my beer. "Yeah. So, I told her I would find out what he wanted since I told her it wasn't right that he was calling."

"And you can't find out shit."

"Here's the fucking thing…I have a connection to the prison, and he told me Handel got sent to the hole the same night that he managed to get a call out to Karmen."

"And now you can't get to him at all."

Pipe hit the nail right on the head. "I told Karmen not to worry about her dad, but something is telling me that shit ain't right, and I'm afraid it's going to fucking blow before I figure out what's going on."

He nodded. "I'll see what I can do when we get back to the club. I think Wrecker knows a few members from other chapters that are in there. They might be able to get word to Handel or figure out why he's in the hole."

Well, that was at least some good news. "I'd appreciate it, brother. I hope it's nothing, but I'd rather be safe than sorry."

"Nickel, Pipe!"

I looked over my shoulder and saw Jenkins sitting at a table in the corner calling us over.

"Put a fucking lid on it, brother, and just listen to what he has to say."

We both lumbered over to his table and took the two empty chairs.

"Figured you would want to meet Cora before she hops on the back of your bike tomorrow morning."

Pipe cut me off before I could tell him she wasn't riding on the back of my bike. "She'll be on my bike tomorrow. Nickel has an ol' lady."

Jenkins nodded his understanding that the only chick who was going to be on the back of my bike anymore was Karmen. "I didn't know you had settled down."

I leaned back in my chair. "It's new, but it's for real." I didn't want him getting any ideas that I was going to hook up with his sister.

"Good. I'm sure it'll be hard for Cora to adjust to a new place. Hopefully, your ol' lady can help her settle in."

"I thought that this was just temporary?" I didn't want this chick living with me forever. Hell, I didn't want to be responsible for her at all.

"She'll need to stay as long as she does."

Well, if that wasn't a shit answer.

"You think you can tell us why she needs to hide out in Weston?" Pipe asked. He was also annoyed with the minimum information that we were getting.

Jenkins looked to his left and right. "There is some shit brewing here that I think it would be best for Cora not to be around when shit hits the fan."

"So that shit isn't going to follow her back to Weston, right?"

"As far as I know, it shouldn't."

That wasn't exactly a solid yes. "So, where is she?" I wanted to see who the hell I was being forced to take home with me tomorrow.

"Ryker," he called out, "go find out where the hell Cora is."

"She said she's not coming out," a guy, who I assumed was Ryker, called out.

Jenkins slammed his bottle down on the table. "Damn her. Why the hell can't she see I'm just trying to keep her safe?"

The three guys who were sitting at the table snickered at a joke that Pipe and I were not a part of.

"You know how she is," the guy to my right said. Although I had been to the River Valley chapter many times before, I was never able to remember any of their names. Maybe it was my brains way of saying none of these guys were important enough to remember. I managed to glance over and see his patch said Mercy. I could imagine the story that went along with his name.

"Well, she can hide out in her room all night, but come morning, she better have her ass on the back of his bike, or there will be hell to pay," Jenkins warned. He pushed away from the table and stood. "I've got some shit to take care of. I doubt I'll see you before you leave in the morning. I'll be in touch if there is anything more you need to know."

Jenkins stalked past the bar and out the front door. "Well, that answered absolutely none of the questions we had," Pipe muttered under his breath.

Not like I expected Jenkins to actually give us any information that was useful. "I'm just gonna head to bed. The morning is going to come quickly."

Pipe nodded. "Night, brother. I'm gonna finish my beer and maybe play a game of pool."

I wasn't surprised that he wasn't going to call it a night. Pipe was always the last one to fall into bed, but he was also the first one to be awake in the morning. I didn't know how the hell the fucker did it. "Try to get some sleep, brother." I clapped him on the shoulder as I left the table and walked down the hall to the bedrooms.

River Valley's clubhouse was twice the size of Weston's, but it was run down and in need of a good cleaning. Pipe had made the comment that you got the original MC feel here and, more than likely, some of the dirt leftover from the original members.

I fell onto my stiff as hell bed and pulled my phone out of my pocket. I had been trying to call or text Karmen when I had the time, but that wasn't often. She had told me that she had a night in with her girl last night, but tonight, she just planned on doing nothing.

That was where Karmen and I were different. I had to be doing something. Even if it was just hanging out with the brothers shooting pool, it was still doing something.

I swiped across her name and put the phone to my ear. It was half past eleven, and I didn't know if she would be sleeping or not.

"Nickel?" she answered sleepily.

Fuck, I missed her. "Baby girl, you asleep already?"

I heard her light sigh and the covers moving over the phone. "It's late, and I was tired."

"How was your day?" I, unfortunately, hadn't been able to talk to her at all today and only sent three or four texts back and forth.

She hummed under her breath. "So busy. Two residents passed away today."

"I'm sorry, babe."

"Yeah, they were both totally unexpected, too. I hate having to call family to let them know they're loved one has passed away. Thankfully, Nikki worked with me, so she helped."

"That's your girl, right?" I had never really paid attention to anyone besides Karmen. I could pick her friend out of a lineup, but I didn't know her name.

"Yeah, we were both a bit hungover from drinking too much cheap wine last night, but we snapped right out of it."

I chuckled. "At least it wasn't Jack like the other night."

Her light giggle floated through the phone. "I don't think I'll be doing that again anytime soon."

"Don't make promises like that. I like when you get a little tipsy."

She groaned into the phone. "You just like that my brain completely shuts off when I drink."

"That might have a little something to do with it. You manage to overthink everything enough for the both of us."

"Sometimes, I think people wish I was brain dead," she growled softly.

I laughed and covered my eyes with my forearm. "You know that's not what I want."

"I know. How is whatever you're doing going?" she asked, changing the subject.

"All done. We'll be heading back in the morning. Pipe is living it up with the guys, but I thought I would come back to my room and wake you up."

"Well, you succeeded on that."

"You got work in the morning?"

"No, thank goodness. I don't think I could manage working tomorrow."

"Nice," I mumbled. "I'll be over after I get back to the clubhouse."

"You could just come straight to my house," she replied coyly.

"I could, but I have something I need to drop off at the clubhouse, and I need to go over some things with Wrecker before I'm able to come over."

She sniffled into the phone. "Well, hopefully, I'll be home when you get here. I need to go grocery shopping and pick up some new scrub tops at the mall."

"You better be there when I come over or I'll find you, baby girl."

"Promises, promises," she tsked. "I guess we'll find out tomorrow if I'm there."

"You're kind of sassy when I wake you up."

I couldn't see her, but I knew she had just rolled her eyes. "Then I guess I better go back to sleep. I'll maybe see you tomorrow, Nickel."

"Oh, Karmen. You're definitely going to see me. I should be there around three."

She hummed. "Well, I guess I can get all of my errands done before then."

"And if you can't, wait for me, and I'll go with you."

"You wanna go to the mall with me?" she asked, shocked.

"Pretty sure I'll go anywhere as long as you're with me. We could hit up that fancy bra store, and you could do a little modeling for me."

Karmen laughed and damned if my dick didn't harden. "You mean Victoria's Secret?"

"Yeah, baby. You and I could have some fun in those fitting rooms together."

"And this is where I get off the phone, Nickel. You being in a fitting room with me is too much to think about at this time of night."

"I'll let you go only if you promise to wait to go to the mall." I was liking the idea of having my way with Karmen in a tiny fitting room.

"You're a dirty man, Nickel. I'll see you tomorrow."

"Night, baby girl."

She hung up before I could bug her more about waiting for me. I dropped my phone on the bed next to me and looked up at the dingy white ceiling. I was in a shit hole bedroom, but talking to Karmen on the phone had made all of this shit disappear, and I wasn't even pissed anymore.

Having Karmen around was going to be good for my sanity. I just hoped she decided that she wanted to stick around.

****

Karmen

"You're early."

"I said it would be around three."

"It's one-thirty. That isn't around three. That's more like around one or two." I peeked out at Nickel through the three-inch gap I had opened the door. I wasn't ready. Well, physically I was ready, but I hadn't been able to give myself a pep talk yet. "Come back at three." I moved to shut the door, but Nickel stuck his foot in the way.

"I see me being gone two days fucked up all the progress we made last week."

Ha, that was the damn truth. "Just give me an hour, and I'll be ready."

He pushed open the door and looked me up and down. "You look ready to go to me. Grab your purse or whatever you need to bring and let's go. We can take the bike."

I scoffed and shook my head. "We can't take your bike. I need to buy stuff. How am I supposed to hold onto you and a bunch of bags?"

"We'll put your shit in the saddlebags."

"How big are they?"

"Big enough."

"Hmph, every man says that," I whispered.

Nickel wound his arms around my waist and pulled me flush against his body. "You know it's big enough, baby girl."

I couldn't control myself not to roll my eyes. "I think we established many times over that it is more than big enough," I looked down between us at his crotch.

Nickel's body shook as a chuckle rumbled around me. He brushed my hair out of my face and tilted my head back to look up at him. "What's it going to take for me to get you out of this house now and not an hour from now?"

My eyes traveled over his handsome face, taking in his stubbled skin. "I like this," I whispered as I stroked his cheek. A smirk spread across his lips, and I was mesmerized. God damn, this man was handsome. Every time I looked at him, I found something new to focus on.

"Thank you, baby. Now answer my question." Nickel wasn't messing around.

"You keep the scruff, and we take my car." I wasn't budging on the scruff. If he really tried, he could get me on the back of his bike, and I would just go shopping after work to get the rest of things I wouldn't be able to fit in the saddlebags.

"Deal, but I get to drive."

A smile spread across my lips, and I bobbed my head. "You've got a deal, Outlaw."

"Outlaw?" Nickel laughed. "You giving me another road name?"

I tilted my head to the right. That reminded me of the question Nikki asked me before. "What's your name?"

Nickel smiled hugely and shook his head. "I think it's time to go."

I gripped his biceps., "Not so fast. I don't leave until I find out what your real name is."

"I've been called Nickel for the past fourteen years of my life. That is my real name."

"Nope, that's not gonna fly. I wanna know what your name was before you became Nickel, the outlaw."

"I am not an outlaw."

I waved my hand. "Ignore that then, just tell me what your name was the day you were born."

"You aren't going to let this go, are you?"

Hell no. I knew the bare minimum about this man, and I was going to start finding out more. "Spill it, or I keep calling you Outlaw."

"You find out what it is, you keep that shit to yourself, Karmen. The only other person that is alive who knows my name is Pipe."

There was another little nugget of information about Nickel. His parents were both gone. I held up my hand and smiled. "Scouts honor. My lips are sealed."

"Grab your keys. I'm not telling you until your ass is sitting in the car."

Leave it to Nickel to still be in charge when I had the upper hand. "Your alpha drives me crazy sometimes," I mumbled as I hitched my purse over my shoulder and grabbed my keys.

"No idea what the hell that means."

"You're bossy. Too bossy."

Nickel scowled, grabbed my hand, and pulled me out of the apartment. "Don't act like you don't like it, baby girl."

He didn't let go of my hand 'til we reached my car and I beeped open the locks. "I like it, but sometimes, it's a bit too much. I'd like to make my own decision sometimes."

"Okay, I'll let you decide if I'll kiss you here or when we get in the car."

I rolled my eyes and reached for the door handle. "How kind of you."

He shrugged and knocked my hand out of the way. "I'm assuming we're gonna make out in the car. I'm good with that." He pulled open my door and motioned for me to get in. "It's been two days since I kissed you. Get your ass in the car before I put you in the car."

I ducked into the car and slammed the door shut. The man was absolutely insane. I was half tempted to lock the doors and not let him in.

Nickel moved around the front of the car and pointed at me through the windshield. "Don't even think about it," he hollered.

"Damn man," I mumbled as he got on the driver's side.

"Remind me why you need to be the one to drive."

Nickel stuck the key in the ignition and turned in her seat to look at me. "I like to be in control. You know this."

"I didn't know that dealt with everything."

"It does," he replied.

"I don't know if I can handle that, Nickel."

He threaded his fingers through my hair and pulled me close. I was pressed against the center console, and I braced my hand against his chest. "You'll get used to it," he promised against my lips.

My fingers balled his shirt up in my grasp as his tongue swept through my mouth, and I did the only thing I could—hold on. Nickel kissed me thoroughly while his hands drifted from my hair and over my body.

"Do we really need to go to the mall?" His mouth moved from my lips to my neck, and I tilted my head to give him better access.

"I...uh...there is stuff...Jesus Chri—" I pressed against Nickel's chest and moved toward the door, out of Nickel's reach. My face felt hot, and I knew I was blushing all the way down to the tips of my toes. "I need more scrubs for work. I've been washing the same two tops every other day the past three weeks. I'd like more than one day where I don't have to do laundry."

He grabbed my hand and tried to pull me closer. "I'll do your damn laundry for you as long as you get your sweet ass back over here."

I shook my head and buckled my seat belt. "No. Not happening." Even though my body was screaming for his touch, I had to say no. I was horribly terrified that Nickel didn't want to be seen with me in public, and this was going to be the test to see if that was true or not. "Drive." I looked forward out the windshield and saw Nickel out of the corner of my eye. He was still turned toward me, and he looked like he was ready to scream.

"You get one hour at the mall. That's it. I've been waiting to have you underneath me the whole ride back to Weston, and I'm not going to let you make me wait too long. Don't forget your body belongs to me, baby girl."

I turned my head toward him and watched him buckle his seatbelt and start the car. "How gracious of you to give me an hour to shop. Maybe you should just wait in the car while I get everything I need."

He shook his head and drove out of the parking lot. "You're not going to be out of my sight in those shorts. Here I thought you were some quiet, shy girl but, when you have those shorts on, you are anything but a girl."

"Then why do you call me baby girl?" I sassed. I loved when he called me that, and I would honestly be upset if he ever quit, but I was apparently in a mood to argue with everything he said.

"Because it's what I call you."

I rolled my eyes and turned the radio up a bit. "Speaking of what people are called, spill your name, Outlaw." It was a twenty-minute drive to the mall, so that gave me plenty of time to find out a little bit more about Nickel.

He glanced at me but kept his lips sealed.

Nickel smoothly merged onto the highway and didn't talk 'til after he reached eighty and turned on the cruise control. "You wanna tell me why you need to know so bad what my name is?"

I managed to shift in my seat and turn to face him. I didn't run the risk of him pulling me into his lap when he was driving. Although, I really shouldn't put it past him that he might not try something at a stop light. "Because I like you, Nickel, but I feel like I know nothing about you and that scares me."

"Why does it scare you?"

"Because I only know the basics about you, and somehow, I feel things I shouldn't."

He eyed me up and down and reached for my hand. His laced his fingers through mine, and rested our hands in his lap. "I mean it when I say you can't tell anyone what it is, Karmen."

I nodded. Looked like I wasn't going to be able to tell Nikki what his real name was, but I could at least tell her that Nickel was his road name. "I promise."

My answer satisfied him, and he sighed deeply. "My full name is Augustus Callum Cunningham."

"Well, that's a mouthful." I tried my hardest not to laugh, and I thought I was doing okay until Nickel looked over at me, and I tried to think of him as Augustus.

"See, that right there is the reason why I didn't want to tell you," he said, outraged.

I covered my mouth with my hand and turned to the windshield.

Augustus Callum Cunningham.

I was never going to be able to call him that. Augustus was far from a badass biker name. "Did your mother hate you?" I managed to get out in between giggles.

Nickel scowled and squeezed my hand. "You can now see why I was more than happy to get my road name."

I leaned my head back against the headrest and turned toward Nickel. "And why did you get the name Nickel?"

"Hey, I just agreed to tell you what my real name is."

My bottom lip pouted out, and I gave him my best puppy dog eyes. "Please? I promise if you tell me, we can make a stop in Victoria's Secret."

Nickel glanced at me with heated eyes. "I get to go in the dressing room with you?"

I rolled my eyes. "You're going to get us kicked out of the store, though."

Nickel shrugged his shoulder and exited the highway. "That may be, but it'll be a hell of a story to tell."

"I roll my eyes way too much when I'm around you," I muttered under my breath. "Now spill why you got the name Nickel before we get to the mall."

He sighed and gripped the steering wheel. "I was drunk."

"Gee, that's hard to believe that this is how this story starts," I mumbled.

"You wanna hear the answer or not?"

Nickel glared at me, and I held up my hands. "Sorry, sorry. Continue." Jesus, the man was little sensitive today.

Nickel drove for a few minutes before he finally spoke. It took everything in me not to pounce on him and demand he tell me why he was called Nickel.

"So, I was drunk."

I couldn't hold back the snicker that escaped. He side-eyed me, and I got my shit under control.

"Pipe and I were playing pool. We were both prospects and were right in the thick of doing every little bullshit thing we were asked to do. You know what a prospect is?"

I shook my head. "I think I know, but I doubt I know exactly what it means."

"It's basically me having to do absolutely anything asked of me to prove to the other club members that I will do anything for the club. Proves loyalty."

That made sense. Although, couldn't one prove loyalty by not being a slave? "So what were some of the things you had to do?"

"Keep the clubhouse clean, no matter the time of day answer the phone and do whatever they asked. One time, Pipe had to drive to Chicago to get a deep dish pizza for Wrecker and be back in three hours."

"That's impossible," I insisted. It took two hours one way to get to Chicago from Weston.

"I know, and so did Wrecker. But Pipe somehow managed to do it."

I looked out the windshield and saw we were only minutes away from the mall. "Now spill why you're Nickel." I wasn't letting him out of the car until he told me.

"So, we were playing pool, we were both drunk off our asses, and Wrecker walks out with a jar full of change under his arm. I'm talking a huge fucking jar. He sets it on the pool table and looks at Pipe and me. He twists off the lid to the jar and tosses it to me. He tells us that there is three hundred twenty-one dollars and seventy-nine cents in the jar."

I slapped my hand over my mouth and think I know where this is headed.

"That fucker takes that jar, holds it over his head, and smashes it down on the floor." Nickel sounded amused and had a smirk on his lips. "He then tells us we need to find every last penny or we are out."

"Holy crap," I whisper. That was a hell of a lot of change.

"You've never met Pipe before, have you, baby girl?" I shook my head. "Well, imagine me and a guy bigger than I am, drunk off our asses, down on the floor on our hands and knees trying to count change while we shove it in our pockets."

"Why didn't you go get a bowl or something?"

Nickel smirked and turned into the mall parking lot. "We were drunk, babe." Good point. "Pipe took his jacket off and laid it out on the floor. We piled all of the change on it, and painstakingly counted every quarter, dime, nickel, and penny."

"So then what happened?"

"It took over two hours and us recounting the money eleven times before we were close."

"Close?"

"Yeah. We were so close, but we were missing a nickel."

"No way!"

Nickel laughed and pulled into a parking spot that was surprisingly close to the entrance. "Yes."

"So what did you do?" This was absolutely insane. Who in the hell does this to people? It was like hazing in a fraternity, but fifty times worse.

He shifted the car into park and turned his body toward me. "At this point, Pipe and I had sobered up and knew that we were screwed. Neither of us had any change on us and were back to crawling all over the floor looking for a fucking nickel."

I covered my mouth with my hand and tried not to laugh. Nickel being at the mercy of anyone was something that I just couldn't picture.

"You laugh, but back then, Pipe and I were frantic as hell."

"So what happened?"

He shook his head and threaded his fingers through mine. "Wrecker lied."

My jaw dropped, and I got pissed on Nickel's behalf. "You are kidding me!"

"Nah. That fucker wanted to see how far we would go until we gave up."

"So after hours of searching, you finally gave up and then he told you."

"Nope, we never did give up. Wrecker told us while we were both still on our hands and knees on the floor, but neither of us believed him. Pipe was the first one to stop looking, but I was convinced that there was a nickel on the floor and Wrecker was just testing us."

"You got the name Nickel because you wouldn't stop looking for the damn nickel," I laughed.

He pressed a kiss to the back of my hand. "Yup, more or less. They just did it making fun of me, and then it just stuck."

I leaned forward, a breath away from his lips. "Well, I think that's a good story. It shows you never give up. Or it could mean you never listen."

Nickel chuckled and pressed a kiss to my lips. "I think you're right on both counts, baby girl."

I hummed under my breath and pressed my forehead against his. "I missed you." I held my breath, terrified that I sounded like a love-sick teenager. He had only been gone two days, but it had felt like a month.

"You were on my mind the whole time."

My heart sang, and my breath whooshed out. "Thank the Lord," I mumbled. It wasn't a promise of his undying love, but it was better than if he had said okay.

"Time to shop. I hate the mall, but if this is where you need to be, this is where I need to be." He pressed a quick kiss to my lips and slipped out of the car.

He opened my door and held his hand out to me. I looked up at him, my mind wondering how in the hell I was lucky enough to find a man like him. I was still getting to know him, but everything I did know made me want to find out more. Even his goofy story of how he got his road name made me eager to learn about his MC and the other members.

"Get out of the car, or I'll put you over my shoulder and carry your sweet ass into the mall."

I put my hand in his, and he pulled me out of the car. "And there comes the demanding Nickel."

He wrapped his arm around my shoulders and pulled me to his side. He beeped the locks on the car and guided us to the entrance. "Don't act like you don't like it, baby girl. I'll have to remind you in the fitting room just how much you like me telling you what to do."

As much as I was acting like I didn't want him to come in the fitting room with me, my body flushed at his words, and I hoped like hell he was able to sneak in.

I was up for a reminder of all of the things I secretly liked about Nickel.

****

Nickel

"I like red."

"Well, I like green."

I grabbed the lime green panties that looked like snot and tossed them on the shelf in front of her. "I'm the one who has to see you in them, so I'll decide."

"You did not just say 'I'll decide.' Could you be more of an ass?" she seethed at me.

I grabbed a handful of red underwear with one hand and Karmen's arm with the other. "You like my ass."

She stumbled as I pulled her into the fitting room, and I managed to grab her around the waist while I kicked the door shut. "Ass," she hissed.

I could pinpoint exactly where in our shopping trip that Karmen kicked up her attitude and decided she was going to disagree with everything I had to say. Even when I had suggested we swing by the food court to get a drink, she said she didn't want to.

She collapsed on the bench in the fitting room and glared at me. "You wanna tell me what the hell your deal is right now, babe?"

A low growl slipped from her lips. "I'm fine."

"You're going to make me fuck it out of you, aren't you?"

She crossed her arms over her chest, and I didn't think it was possible, but she glared even harder at me. "Try it."

"Does this have to do with the sales clerk?"

Her face turned bright red, and she stomped her foot. "Damn straight, it does! It also has to do with the blonde at the uniform place, and the pretzel girl who started it all."

Pretzel girl? What in the hell was she talking about? I slipped my cut off and tossed it on the bench next to her. "You lost me at pretzel girl."

She pointed at my cut like it was a snake ready to bite her. "That thing right there is the reason why every girl we walked by undressed you with their eyes then screwed you in their minds."

Oh, Jesus Christ. I couldn't help that people looked at me. It happened wherever I went, and it wasn't just me it happened to. Every member of the club got stares and random women flirting with them. It was one of the perks of wearing a cut, but when you had an ol' lady, it became a curse. "You're going to have to get over it."

She stomped both of her feet on the floor and looked absolutely outraged. Even pissed off, Karmen still looked hot as hell. Ready to rip my balls off, but still hot. "Or I stop seeing you because I shouldn't have to deal with this."

I pulled my shirt off over my head and tossed it on top of my cut. "That's not an option."

"Why the hell are you taking your shirt off?" She scooted back as far as she could on the bench, pressing her back against the wall.

"Because you're obviously going to make me fuck this out of you."

She shook her head and held out her hand to me. "Hold on there, Outlaw. That is not about to happen. What's going to happen is you're going to put your shirt on, your vest thingy on, and then we are getting the hell out of here."

My fingers went to the button on my jeans. "No. That is not what is going to happen at all. You're pissed off at me for something that I can't control."

"Pfft, you can totally control this."

I popped open the button and pulled down the zipper. "And how the hell am I supposed to stop people from looking at me?"

"Stop looking so dangerous and handsome. Wear a potato sack. Hell, wear a damn bag over your head! Or, I just won't go out with you anymore."

Yeah, none of those were going to happen. Karmen was going to have to get used to it. I chuckled and pulled my pants down. "You know what's really messed up about this whole thing? You have guys checking you out too, baby girl, but it ain't pissing me off."

"Now you are just making stuff up. There isn't anyone looking at me. If anything, they look right through me to see you. The one man that did look my way was gay and trying to sell me hair extensions."

I had noticed the guy she was talking about, but that wasn't who I had seen checking her out. "No. You need to open your eyes and realize you're a fine piece of ass that any man would be glad to have. Unfortunately for them, you're my fine piece of ass, and all they can do it look."

"Stop trying to spin this. I shouldn't have to stand by and watch all of these women drool over you."

I toed off my boots and kicked them under the bench. "Then don't pay attention to them. I sure as hell don't."

She rolled her eyes and crossed her arms over her chest. "I don't know why you're undressed. I'm pretty sure red lingerie wouldn't look the best on you."

I quirked my eyebrow at her.

She threw her hands up in the air. "Oh, who am I kidding? You would probably somehow make it look good."

My eyes landed on the pile of red fabric I had dropped on the floor. "That shit ain't never going to happen. You can buy me red boxers, that's it."

Her eyes landed on the gray boxers I had on. "You can get one of your adoring crowd to buy them for you."

Yup, I was definitely going to have to fuck this out of her. "Stand up," I ordered.

She shook her head. "Nope, demanding Nickel isn't going to make this better."

I crossed my arms over my chest. "Who am I in this dressing room with?"

"Me, but who knows how many women have been here before me."

Jesus Christ. "Karmen, stand your sexy ass up right now before I make you stand up." She wasn't going to piss me off. She was trying, but it wasn't going to happen. I was throwing her into shit that she wasn't used to, and I knew there were going to be things that were going to be hard for her to accept. This was apparently going to be the first thing.

She stood up and glared at me.

"Take off your shoes."

"Nickel, you don't have to do this."

"Karmen, no one tells me what I do and don't have to do. Now, take off your shoes and stop talking." Her mind was working overtime on a new reason why we weren't going to work.

She kicked off her white sneakers and dropped her arms to her side. "Now what?"

Fucking attitude. I was going to enjoy this. Karmen tossing attitude made me want to put her over my knee and show her exactly what attitude would get her. "Shorts and panties off."

Her eyes rolled again, but she listened to me without protest.

I bent over and picked up a pair of red panties. "Put those on." I tossed them to her, and she caught them mid-air.

"Nickel, you're not supposed to take off—"

I shook my head. "No talking. We're buying them so you can put them on." She was going to try anything to stop what I had planned.

My gaze followed her hold them out in front of her, then gingerly step into them. She shimmied them up her legs and tugged her shirt down over them.

"Shirt off." She wasn't going to hide from me.

She mumbled under her breath as she tugged the white t-shirt over her head, but I let her have her complaining.

"Bra off." She looked hot as fuck in her mismatched bra and panties, but I just wanted to see her in the panties.

She reached behind her, unhooked the bra, and tossed it on the floor. "Happy?" she sassed.

More than she would ever know. Karmen was made for me, and I was never going to let her go. She could bitch at me every day for the rest of my life, and I knew I would still be a lucky mother fucker for having her. "Yeah, baby girl." The red panties rode low on her hips and fit her perfectly. I was going to buy twenty pairs of them and make sure she wore them every day.

I moved toward her and cupped her breasts. "When we're out in public, I'm yours." She rolled her eyes. "You roll your eyes one more time at me and I'm going to put you over my knee."

She tipped her head back and stared me down. "Try me," she whispered.

Fucking fearless when she was pissed off. I was either going to have to keep her in bed or pissed off so she would stop overthinking everything. "Oh, don't test me. That'll happen, just not right now." My hands traveled down her sides, and I wrapped my arms around her waist. I pulled her flush against me and spun around to press her against the wall. "Try not to be too loud. You might get us kicked out of here," I warned.

"I'm not the one who's going to get us kicked out of here, it's going to be you. We can't have sex here," she insisted.

"We can, and we are. Just try not to moan my name too loud like you normally do. It's hot as fuck, but now probably isn't the time for it."

She smacked my shoulder and tried to wiggle out of my arms. "I can't believe I missed you."

My fingers of one hand circled around her tiny wrist, and I pulled her arms over her head with the other. "You can't take that back."

"What, are you five years old telling me no take backs? I can take it back if I want to."

I rubbed my body against her and pressed her into the wall. "No. You can't take that back. It means too much to me." I was a dick, but I didn't want Karmen to think that was all there was to me.

She closed her eyes and shook her head. "Do you know how hard it was to walk next to you?" She buried her face in my neck and wrapped her arms around me.

I had my sweet Karmen back. "I don't know what to tell you. You need to just focus on me and not anyone else."

"And what happens when one of those many women happen to catch your eye, and suddenly I'm out, and they are in?"

I didn't know how to make this woman believe me that I wanted her and I wasn't going anywhere. "You're just going to have to trust me. I could tell you until I'm blue in the face that I want only you, and you still wouldn't listen to me. You may say that I don't listen, but neither do you, baby girl." Replacing Karmen with some average pussy was not going to happen.

"Why do you have to be so good-looking," she mumbled. "And make sense."

Thank Christ, she was finally listening. I didn't know if it was going to stick, but for now, she was hopefully over whatever bullshit she had in her head. "Now that I convinced you not to kick me to the curb, are you going to let me have my way with you?"

"Jesus, Nickel. What the hell am I supposed to do with you?"

I shrugged and tilted her head back. "Let me fuck you, buy you sexy as fuck panties, and let me be me."

"I think there might be a bit more to that, but that should cover the next two hours or so," she laughed.

"You about right about that."

She wrapped he arms around my shoulders and reached up on her tiptoes. Her lips were an inch away from mine, and she whispered low, "I'm sorry I'm such a spaz. One half of my brain tells me just to chill out and enjoy whatever time I have with you, and then the other half is, well, just crazy."

My hands traveled down and grabbed a handful of her sweet ass. "Wrap your legs around me," I ordered. I lifted her up, and her legs awkwardly clung around me.

"Did you even hear a word I said?" she gasped.

I ground my rock hard dick into her panty covered pussy, and I regretted telling her to put the damn things on. "I heard you."

She rolled her eyes. "You have a one-track mind right now, don't you?"

"Baby girl, it has been well over ten minutes of me watching you standing in nothing but a pair of red underwear, and I have to say, I have had some damn good self-control. I don't know any man who could keep his cool and his hands off you like I just did." And that right there was the damn truth. I could only go so long with Karmen standing in front of me almost naked before I said fuck it and just fucked her. "Tell me you don't want this as bad as I do."

She bit her bottom lip then pressed a kiss to my lips. "I mean, seeing as we both only have underwear on and," her hand snaked down between us, and she gripped my dick through my boxers, "you are more than ready, I don't think we should let this go to waste."

"Can't argue with that reasoning," I agreed.

Her hand slid into my boxers, and her fingers wrapped around my dick. "This is gonna be fast, right?" she whimpered as she stroked me up and down.

"Yeah, but I promise it's gonna feel fucking great." I pressed her against the wall, one hand grabbing her ass, and the other slid into her panties and pushed them aside. I grabbed her hand that was stroking my dick and placed it on my shoulder. "Better hold on," I whispered.

She opened her mouth to talk, but I thrust deep inside her, and she snapped her mouth shut. Her head rolled to the side, and she closed her eyes. I loved watching Karmen when I fucked her. She didn't hold anything back. I fucking loved that.

Each time I thrust deep, a quiet moan slipped from her lips.

I had told her this was going to be quick, but that didn't mean that she wasn't going to come with me. My hand sought out her clit, and a loud moan fell from her lips as my finger circled her bud. "Quiet, baby girl, or we're going to have an audience."

She bit her lip and nodded. Her eyes were filled with desire, and I knew it was hard for her to be quiet. This was all me. I was the one doing this to her, and all I wanted was to fill her sweet pussy with my cum then beat on my chest because I was the only one who could do that to her.

"Nickel, please," she panted in my ear. She buried her face in my neck and wrapped her body around mine.

My finger flicked her clit, and her pussy gripped my dick like a vise as she fell over the edge. "That's my girl," I growled.

I thrust one last time, her pussy milking every last drop of cum from my dick. Holy fucking shit. I was never going to get used to this. Karmen made me come so hard that I was completely drained but was always ready to go again

"Holy…Jesus…that was…" Karmen couldn't even string a sentence together.

I wrapped my arms tightly around her, walked over to the bench, and sat down with her straddling my lap. "You are so buying these panties," I whispered.

Karmen busted out laughing and smiled down at me. "I'll tell the cashier to ring them up…and every other pair of red panties they have."

I brushed her hair from her face. "Finally seeing things my way?" There wasn't a chance in hell I was going to let her buy those other ugly ass panties she wanted.

"You do have a teeny tiny point when you say you're the only one who's going to see them," she admitted.

I chuckled and leaned back against the wall. "It was only a matter of time before you saw things my way."

"You have to win every now and then, Outlaw." She pressed a kiss to my lips and slid off my lap. She yanked the tag off the panties she was wearing and pulled her jeans on. I watched her get dressed while my dick hung out of my boxers, and I couldn't help but think she was right.

Everyone ends up winning every now and then, and I was lucky enough to hit the jackpot and get Karmen. I was one lucky son of a bitch.

****

Nickel

"Where the fuck have you been?"

I swung my leg over my bike and stood. Pipe was barreling down on me with a shit-eating look on his face. "With Karmen."

"Well, maybe you should answer your fucking phone when I call. You asked me to look into her father, but when I find shit out, you can't be bothered to answer the fucking phone."

"You think you can cool it with ragging on me like my mother?" I really wasn't up for being bitched at. It was late Monday night, and I was only at the club to grab a change of clothes, and then I was heading back over to Karmen's. With Cora taking up residence in my room, I had an excuse to be over at Karmen's every night.

"You think you could act like you maybe care a little bit about this club anymore? I was the one who had to fucking bring everyone up to speed with Cora being here when I'm not the one who is supposed to be taking care of her."

"She's fucking twenty-eight years old, Pipe. You really think I need to be taking care of her? As long as she stays in the clubhouse, nothing is going to happen to her."

He shook his head and pulled a cigarette out of the crushed pack he removed from his pocket. "You know," he mumbled, "I'm real glad you were able to hook Karmen, but do you think you could take your head out of your ass and not disappear for days?"

I had been gone for twenty-four hours. He was acting like I had taken off for weeks. "You gonna tell me why you were trying to get in touch with me, or just keep nagging me?"

Pipe growled and lit the end of his cigarette. "I shouldn't even tell you."

I rolled my eyes and crossed my arms over my chest. "Look, Karmen had no idea about Cora, and I'm not sure how the fuck to tell her. So if this has to do with Cora, just give me some time to figure out how to tell Karmen. She's already insecure as fuck and telling her I have a chick staying in my room really isn't going to go over well." I hated not telling her, but honestly, I had no idea where to start.

"No, she just sits in your room, comes out to eat twice a day, and that's it. She's only spoken two words to me, and they were yes and no." Pipe exhaled and blew a cloud of smoke in my face. Fucking prick. "It's about her dad."

"You work fucking fast." It had taken me close to a week just to find out that he had been tossed into the hole.

"I get shit done. That's why I'm VP." Prick loved to throw that shit in my face.

"Plus you don't ever sleep for longer than two hours."

"You wanna hear what I know, or talk about me sleeping?"

I nodded. I needed to know what he knew. I still hadn't shaken the feeling that something more was going on than what we thought. "Fucking spit it out."

"Your girl who you thought was sweet, quiet, and innocent? Well, she's got a shit ton of hell about to rain down on her thanks to her good ol' dad."

"You're fucking kidding me." I ran my hand through my hair and sighed. I knew that things with her dad weren't going to be easy.

"Seems the family he plowed into when he was drunk had a son that lived. He's out for blood."

"Against the dad, right?" I knew the answer, but I was praying that I was wrong.

Pipe shook his head. "Seems he's out to erase the whole Handel name, and he plans to start with Karmen. Her dad got wind of what was going on, and that's why he called her the other night. He was trying to warn her."

"Mother fucker." Her dad was a complete douchewad, but he was at least still trying to look after his daughter. "So this guy had connections in Winchester and got Handel thrown in solitary so he couldn't talk to Karmen anymore."

"Ding, ding. The guy's name is Ryan Morski. The little bit of digging I did on him doesn't bode well for us. He was seventeen when his family died, and he managed to escape the system since he was close to eighteen. He's been bouncing around most of his life, getting into trouble but nothing major. He used to run with a club over the border, but as far as I can tell, he left there and hasn't been seen for six months."

"What club was he in?"

"Hell Captains."

I scoffed and leaned against my bike. "They're just a bunch of wannabes who drive around on Kawasakis and do wheelies." Hell Captains were a joke when it came to the MC scene.

"I know, brother. What I'm worried about is the fact that no one has seen him in a long fucking time."

I crossed my arms over my chest. "Then how the hell do you know that he is coming after Karmen?"

"Because the fucker is done hiding."

Jesus Christ. I didn't need this bullshit in my life right now. I just wanted the club to go back to the way it was when I first joined and have Karmen be my ol' lady. Nothing more, nothing less. "So I'm assuming he has connections in Winchester since he got Handel thrown in the hole."

"Got a friend who is a guard. He made up some bullshit story about Handel taking a swing at him. From what I saw and heard about Handel, the guy has been a model prisoner and doesn't cause trouble. He was up to be paroled next month when the shit with the guard went down. Now he'll be lucky to get out early at all."

"Shit." I didn't know what the hell Morski was up to. If he wanted Handel dead, he was going to have a hell of a time getting it done now if Handel was going to be locked up for the rest of his sentence.

"We have church in ten minutes. Be there. You're going to need the help of the club if you want to keep Karmen safe."

Son of a bitch. "I left her all alone at her apartment."

Pipe mumbled under his breath about me not answering his phone. "I'll send Boink over to keep an eye on her."

Fucking Boink. He better pull his head out of his ass and keep Karmen safe. "You really think Wrecker is going to help with this?"

Pipe moved to the front door, and I fell into step beside him. "I know you don't have much faith left in this club anymore, Nickel, but you have to know that Wrecker has our backs, no matter what."

We walked into the room off to the side of the common area and took our seats. Pipe sat to Wrecker's left, and I sat on his right. All the other brothers were gathered around the table waiting for us. "I thought you said church was in ten minutes."

Wrecker grinned. "That was the longest we were going to wait for you."

"Yo, Boink," Pipe called down to the end of the long ten-foot table. "Head over to Nickel's ol' lady's house and keep an eye on her."

Boink slipped out of the room.

"Don't you think I should have told him where she lived?"

Pipe smirked and shook his head. "We already know where she lives."

Of course, they fucking did. I'm sure when Pipe was doing his digging into Handel, he found out more about Karmen than I knew.

Wrecker leaned back in his chair and looked me up and down. "Pipe tells me your ol' lady has some shit coming down on her, thanks to her dad."

I nodded and clasped my hands in front of me on the table. "Yeah. She got a call from him the first night I was with her, but I wasn't able to get in touch with him after. Pipe was able to pull some strings to find out info."

A slick smile spread across Wrecker's lips. "I think you mean I pulled a few strings."

Aw hell. "I had no idea it was you."

"It was. You know I don't like shit going on behind my back. Thankfully, Pipe was smart enough to clue me in."

"I appreciate that, Wrecker." Wrecker was not in a good mood, and I had a feeling I was the reason he wasn't.

He inclined his head. "I'm surprised you appreciate anything anymore, Nickel. I know you've been having some problems accepting where the club is headed."

I made eye contact with Pipe, and he nodded at me. There wasn't any use in beating around the bush. "I don't like the shit we have to do now. You knew I voted against it, so you have to understand that I'm not going to be happy making all of these bullshit runs."

Wrecker tapped his fingers on the table, and his gaze traveled around everyone in the room. "I can tell you right now, that you are not the only one who feels that way. Unfortunately, things are happening that we have no control over."

That was the exact same thing that Pipe had told me. "I didn't know the extent of how far things were out of our control. Pipe was nice enough to clue me in the other day when we were in River Valley."

"I can't have my Sergeant at Arms going off half-cocked when he doesn't know the facts. Just like I also don't want my Sergeant at Arms taking care of a dangerous situation on his own."

Fuck. "I didn't know that it was a situation until Pipe found out for me. Karmen figured it was just her dad trying to get her to vouch for him for parole. She hadn't talked to him for years before that."

Wrecker nodded but stared me down. "I understand why you did what you did, but next time, use your fucking head and realize that a guy from prison calling in the middle of the night isn't something to wait a week to figure it out."

Point fucking taken. "I got it," I gritted out.

"Now that we got that taken care of, you wanna hear what else we were able to find out?"

I sometimes hated Wrecker. The damn asshole knew what the hell he was doing but was such a dick about it. "Yeah," I mumbled.

"Your girl herself is clean as a whistle. Never even got a speeding ticket. The same cannot be said for the rest of her family."

I crossed my arms over my chest. "I know all of this, Wrecker."

"He's letting the rest of the guys know," Pipe chimed in.

I shifted restlessly in my chair. I didn't want these fuckers to know anything about Karmen. All this bullshit made her look different in their eyes.

"Drunk driving. Smashed into a family of four. Killed them all except for one," Wrecker went on. "He's doing time in Winchester and got thrown in solitary after he reached out to his daughter. The kid that didn't die, Ryan Morski, is now going after Handel and anyone related to him. His first target is supposedly Karmen."

My phone dinged in my pocket, and I pulled it out to see Karmen had texted me.

Scary looking biker dude sitting at my curb looking at my apartment. Do I have a sign hanging on my house for all badass bikers to come over?

A smile spread across my lips. **Only I'm allowed to come over. That's just Boink keeping an eye on you. Shit came up at the club.**

"You done smiling at your phone like a fucking schoolgirl?" Wrecker asked. He was riding my ass hard right now.

I set my phone down on the table. "Look, I can tell you really don't want to fuck around with this, so just tell me what you found out, and I'll get it taken care off." All I needed to know was where the asshole was and shut him the hell up. It was a shit hand he was dealt losing his whole family, but it wasn't Karmen's fault. He was more than welcome to go after Handel, but he wasn't going to touch Karmen.

"We don't have a problem helping you. The problem I had was you thought you were going to take care of this shit yourself. We cleared that up, and now we are moving the hell on, right?" Wrecker stared me down and leaned forward in his chair, resting his elbows on the table. "We're brothers, Nickel, and myself and everyone in this room is going to help you and your woman take care of this shit. Got it?"

I looked around the table and bobbed my head in understanding. "Fine."

Pipe opened a file folder he had in front of him and pulled out a picture. He held it up for everyone to see. "This is Jeff Sanders. This is the guard who fed Morski the info on Handel. From what I gathered, he went to school with Morski and is just doing the friendly thing of helping ruin Handel."

"A real regular saint, huh?" Slayer mumbled from the other end of the table.

"So why don't we grab Jeffy boy and have him tell us where Morski is hiding out and finish this shit tonight," Clash suggested.

Pipe pulled out another piece of paper and pushed it across the table to me. "That is his last known address. He works the graveyard shift." He looked over his shoulder. "He's sleeping right now but should be up in about two hours."

Wrecker nudged me with his elbow. "You wanna go back to doing this shit on your own again?" he jested.

Pipe and Wrecker had known about Karmen's father for twenty-four hours and already had found out more information that I had been able to collect in a week.

I shrugged and looked at the piece of paper. "There's no sense in y'all backing out now."

Everyone snickered, and I knew I wasn't going to hear the end of this for a while.

"So let's go wake this fucker up," Brinks growled from the corner.

Pipe and Wrecker looked at each other. "I told you as soon as we told them they were going to want to wreck shop and kill the fucker," Pipe laughed.

"Clash, Slayer, and Maniac, I want you three to go with Nickel and find out everything you can from this guard."

Slayer and Maniac high-fived while Clash cracked his knuckles.

"I've been looking for a reason to beat the shit out of someone lately," Clash said with a twisted smile on his face. He was one guy I didn't mind having ride with me.

Wrecker's eyes landed on me. "Call your girl and tell her to pack a bag. Until we figure out where Morski is, here is where she needs to be."

"She's not riding on the back of Boink's bike," I growled. She was only going to be on my bike. Period.

Wrecker and Pipe both laughed. "Have her drive her damn car then, just tell her to get here."

"Wrecker and I will keep an eye on her while you are gone," Pipe said with a wink.

Jesus Christ. I could only imagine what these two had up their sleeves. "I'll lock her in my room."

"With Cora?" Pipe questioned.

"Fuck," I hissed. "We're gonna have to wait until she gets here before we head over to the guard's house."

"Gotta get your ol' lady's permission?" Maniac said, and the rest of the guys laughed.

I grabbed my phone off the table and pushed my chair back. "Laugh all you want fuckers, but I'm the only one here who's getting laid regularly.'

They all flipped me off but didn't argue the fact.

"Call your woman, figure shit out with her, and then I want you out of here within the hour. Morski lives twenty minutes away."

My finger swiped over Karmen's name, and I put the phone to my ear as I walked out of church. I had twenty minutes to get Karmen here, explain to her why I had another chick staying in my room, and I hoped she didn't freak the fuck out and run.

I was fucked.

****

Karmen

This was crazy.

Nuts.

Insane.

Asinine.

I looked down at the suitcase on the bed and wondered if I could fit a pair of slippers inside. I didn't want to walk around the clubhouse barefoot. Seriously, I had seen a couple episodes of that MC show, and the floor looked none too clean.

"Slippers are a must," I mumbled under my breath.

Nickel had called me five minutes ago and told me there was some shit going down and the only way for me to be safe was to come to the clubhouse. He also insisted that I was supposed to drive my car no matter how many times Boink—what kind of name was Boink by the way?—tried to convince that it was okay to ride on the back of his bike.

He also told me I needed to hurry up and be there fast. Fast packing was something I was apparently not good at.

I was frantic trying to figure out what I needed since I had no idea how long I was going to be there. I also worried that I had to leave my place, and Nickel wouldn't tell me why.

"Come on, sugar," Boink called from the living room. "Nickel is blowing up my phone wondering where we are."

I rolled my eyes and grabbed my slippers off the floor. Even when Nickel wasn't here, he was still telling me what to do. I managed to cram the slippers into the side of the suitcase and zipped the case shut.

I had no idea what was going on, but I had to say that I had tried to pack for every possible situation. As long as during those situations I could wear jeans and a t-shirt.

"Tell me again what's going on." I dropped the suitcase at Boink's feet and slid my feet into a pair of flip flops I had left by the door.

"You might want to grab a pair of tennis shoes, too, sugar if you plan on riding on the back of my bike."

A laugh bubbled out of my lips, and I shook my head. "Nice try, but that's not going to happen. Nickel managed to warn me about you."

Boink scoffed and grabbed the suitcase. "That asshole manages to take away all of my fun."

"But thank you for reminding me to bring shoes for when I ride with Nickel." Thank goodness Nickel had warned me about Boink, or I might have fallen for his ploy to get me on his bike.

"You regularly try to get women you don't know on the back of your bike?" I grabbed my wallet off the counter and my keys.

"Just the ones that are interested in Nickel."

I bit my lip and quirked my eyebrow. "And how many exactly has that been?"

He shook his head and laughed. "Nice try, sugar."

Hey, it was worth a shot. I just wanted to know if that number was in the tens or higher. "Well, I think I'm ready for my adventure to Lord knows where."

"Just to the clubhouse."

The word *clubhouse* terrified me. I had no idea what to expect, and from the sound of it, Nickel was leaving as soon as I got there. "Are there any other girls at the club?" I asked Boink as I locked the door behind me and followed him down the stairs.

"Not like you."

"But there are girls there?"

Boink pushed open the main door to the apartment complex and walked out into the setting sun. "Sugar, I'm not sure there is a right answer here."

"It's really a simple question, Boink." Boy, did that sound weird coming out of my mouth.

"Look, there are girls there, but they aren't you. That's all I can say. There's Cora, but we haven't actually talked to her. She tends to stay to herself."

Huh? What? They had a girl living at the club, but they hadn't talked to her? I thought any girls who were in a club who weren't with a member were kind of like free range.

I pictured girls wandering around like chickens as they pecked at the ground looking for food.

"What's with the goofy smile, sugar?" He stood at the trunk of my car and motioned for me to pop the back. He tossed in the suitcase and slammed it shut.

"Just a funny thought I had."

He looked me up and down and shook his head. "Goofy as hell but hot. Totally Nickel's type."

"Nickel has a type?" Here I thought I was out of the box for him.

"Yeah, you."

Well, okay then. "Have there been ones before me tha—"

Boink held up his hand and shook his head. "You can stop right there, sugar. I'm not saying anything."

I sighed and wrinkled my nose. "You're no fun." He shrugged and leaned against my car. "I have no idea where I'm going or why I'm doing this."

"Follow me, and you're doing it because you've got it bad for Nickel, just like he has it bad for you."

"How do you know that?"

Boink straightened up and looked down at me. "Because he's moving Heaven and Hell to keep you safe. Open your eyes, sugar." He walked over to his bike he had parked across the street and threw his leg over the seat. "Get in your car unless you plan on riding behind me," he called.

I stomped my foot. Damn that man. "Not happening," I yelled back. I slid into my car, started it up, and managed to get behind Boink as he rocketed off the curb.

The clubhouse was on the other side of town, and it took a little less than ten minutes to get there. It was a low-slung brick building that was pretty damn big. The gravel parking lot was littered with various cars and trucks, but there were at least fifteen bikes parked in the first row by the front door.

I shifted my car into park, and my door swung open before I could even pull the keys from the ignition. "Took ya long enough."

Nickel held his hand out to me and pulled me from the car. "You don't really give a girl much time to get ready. I was about to order Chinese when you called."

He wrapped his arms around my waist and pulled me close. "You can eat here."

"And why am I here?"

Nickel sighed and looked around. "I got some info on your dad."

I tensed at his words. "What info would that be? Is he okay?" The man hadn't given me the greatest childhood, but when it came down to it, he was still my dad.

"As far we know, he is fine."

I breathed a sigh of relief. "So what is happening if he's okay?"

Someone called Nickel's name, and he glanced over his shoulder. "Shit, I gotta go, baby girl. You think you can get inside?"

I mentally freaked out but nodded my head. Something bad was apparently happening and me losing my shit was not going to help. "Um, yeah. Boink can show me around."

Nickel laughed and pressed a kiss to my forehead. "I shouldn't be gone long. Pipe and Wrecker said they would entertain you, but I gotta be truthful and tell you that scares me a little."

I gulped. "You're really inspiring confidence in me right now."

Boink walked over and tipped his chin towards Nickel. "Whatever she's saying about me, it's probably true."

Nickel pressed a quick but hot kiss to my lips and walked over to his bike. Boink grabbed my keys out of the ignition and popped the trunk.

Nickel roared out of the parking lot with three other guys on bikes following him. "Something bad is happening, isn't it?" I asked Boink.

He grabbed the suitcase and slammed the trunk. "He'll be fine. He's got Clash, Slayer, and Maniac at his back. Nothing is going to happen." He sauntered to the front door, and I scrambled to grab my tennis shoes and wallet from the front seat. "Wait for me," I called.

Boink opened the door and held it for me. "After you, sugar."

I ducked under his arm and slipped through the door. It was much brighter than I had imagined. I had pictured dark and dirty.

I was off about the dark, but the jury was still out on the dirty.

Two guys sat on a couch in front of a huge TV while another lounged in the corner with a lit cigarette hanging from his mouth. On the opposite side of the room, two guys were playing pool while one watched. Only one of the guys look familiar, and I think it was Wrecker.

"I'm damn surprised he let you come in without him," the guy who I thought was Wrecker called from the couch.

I looked over my shoulder at Boink, and he had a huge grin on his face. "Fucker even warned her about riding on the back of my bike."

All the guys roared with laughter.

"You can put her shit in Nickel's room. We moved Cora," someone told Boink. Cora? Huh?

"Sounds good." Boink walked around me and slipped down a hallway to the left. I shuffled my feet to follow him, but one of the guys called my name.

"Boink can take care of your bag. I'll introduce you to the guys that are here. I'm Pipe, by the way."

Oh goodie. I was about to be bombarded with six names that I wasn't going to be able to remember. "Um, sounds good." Could I tell these guys no? All I really wanted to do was follow Boink to Nickel's room and wait for him to get back.

Pipe stood and walked over to me. He slung his arm over my shoulder and pointed to the other guy that had been sitting on the couch next to him. "That guy right there is Wrecker."

"Uh, hey," I said. I waved lamely, and he tipped his chin at me. We had met at the fireworks, but it was like he was different guy in this element.

"The fucker in the corner is Brinks. He tends to, well, sit in the corner and be a bastard."

I waved and plastered a fake smile on my face while all I could think was stay away from Brinks and corners. I couldn't really make out what he looked like, but scary was a word that came to mind.

"The two playing pool are Warrior and Snapper, and the one holding up the wall is Freak. Freak is a prospect and will get you anything you need, Karmen. Ain't that right, Freak?" Boink asked, laughing.

Freak laughed, but I could tell that he wasn't thrilled about helping me. "I shouldn't really need anything. Just show me where Nickel's room is, and I'll just keep to myself."

Wrecker rose from the couch. "You can't go to your room without dinner. Nickel would have our asses."

I looked around and tried to figure out the best way to convince Wrecker to let me go. "I... um... well..."

"You think we can order something other than pizza?" One of the guys who had been playing pool yelled. I, of course, couldn't remember either of the three names.

"Nickel said to order Chinese," Brinks mumbled from the corner.

Of course, Nickel would tell them what to order.

"Hell yeah, I want some of that General chicken shit and those crab cheese things." Boink rubbed his hands together and sauntered over to the bar that ran along the back wall of the, well, I guess you could call it the living room, although I'm sure they called it something else. He was apparently back from putting my suitcase in Nickel's room. "You want a drink, sugar?"

I gripped my wallet in my hand and curled my fingers around the shoes I still had in the other hand. "I'll just take whatever."

"Oh, come on. You can't just say whatever, especially with us. Boink is liable to mix up a batch of Wopatui if you say whatever." Wrecker smiled at me, and a little shiver ran through my body. Each of the guys had an air about them that screamed badass, but Wrecker was different. His dark hair was shaggy, his eyes dark brown, and his face was tanned dark. He was handsome as hell, but I could tell that he was a bit older than Nickel. He had to be in his late forties, but he still looked damn good.

"What's Wopatui?"

Boink hooted from over by the bar and slapped his hand down. "That's it! Time to make some Wopatui, fellas." He started pulling what seemed like every bottle of booze from under the bar and set them on the top. "Boink style."

"Brinks, order the food. Get a little bit of everything." Wrecker tossed Brinks his phone. "Make sure you get what Karmen wants." Wrecker sauntered down the hallway Boink had disappeared down before. I assumed it led to the bedrooms, but I knew I couldn't venture down the same hall and find Nickel's room. Dammit.

Pipe squeezed my shoulder. "Try to relax," he whispered in my ear. He followed behind Wrecker, and I wished that I could disappear too.

"What food you want, princess?" Brinks asked me.

My mind went blank. Normally, I could rattle off what I wanted from the Chinese place, but all I could think of was rice. "Uh, rice?"

Brinks stood up and started pressing buttons on the phone. "If all you want is rice, then I can make you that in the kitchen."

The thought of any of these guys making something more than a frozen pizza was absurd. "Um, shrimp lo mien, egg drop soup, and egg rolls. Oh, and those cheesy things Boink wanted."

"Crab rangoons?"

I knew what they were called, but I didn't think that Brinks would know. "Yup, those."

Brinks wandered out the front door with the phone pressed to his ear, and I was left with no idea what to do next.

"Come over here, sugar, I'll show you how to make Wapatui that is guaranteed to knock you on your ass."

I dropped my shoes by the door, shuffled over to Boink, and sat on one of the stools in front of him. I wasn't sure drinking something that could knock me on my ass was a good idea right now. "You know, maybe I'll just have water."

Boink scoffed and continued to empty various bottles into a huge pitcher. "Water ain't an option when I'm behind the bar."

"I don't think being knocked on my ass is a good idea right now. Nickel wouldn't tell me what is going on, so I think I should try to keep my wits about me."

"Nonsense," Boink replied. "We'll get Cora out here. Try to loosen her up."

"Cora?" I asked.

He grabbed a huge wooden spoon and stirred the concoction he had painstakingly been making. "Jenkins' sister. She's here hiding out too, but none of us know why. She came back with Nickel and Pipe."

Well, that was news to me. "Oh, I had no idea."

Boink shrugged. "Not much to tell. Jenkins told them to bring her back, and they did. Nickel is supposed to be looking over her, but we've all taken pity on him and have been helping out."

Why wouldn't have Nickel told me about Cora? Unless there was something going on, and he felt he couldn't tell me. "How long is she going to be around?"

"Not a clue. I know Nickel's saddle bags were full when they rolled into the parking lot."

Hold on. When they rolled into the parking lot? Did Cora ride on the back of Nickel's bike, but yet, I wasn't allowed to even think about getting a ride from one of the guys. That seemed like a little bit of bullshit to me. "You know what, Boink? I think I will have a glass of Wapatui now."

He eyed me up. "You sure about that, sugar? Maybe this isn't the best idea."

Oh, hell no, it was the best idea I had heard in a long time. Not only did Nickel have a woman he was supposed to be taking care of, but he had also had a woman on the back of his bike. "I think it's the best idea I've had in a while. Grab me a glass and fill it up."

Nickel wasn't here to tell me what to do, so I was going to do what felt right. And right now, it felt right to drink 'til I got knocked on my ass and not worry about Nickel or any of his crazy rules.

I was getting drunk with Boink tonight. Straight up.

****

Nickel

"You've been a busy boy, Jeffy."

"The name is Jeff," he bit off.

This prick was tied up with his arms behind his back, and he was still acting like a royal asshole.

Clash grabbed him by the hair and yanked his head back. "It's Jeffy now," he growled.

Slayer and Maniac were sprawled out on chairs behind me, and they snickered. "I didn't know this was going to be so entertaining," Maniac chuckled.

It hadn't taken much to subdue Jeff. He was still asleep when we had broken down the door, and Clash had managed to get to him before he had his wits about him.

Once we had him tied up, Jeffy seemed to wake up and not shut up.

"I don't even know why the hell you guys are here. I haven't done anything to piss off the Fallen Lords," he rambled.

"Oh, but you have, Jeffy boy," Clash gloated, releasing his head. "You're fucking with one of our own, and we came to pay a visit to find out why."

Jeffy's eyes darted around the room. "Look, I honestly have no idea what the hell you guys are talking about. This is bullshit," he spit out.

Clash tsked at him. "Why are they always so stupid?" he asked us.

I grabbed a chair from the kitchen table and spun it around in front of Jeffy. I sat down, straddling the chair, and rested my arms on the back. "Do you have a girlfriend, Jeffy?"

He shook his head. "No. Is this what this is about? Did I hit on your girlfriend or something? Was it the blonde at the bar the other night?"

Clash looked down at me. "Can't we just beat it out of him? All of this talking is boring."

I shook my head. I needed to get Morski's location first, and then Clash could have his way with him. "No, this has nothing to do with the blonde. This has to do with Fritz and Karmen Handel."

Jeffy's face paled, and he gulped. "Um, I have no idea who that is."

I shook my head. "You're a horrible liar, Jeffy. If you're going to be a scheming, no good prison guard, you're going to have to learn how to lie. Watch this." I winked at Jeffy and turned to Slayer. "What job did your dad do?"

Slayer didn't even blink. "He was the forty-second president of a small island off the coast of Belgium. He was assassinated right after I was born and the island was in turmoil, so my mother decided to burn the island and move to the US."

"What?" Jeffy tilted his head. "Does Belgium even have a coast?

"I haven't a fucking clue, but you fucking believed me, didn't you?" Slayer laughed.

Maniac elbowed Slayer and shook his head. "Belgium does have a coast, you dumbass."

I turned back to Jeffy. "If you're gonna be a prick and do shitty things, you're going to need to lie a hell of a lot better than that. You know exactly who Fritz and Karmen are because I know you're a guard at Winchester."

I didn't think it was possible, but Jeffy paled even more. "I didn't know what he had planned. I thought he just wanted me to get him put in solitary because he wanted to make his life hell. I had no idea he had other plans."

"Who had other plans?" Clash demanded.

Jeffy looked over his shoulder at Clash. "Um, Ryan."

Clash grabbed his hair again and yanked his head back. "Ryan who?"

"Morski. Ryan Morski," Jeffy rambled. "I went to school with him. He dropped out before graduation, but we were friends. I hadn't heard from him for a few years, and then he called me about six months ago. He said he just wanted me to find out some info on Handel. I knew his family had been killed by the guy."

"So you thought you would just feed him all the information he wanted, right? What was in it for you?" I asked.

"He, uh, said if I told him shit, he would deposit ten thousand dollars into my checking account."

Clash whistled low and released his hair. "That's a pretty fucking penny for just gathering a bit of information that is all public knowledge, huh Jeffy?"

I rubbed my chin and squinted at Jeffy. "Something tells me you helped more than just telling him about Handel. I think you got Handel thrown in the hole so he couldn't get word to his daughter that Morski was coming after her. But you wouldn't do something like that, would you Jeffy? I mean, you're a man of the law. That would go against your moral code."

Jeffy squirmed in his chair, tugging on the binds around his wrists. "Look, I had no idea he was going to go after his daughter. Ryan just told me bare minimum details. He said he just needs Handel quiet and unable to reach out. That's all I knew. I fucking swear. I'd never help someone hurt a woman."

"But you're okay helping hurt Handel?"

He kept squirming but tried to talk his way out of getting his ass kicked. "He's a piece of shit that killed a bunch of people. Did it really matter what happened to him?"

"I see where you're coming from, but I also see that you helping Morski is in return fucking with my woman."

It finally hit Jeffy why we were here. "Karmen is yours," he mumbled.

"Ding, ding. Tell him what he's won, Slayer," Clash rang out.

Slay cleared his throat and gave it his best talk show host impersonation. "Well, Clash, he's won an all-expense paid ass-kicking, but not before he spills his guts and tells us where Morski is."

I leaned back and crossed my arms over my chest. "Tell me where to find Morski, get Handel out of solitary, and maybe I'll tell Clash to go gentle on you."

He looked over his shoulder at Clash who was cracking knuckles and gulped. "I only have his phone number. When I met him in person, it was at a bar near the prison. I'm not sure where he is staying, but I think it's somewhere near."

"Name of the bar," I demanded.

"Locke's. It's on Cram street. We met there a few times."

"You two planning on meeting up soon?" If we could set up a meeting between Jeffy and Morski, we could get the jump on Morski and finish this shit quick.

Jeffy shook his head. "He hasn't mentioned anything lately. He said I would get paid after he takes care of Handel."

Maniac chuckled. "I hate to break it to you, fucker. But you ain't getting shit from Morski after we finish with him."

I stood up and pushed the chair out of the way. "Get the phone number from him. We can see if we can get anything off of it, but it's doubtful." Clash nodded. I crouched down in front of Jeffy. "Oh, and if you tell Morski anything about what happened here tonight, what happens to Morski will be nothing compared to what we do to you." I slapped his cheek and tipped my chin to Clash.

Slayer slid up next to me. "You're not going to stay and have a little fun with us?"

I watched as Slayer reared back and punched the hell out of Jeffy. Poor fucker. "I'm gonna head back to the clubhouse and check up on Karmen. She's probably hiding out in my room wondering what the hell is going on."

Clash landed another punch to Jeffy's gut, and his chair rocked back. "I'll make sure Clash doesn't kill this fucker. We might still need if him we aren't able to find Morski."

Maniac moved behind Jeffy and untied his hands. Clash yanked him from the chair and pinned him to the wall. "That'll probably be a good idea." I clapped Slayer on the back and ducked out the door.

We were a little bit closer to finding Morski and, hopefully, would have him in the next day or two.

I swung my leg over my bike and cranked it up.

Now I needed to get back to the clubhouse and make sure Pipe and Wrecker hadn't terrified her and sent her running.

****

Karmen

"One more."

"Hell no. Nickel is going to kill me when he gets back. I'll never be able to talk to you again."

I giggled and waved my glass in Pipe's face. "This is all his fault anyway." At least, I think it was. I wasn't even sure why I was still drinking. I had moved way past tipsy and had two feet firmly planted in drunk land.

Pipe hung his head and grabbed the glass from my hand. "Fill it up, Boink." He set the glass on the bar, and Boink filled it with rum and cola.

I reached out and petted Pipe's head. "That's a good boy."

Yup, totally drunk. We had managed to finish the Wapatui an hour ago, and I had moved on to rum. "We are totally living the pirate life," I hiccupped.

Pipe finished his beer and tossed it in the garbage can. "Nickel know how crazy you are?"

I shrugged. "He appears to like it." I twirled the tiny straw in my glass. "That'll change soon." Oh Jesus. That was another thing that happened when I drank. I talked…a lot.

"Don't know why, babe. You got everything he wants and probably more. He'd be a fool to let a girl like you go."

I propped my arm on the bar and rested my head on my hand. "That's so sweet you to say." Sweet hell, I knew what I wanted to say, but it wasn't coming out right. "I have rum tongue."

Pipe smirked and shook his head. "I'm not going there, babe. I'd be sitting here dead if Nickel heard me talking about your tongue."

"Too fucking late."

My eyes focused over Pipe's shoulder and saw Nickel standing there, pissed off but hot as hell. "Nickel is behind you," I informed Pipe.

"No shit, babe." Pipe stood up and moved away from Nickel with his hands in the air. "I was just keeping an eye on her, brother."

"Your way of keeping an eye on my woman is getting her drunk and talking about what she can do with her tongue?" Nickel boomed.

"Hey," I protested. I slid from my stool and stood on wobbly legs. I held onto the stool Pipe had just left and pointed at Nickel with the other hand. "I am my own woman, so I decided to get my woman drunk." I quirked my eyebrow and ran through my head what I just said. "Fiddle sticks," I mumbled. "That wasn't right."

"You couldn't have just shown her my room? You had to get her drunk?"

"Hey again." I pointed my finger over my shoulder at Boink. "This was all his idea. He gave me his waptilatomy thing-a-ma-bob."

Nickel crossed his arms over his chest and glared at Boink. "You gave her what?"

"Wapatui, man. She liked it," Boink explained.

"Seriously, I am never leaving my woman with you guys again. I was gone for two fucking hours."

Huh, it had felt way longer than two hours. I fell back onto my stool and braced my arm on the bar. "I don't know how to say this, but I think I might puke." Yup, I was totally going to call some dinosaurs on the porcelain phone. "I hate puking," I whined.

Pipe and Boink scattered, not wanting anything to do with the aftereffects of too much Wapatui and being a pirate.

Nickel lifted me off my stool and cradled me in his arms. "Time for bed."

I patted his chest and rested my head on his shoulder. "I'm not cut out to be a pirate, Nickel," I mumbled.

"That's good to know, baby girl." The gruff in his voice had disappeared as he moved through the clubhouse.

"Are we going to have to share the bed with Cora?" Yes, I knew who Cora was, and I was more confused than ever.

"What do you know about Cora?"

I hummed and closed my eyes. The walls passing by were making my effort to not puke nonexistent. "She's staying in your room, and you have to keep her safe." At least, that was the condensed version. Boink had spilled the beans about Cora, and I had insisted he tell me everything he knew. It wasn't a lot, but it was enough for me to start wondering where I fit into Nickel's world.

"She's club business that I had no choice in." He turned down a hallway then set me down so he could dig in his pocket for a key. "Telling the chick I just made my ol' lady that I have another chick staying in my room isn't really something I wanted to do." He opened the door and gently pulled me in.

My head was swimming, and I was struggling to keep up with Nickel was saying. "So, if I wasn't here here, would you have ever told me? There was too many here's in there, I think," I mumbled. Maybe getting drunk wasn't my best idea.

Nickel emptied his pockets onto a small table next to his bed. "Honestly? No, I wouldn't have told you. She means nothing to me and is just something I need to do for the club."

"But you're not doing her." Oh hell, did I really just ask that? I never would have said that if I were sober.

Nickel chuckled. "No, not at all. The only time I saw her was when she walked out of the River Valley clubhouse and got on the back of Pipe's bike."

"Boink made it sound like she rode on the back of your bike."

Nickel looked over his shoulder at me. "Did he now?" His eyes were dark, and he was back to being pissed.

Uh oh. I might have just gotten Boink into a whole load of trouble. "He didn't say those words exactly." I felt Boink and I were pretty close, and here I was, throwing him under the bus. "Please don't hit him for me."

He shook his head and moved toward me. "You trying to make me laugh, baby girl, so I don't put you over my knee for getting drunk?"

That wasn't my intention, but if it was working, I wasn't going to stop. "If I were doing that, the thing you just said, would I be able to go to sleep? Like, now-ish?" Now-ish. Good lord.

"No, because we need to talk." He rested his hands on my hips, and I tilted my head back to look at him.

"You're tall." Where in the hell did my filter go? These were the things I normally thought but never said out loud.

"Have been all my life."

"Even when you were younger?"

"Yes. That okay? Probably means when we have kids, they're going to be tall."

I blinked slowly. "Say what?" Kids? With Nickel? I looked around, trying to figure out if we had fallen into the twilight zone when we had walked into Nickel's room.

He wrapped his arms around my waist and pulled me close. "Kids. As in with me and more than one."

"Uh…um…okay." Had the thought of having kids with Nickel crossed my mind? Yes, it had. But as soon as I had thought it, it had flitted away because how do you raise a kid in an MC? More importantly, I had no idea how to be a mom since the example I had as a mom left before I could even know her.

"Tell me where you are in your head right now."

My eyes focused on Nickel, and I gulped. "You wanna have kids with me? I don't know how to do that. I can't even figure out how to be a pirate."

Nickel chuckled. "We can figure it out together, baby girl. I'm not sure about the pirate thing, though."

I sighed and face-planted into his shoulder. "Why does it seem like being a pirate would be easier than having a baby?"

"Well, I'm sure they both involve the same amount of alcohol."

My arms wrapped around his waist. "I'm supposed to be mad at you for not telling me about Cora, not talking about babies and pirates," I mumbled.

"You can be mad at me as long as you agree to have babies with me."

I leaned back and pressed my finger to his lips. "And since neither of us are going to remember this tomorrow morning, I can tell you that I'm falling in love with you and I'm terrified that I won't fit into your world."

He swept me up in his arms and tossed me on the bed. The world swayed as I bounced up and down. Nickel threw his cut on the dresser and pulled his shirt over his head. "How drunk are you?"

The world stopped spinning, and I laid my head on the bed. "Um, I think if I don't move, I should be good."

"Guess I'm going to have to do all of the work."

I closed my eyes and heard the zipper on Nickel's pants go down. Thank God, I wasn't going to remember this in the morning. The bed moved under Nickel's weight, and he laid next to me. "Shh, my pirate isn't ready to come out and play."

Nickel chuckled and brushed my hair from my face. "Baby girl, I ever tell you how much you make me laugh?"

I cracked open one eye. "You smirk and rumble." That's exactly what he had just done.

"Well, I can tell you right now, I don't do that much when you aren't around."

I closed my eye, realizing dark was better for me right now. "Glad to be the source of your smirk and rumble." I tossed my arm over my eyes. "You think we could kill the lights. I'm past the fun part of being drunk." Gah, I couldn't remember the last time I had drank so much and felt like crap.

"I'm gonna have to move."

"Ugh, you're going to rock the bed like a ship. Try not to shiver me timbers, Captain Outlaw."

Nickel buried his face in my neck and busted up. I was apparently better at bringing out the smirk and rumble when I was drunk.

"I promise not to shiver your timbers until you sober up."

"Much obliged," I muttered.

Nickel gently rocked the bed as he rolled off. I heard him move around the room, shuffle through papers for a second, and then the room went dark. "Thank you, sweet baby Jesus." I opened my eyes, and it was pitch dark in the room except for Nickel who was standing by the desk with his face lit up by the glow of his phone. "What are you doing?" I asked.

"Turning the alarm off on my phone."

I tsked and closed my eyes. "Bikers do not use alarms." That was absurd. Almost as absurd as bikers having bad days.

The bed shifted as Nickel climbed back in and gathered me in his arms. "Baby girl, where the hell did you get your ideas about bikers?"

"You know, around." I rested my head on his shoulder and trailed my fingers up and down his chest. "But you seem to be smashing all my preconceived notions lately."

"Is that why you ran scared every time I tried to talk to you before?"

I slightly nodded my head and instantly regretted it. "Yeah," I winced.

A rumble rolled from Nickel's chest, and he gave me a quick squeeze. "I had planned on having my way with you tonight, but obviously, the motion of the ocean might be too much for you."

I groaned at his corny pun. "Only I get to make lame jokes in this relationship. You handle the badassness."

"What the hell am I going to do with you?"

"Let me sleep. Sleep sounds perfect right now." I snuggled into him and pressed a kiss to his bare chest.

"Sleep now, we talk in the morning," he grunted.

Ugh, something to look forward to.

I slowly drifted off to sleep tucked into Nickel's side, hoping and praying he would forget every word I said tonight.

****

Nickel

She was out in minutes, and her body relaxed into me.

How the hell did I get to be such a lucky bastard?

This rum drunk pirate had told me she was falling in love with me and agreed to have my babies.

If I wasn't already in love with her, you could damn well guarantee I was now.

****

Karmen

Ugh.

I rolled over and reached for Nickel but found his side of the bed empty.

Double ugh.

Not only was I hungover, but Nickel was gone, and I wasn't up to doing more than rolling over and going back to sleep.

"Scale of one to ten, how miserable do you feel?"

Nickel was sitting on a recliner in the corner, holding a coffee cup in one hand. "I'd be way better if you let me have your cup of coffee."

"Something wrong with the one I have sitting next to you?"

I looked toward the nightstand and smiled. "You're a god," I mumbled. I reached out, and half sat up, leaned against the headboard, and took a hesitant sip. I felt like ass, but not to the point of puking. Thankfully, after I had passed out, I slept the whole night and didn't toss my rum and cookies.

"I figured Captain Karmen would need her coffee this morning."

Gah. "I'm never going to live that down, am I?" Most of last night was a blur, but I did remember trying to be a pirate.

Nickel chuckled and shook his head. "Doubtful. Pipe and Boink asked me how the Captain was doing when I got your coffee."

"Jesus." Yup, never going to hear the end of this. "I bet all you did was laugh and didn't even defend my honor."

"Baby girl, your honor wasn't on the line. You somehow managed to get a road name without even being in the club." He held up his cup to me. "You just became the first ol' lady of the Weston Chapter, Captain."

"Does this mean I get a tiara?" I could so rock a tiara. Or I would even settle for a sash.

Nickel stood up and walked over to the bed. He gazed down and me with a sexy smirk on his face. Would I ever get used to the way this man looked?

"I don't think a tiara would stay on when you're riding my bike."

"I'll settle for a sash. I'd like it to be pink and say 'Badass Ol' Lady.'"

"How about a cut that says, 'Property of Nickel' on the back."

I gulped. "Uh, that's kind of a big deal, isn't it?"

"It means you're mine."

Oh shit. "Um, can I get back to you on that when I'm not hungover?"

A smile spread across his lips. "Okay, Captain, but we both know it's a forgone conclusion."

Ha, maybe to him it was. I didn't know how I was going to fit into his life when he was wild and reckless while I wanted to stay in my own quiet, little world.

"We need to talk. You wanna do that in bed, or do you want to get dressed?"

Err, I didn't want to do either, because I knew we were going to talk about what happened last night, and I really didn't want to hear what my father had done to warrant me to have to quickly leave my apartment and stay at the clubhouse.

"Um, can you take me home and then we can talk?"

"Not happening, at least not yet."

Double crap. "Shower, breakfast, and then we talk?" I was going to push this off as long as I could.

"Shower and then we talk."

"I really think I'm going to need to eat. Help soak up the leftover rum."

Nickel grabbed my cup from my hand and set in on the nightstand. "You have thirty seconds to get your ass out of bed, or I'm joining you in there, and you won't be out of it all day."

Hmm, that really didn't sound all that bad. I could distract him and avoid the talk altogether. "Does that mean we won't talk?"

"Oh, there will be talking, Captain, but there will also be communicating in other ways."

I scrambled out of bed and glared at Nickel. "You seriously don't play fair, Outlaw. Do you have no sympathy for someone hungover?"

He shook his head and pointed behind me. "Bathroom there, and I put all of your clothes in the closet and dresser. I'll be back in half an hour with breakfast, and then we talk." Nickel walked out of the room without a glance at me and shut the door.

Alrighty then. Nickel had put my clothes away. Commence freaking out in five…four…three…

A knock sounded at the door, and I figured Nickel had come back to freak me out even more.

I wrenched open the door, and my sassy retort died in my throat when I saw a tall, slender, redhead standing where I thought Nickel would be. "Uh, hi," I mumbled. Whoever this was, she was gorgeous. It was like a model had walked out of the pages of a fashion magazine, and they had come knocking at Nickel's door. This was the type of woman who should be with Nickel.

"Hey, I'm Cora."

Oh hell. This was Cora? Sweet Jesus. I looked down my body, realizing I didn't have any pants on. Damn Nickel. "Uh, hey?"

"I don't mean to bother you, and I was kind of waiting for Nickel to leave."

She didn't want to talk to Nickel? I figured most women under the age of one hundred wanted to talk to Nickel and just be in his presence. "Oh, well, he's gone." Duh, Karmen.

"I left a couple of things in here before I moved out last night, and I was wondering if I could just grab them quick."

I stood there staring at her, wondering how Nickel had managed to take one look at her and think that he wanted to be with me. She was wearing tight, ripped blue jeans, knee-high black boots, and a purple, flowy top. She was biker chic. Her red hair flowed around her shoulders, and I wondered if it was as soft as it looked. I shook my head and ran my fingers through my rat's nest hair.

Again, I was never getting pirate drunk again.

"Is it okay?"

I pushed open the door and swept my arm. "Yeah, of course. Sorry, I'm a bit out of it. Pipe and Boink tried to make me a pirate last night."

Cora smiled and walked in the room. "I've met Pipe, but not Boink. Lord knows how he got that name."

I nervously giggled and stood back as she walked over to a pile of books in the corner. I'm sure if I had been sober last night when I came in the room, I would have noticed right away that a pile of books didn't belong in Nickel's room. "You like to read?"

Cora crouched down by the books and smiled at me over her shoulder. "Yeah, it's my escape."

I could understand that. When I was growing up, I always had my nose in a book. When I had gone to college, the romance novels I normally read turned into textbooks, and now, I couldn't remember the last time I had read a book for pleasure. "Um, are you okay with where they moved you?" I was the first ol' lady of the Weston chapter. I needed to make sure Cora was being treated right.

She laughed and gathered the books in her arms. "Yeah, basically the same set up no matter what clubhouse you're in. Once the door shuts, it feels like I'm back in River Valley."

I didn't know anything about Cora. Hell, basically all I knew was her name. "You were in a different chapter?" I had no idea women were allowed to be member. I figured it was one big boy's club.

Cora scoffed and stood up. "That would be a big, fat no. My brother is the president of the River Valley chapter. I had to come to Weston because he said so."

"He didn't tell you why?" Jesus, it sounded like her brother and Nickel would get along real well.

"Yeah, you'll get used to that. Especially if you're with Nickel or any of the guys. They have the best of intentions, but it would be awesome if they could share those intentions sometimes."

This woman was preaching to the choir. Although, Nickel was trying to talk to me about what happened last night, and I was avoiding it like the plague. "I'm right there with you, sister."

"I'm sorry I was staying in Nickel's room. I was kind of thrown at him. He didn't stay with me in the room at all. He just followed behind Pipe and me, and then he was gone," Cora explained. "I can guarantee you that I am not here to catch me a Fallen Lord from the Weston chapter. If I had it my way, I would have run away to Hawaii and waited out whatever shit Jenkins had stirred up."

"Jenkins is your brother?"

She nodded her head, juggled her books into one arm, and held out the other to me. "Cora Jenkins," she said with a smile as she shook my hand.

"Karmen Handel. I wasn't expecting your last name to be the same as your brother's." Of course, they had the same last name, Karmen. "I mean, I didn't expect his road name to actually be his name."

Cora laughed. "He has a road name, but he absolutely hates it. If anyone calls him it, he punches them in the face."

"Well, he sounds lovely. I'd ask what his road name is, but with my luck, if I ever meet him, I'd probably call him that and then I would have a black eye."

"Let's just say it's worse than Boink."

And here I thought Boink was pretty embarrassing. Although, he seemed to carry the name well. "So, do you at least know how long you will be here?"

"No, but Jenkins had said in passing that I should think of it as a place to start my life over."

Wow. Something bad must be happening for her brother to say that. "Are you looking for a job? Do you have to live here? Can you get your own place?" I had about ten other questions, but I didn't want to bombard her.

"I'd like to get a job, but I have no idea if I can. I haven't really talked to anyone here because I'm so mad at Jenkins. I know none of these guys have anything to do with me being here, but I can't help but be a little bit salty towards them."

I could understand how she felt that way. She didn't want to be here, and she was being watched over by a bunch of guys she didn't know. "Do you want to hang out later? I need to grab a shower, and then Nickel wants to have a talk, but after that, I'm free." It was my day off, and Nickel was just going to have to deal with Cora and me getting to know each other. I could even see if Nikki wanted to come over. She would be in biker heaven if she came to the clubhouse.

"Sure," she agreed. "That sounds like fun. Just knock on my door when you're ready. I know what it means to have a talk with one of these guys. You could be talking for a while." She winked at me and moved toward the door. "Thank you for being so nice. It's always hard for me to make friends once people find out who my brother is. He's not exactly the nicest guy, and his reputation always precedes him."

"Well, I'm not afraid of him." I'm sure if I were to actually meet the guy, I might think differently, but for now, I wasn't scared. "Just give me a couple of hours, and then I'll find you. Nickel still needs to give me a tour, so I don't get lost."

"Sounds good. It was nice to meet you," Cora called as she walked out of the room.

I shut the door behind her and leaned against it. That was much less painful than I thought it was going to be. Cora definitely seemed like someone I could talk to and hang out with. And it was also a good thing that she wasn't after Nickel. I was already doubtful enough about dating him, if I had to fight for him against Cora, I knew I would be out in no time.

The clock on the nightstand said it was already half past eleven, and I knew I didn't have much time before Nickel came back with breakfast, and our talk would start. I doubted the man would let me eat breakfast before he started talking and telling me how things would go.

I entered the bathroom he had pointed out and immediately searched to see if there was a window big enough for me to jump out of. My hopes of an escape died when the only window I saw was a teeny tiny one above the sink that only one of my legs would fit through.

Just like the sparse bedroom, the bathroom wasn't anything to write home about. A shower stall in one corner, a sink next to it, and then the toilet on the wall next to the sink. Minimal, but everything you needed. It definitely needed a woman's touch to jazz it up a bit. Nickel was going to regret bringing me here once I started asking to decorate.

After I hopped in the shower and rinsed off my night of pirate antics, I stepped out and wrapped a towel around my head and one around my body.

"You just getting out of the shower?" Nickel called.

I opened the door and stepped into the bedroom to see Nickel set a plate piled high with eggs, bacon, and toast on the coffee table he had in front of the TV. "Um, Cora stopped by. I didn't get to hop in the shower right away." Plus, I hadn't exactly been quick in the shower. I had spent the time lathering my hair to think about what other than my father Nickel and I had to talk about. I think I might have told him that I loved him last night, but I wasn't sure. I was falling in love with him, but I didn't want him to know that.

He wasn't acting any differently, and you can bet your ass I wasn't going to ask him if I had said it.

"Oh, how did that go?" He looked at me concerned that I was about to freak out.

I tightened the towel around my chest and moved to the dresser. "She seemed really nice. She came to get a stack of books that she had left in here. I told her we could hang out together later since we are both prisoners for the time being."

Nickel chuckled and shook his head. "You are far from a prisoner, baby girl. I don't know how many prisoners have access to all the rum they can drink, and a warm, comfy bed to sleep at night."

"Good point," I mumbled. "It's more that we're here and we might as well make the best of it and hang out. You think I can invite Nikki over? She would freak out if she got to see the clubhouse and the guys."

"I don't really care. I can have one of the guys pick her up after we talk."

I tugged open the top drawer on the dresser and pulled out panties and a bra. I managed to shimmy the panties up my legs under the towel but had to drop the towel to hook my bra. "A ride on the back of a bike? Nikki will love me for life."

Nickel's eyes heated as he watched me hook the bra and pull the straps over my shoulders. "That was pointless to put on. I'm just going to take it off after our talk."

"That's what you think, Outlaw. Maybe our talk isn't going to go the way you hope." I snagged one of Nickel's Fallen Lords shirts out of his drawer and pulled it over my head.

"Now, that right there is sexy as hell." Nickel reached out, tagged me around the waist and pulled me flush against his chest. "Never seen the Fallen Lords look sexier than they do right now."

I smacked him on the chest. "We might need to get your eyes checked, Outlaw." I pointed over his shoulder at the mound of food he brought in. "Is that for me?"

"That is for both of us, baby girl. We can eat while we talk."

I pulled out of his arms and collapsed onto the couch he had along the wall opposite of the TV. "You sure are hell-bent on having this talk, aren't you?"

Nickel grabbed the plate of food and sat down next to me. "You need to know what's going on with your dad." He scooped up a pile of eggs and held it to my lips.

My stomach growled. I was apparently over being hungover and was now needing sustenance. "We're only going to talk about my dad?" Nickel stuck the fork into my mouth, and I moaned around the delicious tasting eggs. "Did you make this?"

Nickel shook his head. "Nah. Brinks was making breakfast, and I snagged his plate when he wasn't looking." Nickel shoveled in a pile of eggs into his mouth and smirked.

"So, we're eating stolen breakfast? You really are an outlaw when it comes to everything, aren't you?"

He shrugged and offered me a piece of bacon. "My woman needed to eat, and I'm shit in the kitchen. Brinks always makes too much anyway, so he'll be fine."

"Brinks is the one who sits in the corner and grumbles at everyone."

"That would be him," Nickel laughed.

"Charming," I muttered. I nibbled on the piece of bacon and watched Nickel devour half of the eggs in four bites. He handed me the plate and grabbed both of our cups from the night stand. "Eat and listen." He set my cup in front of me and sprawled out in the corner of the couch with his coffee cup in one hand.

Maybe I could just listen and not have to be active on our talk. At least, that was what I was hoping for.

"Pipe and Wrecker were able to get a man to your dad and find out what is going on. He got thrown into solitary by a crooked-ass guard."

"But why?" Whoops, there went my plan of just listening.

"You know the last name of the people your dad smashed into?"

I had heard it when I was younger, but I couldn't think of it now. "I know it starts with a 'M' but that's all I remember."

"Morski."

Yup, that was it. But why would Nickel know that?

"The only survivor of the crash was Ryan Morski, and he's got a hard-on for your dad to make him pay for what he did."

"Oh, my God," I gasped.

"Yeah. Apparently, that also includes you, too. He's trying to take away everything from your dad, and he's going to start with you. The night your dad called you, he was trying to warn you that you were in danger. The guard that was helping Morski found out and had your dad put in solitary so he couldn't call you again."

"But my dad doesn't care about me. Why would he come after me?"

"He doesn't know that, baby girl. And I think it's more your dad cares about you but he's fucked up so much that he just leaves you alone so he won't fuck up your life anymore."

"Did you talk to my dad?" I didn't know how to feel about the fact that Nickel might have had contact with him. I had cut my dad off because nothing ever changed with him. He made promises that he was never able to keep, and I was sick of being let down all of the time.

"No, right now, I can't get to him. With him being in solitary, he's pretty safe. We did have a talk with the guard who put him there, though."

"That's where you went last night," I whispered. Nickel had packed me up, moved me to the clubhouse, and then he had gone out to try and fix the problem before I even knew about it. I set the plate down on the coffee table; my appetite suddenly was gone. "I don't want you to get hurt or in trouble dealing with my problems."

Nickel scoffed and took a sip of his coffee. "If you have a problem, so do I."

"That's ridiculous. I can take care of this. Maybe if I had a chance to talk to this guy and let him know that I don't have any connection to my father, he will leave me alone." There had to be something that I could do.

"No, that is not happening. You will not have any contact with this psycho. He doesn't care if you hate your dad or not. He's after anyone with a connection to your father."

"But that doesn't make any sense, either. I wasn't there when my dad ran into them."

Nickel shook his head and pulled me into his lap. "He doesn't care about that. He feels that your dad took away his family, so now he's going to take away your dad's family."

Shit. I guess that did make sense, if you were whacked in the head. "So what happened when you talked to the guard last night? You didn't kill him, did you?" Sweet hell, I didn't know what to do if he answered yes. I held my breath waiting while Nickel took another sip of coffee then leaned forward with me in his lap, and grabbed a piece of bacon off the plate. "Gah! Would you answer my question, man?" I smacked his chest and curled my lips.

A smile spread across his lips, and he shook his head. "No." The butthead had just been playing with me. "Clash and the guys had a little fun roughing him up, but I promise, he was still breathing when they left."

Well, that was one thing that wasn't going to weigh down on my conscience. "So, what happens now?"

"Now we find Morski and have a little chat with him."

I quirked my eyebrow. "Something tells me your kind of chat is way different than the kind of chat I would have with him."

"Yeah, we tend to like to chat with our fists."

I wound my arms around his neck and moved to straddle his lap. "I'd much rather you not use your fists because I don't want you getting into trouble."

"I'm not going to get into trouble."

"I bet every person who is in prison has said the same thing before. Hell, my dad always used to brag about how he never got into trouble, and now look at where he is." It was karma that had finally caught up with my dad. I firmly believed that you could only cheat fate so many times before you got what was coming to you ten-fold.

"And every person in prison did something bad."

"Um, Nickel, excuse me if I'm wrong, but you killing Morski is wrong."

He brushed my hair off my shoulder and pressed his warm lips to the bare skin. A chill ran through my body, and I was amazed at the fact that I was talking about Nickel possibly killing someone yet he touched me and I was turned on.

"My bad isn't bad because I'm doing it for the right reason."

I rolled my eyes. "I believe you're splitting hairs to make things go in your favor."

"You gonna finish eating while we talk, baby girl?"

And now he was avoiding even talking about it. I didn't think I would ever see this the same way Nickel would. "Our talk made me not so hungry."

"Sorry, but you needed to know."

I tilted my head. "But you didn't think I needed to know about Cora until I was on the brink of meeting her?"

"I told you that was club business."

"Not sure I'm going to like this whole club business thing, Nickel. I'm already way out of my element being with you then you throw at me the fact there are going to be times where I'm going to ask a question, and you won't tell me the answer because it's club business. I think that's kind of bullshit." I thought it was complete bullshit, but I didn't want to come off as a full bitch. I was treading the line of half bitch at the moment.

"Just think of it as my job. I don't know everything that goes on with you at the nursing home."

Ha! The man was crazy if he thought that he could compare the club to me working at a nursing home. "I don't know whether to stop or to let you go on making a fool of yourself."

"What?" he smirked.

"Nickel, you just compared a nursing home filled with people over the age of eighty to your club of outlaws."

He was back to the smirk and rumble. "Baby girl, just know if it's something you need to know, you will know."

Ugh. That wasn't enough for me. "How about if I ask, then you tell me."

He shook his head. "You ask questions all the time. That really isn't fair to me."

"Fine. I promise I'll only ask if it's really bothering me. I don't need to know everything, but I would like to know before you're about to go do something dangerous."

"Why? So you can try to talk me out of it?"

I pressed my hands to his chest and shook my head. "No. Well maybe, but also so I know. Just me knowing will help me not be such a neurotic bundle of nerves."

"I didn't tell you where I was going last night and you were anything but a bundle of nerves. You became Captain of the clubhouse and made friends with Boink and Pipe."

"That only happened because I was mad at you about Cora because you didn't tell me about her. You had your friends tell me about her, and I couldn't be a bitch about it in front of them because, well, I didn't want to look like a bitch."

"I thought you are going to hang out with Cora this afternoon? Now you're mad about it?"

I poked him in the chest. "No, I'm not mad at her, I'm mad at you for thinking that you couldn't tell me about her."

"Karmen, I barely had you. Hell, I still feel like I barely have you. I'm afraid you'll get scared, or something is going to spook, and you'll be gone before I even have a chance to blink."

"Did you ever stop to think why I might react that way? I've never had anything good in my life before, Nickel. My mom left when I was a baby, my dad left because he was too selfish to think about anything but himself, and my grandma was just a straight up bitch who wanted absolutely nothing to do with me. Before you took off with me on the back of your bike, the only person I had in my life who hadn't screwed me over yet was Nikki. So you need to realize it's going to take me a bit to actually not think you're going to leave me. I mean, have you seen Cora?"

He chuckled and wrapped his arms around my waist. "Yeah, baby girl, I saw her and knew in your mind you were going to think that you weren't as good as her."

I wasn't sure how I felt about him noticing how gorgeous Cora was. I mean, I had asked him the question if he had actually looked at her, but I wasn't prepared for him to say that he actually did notice her. Stupid, Karmen. I wiggled in his lap, wishing he would let me go. I was retreating hardcore because I had managed to spook myself when I was straddling the man's crotch.

"Where are you going?" he muttered. His arms wrapped tight around me, and I knew that there wasn't any escaping.

I glanced over my shoulder at my plate of abandoned food. "I'm hungry."

"Bullshit," he growled.

"Hey, that is not bullshit." Total bullshit. The man knew me too well.

"I'm gonna lay this shit out for you right now, and I'm not going to beat around the bush or assume you know what I'm talking about."

I shook my head and pushed against his chest. "I change my mind. You don't have to tell me anything. Even if it has everything to do with me. I take it all back." I didn't think I was ready for Nickel to lay all his shit bare.

He stood up, my body instinctively wrapping around him, and he fell into to bed with me on top. "We're doing this right here, right now." He rolled us over, so he was on top, and I had no way to escape. "I'm here."

I blinked slow. "Yes, you're here."

He shook his head. "No, that's not what I fucking mean." He put a finger to my chest. "I mean, I'm here."

I gulped and felt all the blood rush from my face. "Oh hell," I whispered.

"Last night, you were drunk off your ass, and you told me you were falling in love with me. Now, you can say 'til you're blue in the face that you were drunk and didn't mean it, but I'm never going to believe it."

I closed my eyes and wished I could disappear. Dammit all. Why did I have to be so chatty when I drank? "I'm never drinking again." Yup, that was all I had to say about the fact that I was falling in love with Nickel. Hell, it was more like I was actually in love with Nickel, but no amount of rum was going to make me admit that.

"Doubtful," Nickel mumbled.

My lips pressed together.

"You also told me you were terrified to be part of my world. Why? What's so wrong with my life that scares you?"

My eyes bugged out. "Nickel, your world is all wild, bikes, and flying by the seat of your pants. Those are three things I have never had in my life. I saw what being wild and doing whatever you want gets you. My mother couldn't be bothered to stay with me because she was more concerned about where she was going and how much fun it was going to be."

"Karmen."

I rolled my eyes. "Nickel."

"I said I was going to lay all this shit out, right?"

"Yes, but I wish you wouldn't."

He ignored my request and plowed right on. "Never met your mom, and I can tell you right now, if I ever do, she'll be the first woman I ever hit. She screwed with your head so early on that there wasn't any hope for anyone else in your life. Then your father fucking up so bad that you wound up in your grandmother's lap, Jesus, talk about fucked up."

"You're not telling me anything I don't already know." My life was fucked up. Thanks for saying it out loud.

"But you're here, baby girl. You have a good fucking job, a friend that will do anything for you, and a man that will die before anything happens to you. All that bad shit that happened to you growing up left room for when you got older to know what you wanted, and you weren't afraid to take it."

"Did you forget the part where I said I'm terrified of you?"

He brushed my hair off my forehead and shook his head. "No. You're not terrified of me. What you're afraid of is giving me some of that control you've had over the past few years of your life. You think as long as you're in control, nobody can fuck you over. The difference between me and anyone else in this world is that I will die before anything bad touches you. I'm not your mother, not your father, and definitely not your grandmother. They all had the chance to be in your life, and they all blew it. I'm not going to fuck it up."

"You barely know me," I whispered. How long had I been with Nickel? A week? Two? I couldn't keep track.

"Karmen, I've known you for over a year. I saw you take care of my grandmother like she was your own. I saw you laughing in the hallways with your girl thinking no one was looking. I fucking saw you, Karmen. I saw you, and I knew that I didn't deserve you, but I didn't care. You were going to be the quiet to my wild, the simple to my complicated. You were mine from day one, but you didn't even know it. Hell, even with me saying it word for word right now, I can still see that you don't get it."

"I don't get it," I whispered. I wasn't anything he had said. I mean, I was, but all the things he said weren't good enough to fall in love with someone. Everyone does the things he said.

"Jesus, woman." He shook his head and rolled us back over so I was laying on top of him.

I braced my hands on either side of his head and looked down at him. "I'm sorry, but the things you saw are nothing. All of the nurses take good care of your grandma, Nikki laughs all of the time, more than I do. I'm not anything special."

"Let's try this from a different angle."

I blinked. "Um, okay." What other angle was there?

"Tell me what you like about me."

"Uh…um…what?"

Nickel jack-knifed up and sat. "Don't think too hard about it. Just tell me why you're here right now with me."

I looked around his barren room and racked my brain. "Well, I think you're handsome."

"Thank you."

"Uh, I like the close you are to your friends."

"They're my brothers. I would do anything for them, and they would do the same for you and me."

I don't know why he included me in that, but I ignored it. "I like being on your bike."

"I like having you wrapped around me."

"Um, that's all I can think of right now."

He rubbed my back. "You see how I didn't argue with when you told me about all of the reasons why you liked me?"

"Well, that's because all of the things I said were true."

"And all of the things I said about you were true too, baby girl. I could have argued with everything you said, but instead, I took it for what you said and didn't try to convince you otherwise."

I bit my lip and glared at him. "Stop making sense." He was right. I wanted to convince him that he didn't like me every time he told me something he did like. "I just don't see what you see."

"And I don't see what you see when you look at me, either. I'm an asshole who loves to drive my bike, and I really don't care who likes me or not. My club has always come first, but for the first time in my life, I've found something that's more important than the Fallen Lords."

"What?" I gasped. "You can't give up your MC for me."

He chuckled and shook his head. "I'm not giving up the Fallen Lords. I'm just saying if it ever came down to you or the club, I know that I would always choose you. Doesn't mean I don't care about the club, it just means I know at the end of the day, having you in my bed is better than being by myself."

"Why do you have to make so much sense?"

"Because, deep down, you know everything I'm saying in the truth."

He was right, and I hated him for that. "So what happens now?"

"Right now, you stay here with me at the clubhouse until I find Morski, and then after that, we just take it day by day."

That didn't sound very secure to me. Flying by the seat of my pants terrified me. "Um, isn't there a little bit of a plan in there?" I could give up some of the control, but there was no way I would ever be able to just go whichever way the wind blew and not lose my mind.

"You need more, huh?"

I nodded. I needed way more than what he had just said.

"I get Morski. You move back to your apartment. I come over every night. I get you pregnant and move in with you. We're probably going to have to move because, as nice as your apartment is, it's not big enough for a baby and us. I figure we'll get at least a three bedroom because I want two kids, possibly three. Then we'll ge—"

I pressed my finger to his lips and shook my head. "Stop, stop, stop. Way too much. I'm sorry I even asked." Jesus. Next, he was going to tell me what our kids' names were going to be. All I wanted was for him to tell me that he was going stick around even after the whole Morski situation was figured out.

"For telling me you needed more, you sure didn't like to hear what that more was."

"I think the talk about the more that you are referring to should be left to be handled when I'm not hungover. Please." I buried my face in his neck and prayed to God that we were done with this whole conversation.

Nickel wanted to be with me, and I was going to try my damnedest not to push him away.

Try. I was at least going to try.

****

Nickel

"Where's Captain?"

Boink choked on his beer, and I couldn't help but laugh. "She's hanging out with Cora and her girl."

Pipe nodded. "Her girl got a name?"

I leaned back in my chair and crossed my legs in front of me. "Nikki. She works with Karmen." After Karmen and I had our talk, we did a different kind of talking. The kind where when she comes around my dick and tosses her head back because it's so fucking good.

"Maybe I'll swing by and see what they are up to."

I shook my head. "Nope, that ain't fucking happening."

"What? Why the hell not? We're fucking brothers. You should be hooking me up with her."

That shit was not going to happen. At least, not with me pushing them together. I didn't need Pipe fucking over Nikki, and then I had to deal with the aftermath with Karmen. "You want her, then you make it happen, brother. I'm not going to be held responsible when you crash and burn." And crash and burn he would. I had never seen Pipe with the same girl more than twice.

He tilted his head to the side. "We'll see. She might be too much of a hassle if she's anything like your ol' lady. She came with a suitcase full of baggage."

She had, but it wasn't her fault. "Karmen is worth it." She worth a hell of a lot more than the time I had put in so far. Even when she was driving me crazy overthinking and trying to run from me, I still wanted her more than anything. "Now, how about we stop talking about my woman and figure out what the hell we are going to do about Morski."

"Well, since Wrecker let you stay in your room with your woman today instead of coming to church, I guess I better update you on everything that's going on."

"Although, it ain't much," Boink muttered.

"Jeffy didn't give you any more information?" I asked. Jeffy had said that he didn't know where Morski was, but I figured he was lying and Clash would have been able to beat it out of him.

"Fucker really didn't know any more than what he told you. Morski is playing this smart and only feeding people need-to-know information. He's not ready to be found yet." Pipe pulled a cigarette from his pocket and held it between his fingers. "We don't even know if he knows where Karmen lives. I've had Snapper sitting on her house, and he said he hasn't seen anything out of the normal."

"He's had time to figure it out. We have to assume that he's going to make a move. We just don't know when or what it is going to be." This was going to drive me absolutely insane.

"So we go back to Jeffy. Have him somehow get word to Morski that Handel is out of solitary. That'll put a fire under his ass and tip his hand. Force the asshole out, and he's guaranteed to fuck up." I crossed my arms over my chest. Until we found Morski, Jeffy was the only connection we had to him.

"Did we try talking to his old MC? If he had a falling out with them, then maybe they'll be more than willing to help us find him," Boink suggested.

I clapped him on the back. "Even though you have the most ridiculous road name, you definitely got a brain up there, Boink."

He flipped me off and shrugged off my hand. "Y'all are asses," he mumbled under his breath. Boink was one of the youngest members and had only been part of the club for three years. At the young age of twenty-one, he earned the name Boink because he couldn't seem to keep it in his pants. Now at twenty-three, he appears to have his head on his shoulders and thought with that head a little bit more.

Pipe pushed away from the table and stood. "I'll talk to Wrecker and see who he wants to send over to the Hell Captains. You wanna be in on that, or you wanna stick around here?" he asked me.

I wanted to go with, but I also didn't want to be too far from Karmen. "I'm good either way. Wrecker can decide." If Wrecker decided I should go, maybe I could bring Karmen with and get a hotel for overnight. Have a little escape from all the shit swirling around in Weston.

Boink nodded to something over my shoulder. "Your chick just walked into the kitchen."

I looked behind me and saw not only Karmen in the kitchen but Nikki and Cora were with her. "Baby girl," I called. "What are you up to?"

"We're hungry," she answered.

I glanced at the clock on the wall and saw that it was half-past seven. "You're not going to find anything worth eating in there."

The sound of cupboards opening and closing mixed with all three girls grumbling about men and having only beer and condiments to eat.

Karmen stood in the doorway of the kitchen and braced her hand on her hip. "What have you been feeding Cora if there is nothing in the fridge?" she demanded.

I shrugged. "I've been with you since she got here."

"But you're the one who is supposed to be taking care of her. That isn't very cool."

What in the hell was going on? Karmen was looking at me like she was ready to rip my head off, and so was Nikki. Cora was just peeking at us over Karmen's shoulder with a smirk on her lips. I knew Cora had grown up with the River Valley Fallen Lords and wasn't surprised by the fact there wasn't any food in the fridge. "I'll take you shopping if you want." I had no idea what was going to make her happy or set her off.

"Going shopping isn't going to help the fact that I'm hungry right now. If we grocery shop while I'm hungry, we're going to end up buying all of aisle three through nine."

Shopping wasn't the answer she wanted, apparently.

"I'll leave you to figuring out your woman while I talk to Wrecker," Pipe chuckled. He walked past the kitchen, his eyes lingering on Nikki as he mumbled "Ladies," to them. From the looks of it, I wasn't going to have to do anything to get those two together. I was going to have to have a talk with Karmen to warn her girl that messing with a guy like Pipe wasn't like being with any other guy. Pipe had shit hidden away that no one knew about.

"Can we order something?" Karmen asked.

"Yeah. Just tell me what you want, and we can get it delivered, or Boink can go and get it."

Boink glared at me, but he knew he couldn't tell me no. He may be a full-patched member, but he still was the low man on the totem pole.

"Chinese," Karmen called

"Pizza," Nikki disagreed.

"Burgers," Cora added.

Hell, Boink was going to have to run to get the burgers, but we could have the Chinese and pizza delivered, at least. There was no way in hell I was going to tell two of these chicks that they weren't going to get what they want.

"I could go for a burger, too," Karmen said turning around to look at Cora.

"Get 'em both. I could go for some egg drop soup, too."

Nikki clapped her hands together and bounced on the balls of her feet. "It can be a tour of China and Italy ending in America."

Boink and I looked at each other, both of us confused as hell. "Say what?"

Karmen high-fived her and made her way over to me. "It's like a food smorgasbord of the world." She tapped her chin with her finger. "Is there any other place in town we can order from?"

"Baby girl, you want me to order from three places for dinner. I think that is more than enough." I would do anything to make her happy, but I really doubted these three women were going to be able to eat a shit-ton of food from three places.

She pouted out her bottom lip but nodded. "Fine. But I get to order whatever I want."

Boink grabbed a pad of paper off of the bar. "Hit me with it."

The girls rattled off what they wanted, and the list was the whole length of the page.

"You want anything, Nickel?" he asked.

I shook my head. "Just from what Karmen ordered, I know I'll be able to eat off of hers."

"Now, wait a minute. I'm still recovering from being a pirate last night. I need all of the sustenance that I can get right now."

Cora and Nikki looked at each other. "You were a pirate last night?" Cora asked.

Nikki rubbed her hands together. "Here comes the kinky sex stories with Nickel. I totally thought I was going to have to wait a couple of months before she started spilling everything to me."

Jesus. If Karmen was quiet and shy, Nikki was the complete opposite.

"Yeah, totally not what you're thinking. I was with Boink and Pipe." Karmen walked right into this one.

Nikki's eyes bugged out, and even Cora's interest piqued.

Nikki eyed up Boink then turned back to Karmen. "Both of them? At one time?"

"Oh hell! That is so not what I meant," Karmen gasped.

I had to believe that this kind of misunderstanding happened often between Nikki and Karmen. "Yeah, that shit ain't never going to happen," I put in.

Nikki just shrugged. "Hey, I don't know how you bikers are. Plus, with what his name is, you can't be too surprised that I went there."

"No, no, no. Nickel had something to take care of last night, and he left me here. Boink and Pipe helped to entertain me. I drank all of the Wapatui and moved onto rum and coke."

Nikki nodded. "I totally get it now, but what I was thinking in my head was way better."

"I'll get this shit ordered," Boink mumbled. He pulled his phone out of his pocket and walked out the front door.

"Is he dating anyone?" Nikki asked, plopping down in the seat Pipe had abandoned.

"Bikers don't date, darlin'."

Her eyes watched Karmen as I grabbed her hand and pulled her into my lap. "Then what the hell would you call it that you and Karmen are doing?"

Karmen wrapped her arms around my neck, and her smile beamed at me. "Hi," she chirped.

"We're together."

Nikki rolled her eyes. "Which also means you are dating. Boyfriend and girlfriend."

Yeah, hell no. "I'm not thirteen, and I'm not trying to catch a glimpse under Karmen's skirt. I don't date, and I damn sure don't do boyfriend/girlfriend shit."

Nikki looked over at Cora. "I can see why you're turned off by bikers. They can be asses sometimes." Nikki smiled at me. "Although, that assiness is damn hot." She threw a wink at Karmen, and a giggle bubbled from her lips.

"Anyone want to play pool while we wait for the food?" Cora asked.

Nikki jumped at the chance and ran over to the table with Cora following behind her.

Karmen laid her head on my shoulder.

"You okay?"

She nodded.

"You gonna talk to me?" I looked down at her and saw a smile spread across her lips.

"Nikki kind of talked me out," she laughed. "And our little talk this morning didn't help, either."

I brushed her hair from her face and tilted her head back. "It's been pretty hectic for a girl who likes to fade into the background and disappear, huh?"

She face-planted into my chest. "Ugh, I hate that you somehow know me so well."

"If you want, when the food gets here, we can sneak back to my room with a couple plates full and just chill for the rest of the night." I knew Karmen didn't have a chance to process everything we had talked about this morning. As soon as she had woken up from a nap after I had my way with her, Nikki was on the phone saying she was on the way over, and Karmen had to scramble to get ready.

She lifted her head. "No, I can't leave Nikki out here like that. Besides, I like hanging out with Cora, too. She's really nice, Nickel."

Well, that was relief. I had spent barely any time with her and was a little nervous about Karmen wanting to hang out with her before. "Good."

"Did you find out anything more about Morski?"

I shook my head. "No. We're going to follow a couple of leads and see what they turn up."

"Is there anything I can do?"

"Nope. Just go to work and stick with me. I just need you to stay safe."

She sighed and cringed. "Nickel, how am I supposed to work with you following me around?"

I chuckled. "I'll just stay in the parking lot or with my grandma while you're working. I'd like to think that Morski wouldn't try anything at a nursing home, but we really don't know what this guy is thinking."

She sighed, sat up, and put an arm around my shoulders. "But we're safe right now, right?"

"Yeah, baby girl. There is no way in hell Morski could get in here right now."

She smiled and pressed a kiss to my lips. "Then, let's not worry about it right now. There's always tomorrow to freak out and worry about Morski, right?"

I lifted her up and had her swing her leg over and straddle my lap. "Are you trying to tell me to stop thinking right now?"

She tilted her head and smirked. "Yeah, just something I heard before."

I wrapped my arms around her, pulled her close, and couldn't help but laugh. "You're going to drive me crazy, woman."

"There is that smirk and rumble I've come to love," she giggled.

"There's a lot more where that came from," I whispered in her ear.

She pressed her forehead to mine and looked me in the eye. "I think I'll stick around to see that."

Hell yeah.

She was mine.

****

Karmen

I tossed my head back, Nickel thrusting behind me. "Yes, please."

He grunted under his breath, and his fingers dug into my waist.

This is what I loved. This is what felt so damn good that I never wanted it to stop.

"Get there, Karmen. Give it to me."

I loved when he talked to me. Telling me what he wanted was hot as hell, and all I wanted to do was give that to him. "Harder, harder." My body was tense and taut, ready for Nickel to take me to the place he always managed to. Heaven.

"Tell me. Tell me who you belong to," he growled.

My eyes closed. I was unable to keep them open as my orgasm washed over me, and I screamed out his name.

He slammed into me, my pussy milking his dick. My arms gave out, and I face-planted into the bed as Nickel held me up. "So fucking good," Nickel mumbled.

His hands left my hips as he pulled out and fell onto the bed next to me. He gathered me into his arms, my back flush against his front, and I sighed deeply.

It had been the best month of my life.

Just letting go and not worrying about every little thing had been so freeing, and it had let me see exactly what Nickel saw when he looked at me.

"God damn, that was good."

A smile spread across my lips. "You say that every time."

"I don't always say that," he protested.

"Not those words exactly, but it's always something to that extent."

He pressed a kiss to my neck then gave me a little nip with his teeth. "Don't act like you don't like it, woman. I believe you were the one who said you were going to stick around for everything I had to offer."

I laughed and snuggled into him. "I guess I did say that, didn't I?"

"Don't get too comfortable. You promised Nikki and Cora you would be ready to go by six."

I glanced at the clock on the nightstand and frowned. "Yeah, don't think that is going to happen." It was a quarter to six, and I still needed to shower and figure out what I was going to wear.

Nickel slapped my bare ass and rolled away from me. "Get that sexy ass out of bed and get ready for your girls. I asked Pipe to ride along with us tonight, too. I hope that's okay."

I rolled onto my back and watched Nickel stand up and took a minute to appreciate his fine ass. He bent over to grab his underwear, and I almost leapt out of bed ready to jump him again. I was one lucky bitch to have this man in my bed.

"You with me?"

My gaze traveled up his perfect body, taking in every tattoo that adorned his skin and saw he was looking over his shoulder at me. "You were talking?"

He did his sexy as hell smirk and chuckle and pulled his boxers up his legs. Damn, there went my view of his ass.

"I asked if it was okay if Pipe rode along with us tonight."

I waved my hand in the air. "As long as he doesn't call me Captain all night, I don't care." Pipe had taken it upon himself to use my nickname any chance he could. Hell, all of the guys called me it. It had become a game for them to see how many times they could use it in one day. Annoying.

"I'm not sure I can control you three when you're together. I see how you guys are around the clubhouse." He snagged his shirt from the floor and pulled it over his head.

"Please," I scoffed. "Nikki, Cora, and I are not that bad. Besides, we're just going out to dinner." Cora and I were going stir crazy not being able to leave the clubhouse much. I, thankfully, was able to leave when I had to work, but even then, I had one of the guys from the club with me. Cora, on the other hand, barely saw sunlight.

We had to beg Wrecker to let her out of the club to go grocery shopping with me. Nickel told me that no one was sure of what they were keeping Cora safe from, but they knew that with her being in the clubhouse, she would be the safest. Cora and I both understood it, but that didn't mean it still didn't drive us crazy.

"Baby girl, we're trying let you get out more, but we still need to think about your safety first."

I grabbed his pillow and tossed it at him. "If I hear you talk about my safety one more time, I swear to God, I am going to scream. Even in prison, my father still manages to mess up my life."

Nickel caught the pillow in mid-air and tossed it back. "Get up, get dressed, and haul your ass over to Cora's room."

"You're so bossy," I mumbled. I rolled to the other side of the bed and dashed into the bathroom. Being naked in bed with Nickel was different than me being naked just walking around.

"You know, I've seen you naked before," he called as I shut the door.

Yeah, he had, but that didn't mean I needed to parade around naked in front of him all of the time. Now, if Nickel chose to never wear clothes again and stay in our bedroom for the rest of my life, I would be completely okay with that.

He opened the door and barged into the bathroom. I grabbed the bath towel off the rack and covered my body. I was ridiculous, I know.

"You keep running away from me like that, I'll fuck you against the shower wall like I did last week." He grabbed my arm and tugged the towel from hands. "I don't know what's going on in that head of yours, but whatever it is, it needs to get lost. I see you naked every night when you're lying in my bed. Don't hide from me." He rested his forehead against mine, and I melted into his embrace.

"It's just different when we aren't in bed. Gravity and the fact that we're both so into getting off helps distract from all of my jiggly bits," I mumbled.

"In case you haven't noticed, I fucking love all of your jiggly bits."

I slugged him in the shoulder. "You're not supposed to agree that I have jiggly bits!"

His hands slid down my bare ass. "You're perfect, Karmen. Jiggly bits and all." He grabbed my ass and ground his jean-clad dick into me. The rough feel of his jeans against my bare skin drove me crazy.

My body hummed under his attention, and even though I had just had him five minutes ago, I needed him. "I think Cora and Nikki are going to have to wait a little bit longer."

Nickel chuckled and pressed a kiss behind my ear. "Tonight. Maybe you can channel your inner Captain at dinner, and we can sail the seas tonight when we get back."

"What's wrong with right now?" I purred.

He lifted me up, my legs circling around him, and he set me on the edge of the sink. Oh, this was going to be fun.

He kissed me.

Oh Lord, did the man kiss me.

My hands curled around his arms and held on as his fingers delved into my hair and held my head still as he took everything in that one kiss.

"Nickel, please," I moaned.

He ripped his lips away and rested his forehead against mine. We were both panting, trying to catch our breath. "Damn, you can kiss."

I pressed a kiss against his lips and smiled. "I can say the same thing about you."

"Shower, get dressed, and we'll continue this tonight."

I shook my head and tightened my grip on him. "No," I whined. "You can't do that to me. I'm ready. Like, so ready." It was only going to take a few thrusts 'til I was coming around his dick again. "Five minutes, please."

He pressed a kiss to the tip of my nose and untangled himself from my hold. "You know I'm not some minute man, baby girl. If we're gonna do it, we gotta do it right."

"Fine, whatever." I would agree to anything the man said as long as he touched me again.

"We can take half an hour. I know Nikki and Cora will totally understand when I tell them why I was late." I reached for him, but he sidestepped and slid out the door.

"Tonight. You'll want it even more then." He shut the door, and I was left there sitting on the edge of the sink, naked as the day I was born.

My breathing was still labored, and my need for him was still there. This had to be a joke. Bikers didn't leave woman on the edge of a sink, butt ass naked, did they? I mean, I was on display waiting for him, what more did I need to do? "Nickel!"

I waited, figuring he was just messing with me.

Nothing.

Not even a chuckle from the other side of the door.

"What an ass," I hissed. I slid off the sink and peeked out the door. He was gone.

He had seriously left me.

I slammed the door shut and blew my hair out of my face. If this was the way he wanted to play, then I would play.

He wasn't going to know what hit him when I walked out of this room. I knew just what I was going to wear.

Game. On.

****

Nickel

So far, I was going to have to beat the shit out of Pipe and four other guys who were sitting at the bar. Plus, I think there was a chick when we first walked in that I needed to add to my list.

Karmen was playing a dangerous game with me, and I don't think she knew exactly what she was doing.

Let's start with the heels. At least three inches tall, blood red, making her legs even longer and sexier. If I had known she had heels like that laying around my room, I would have made her wear them whenever I fucked her.

Now, the dress is where she started pissing me off. I wouldn't even call the damn thing a dress. It went to her knees, but the bottom eight inches of the dress was damn fringe that swayed and moved every time she walked, exposing her bare thighs.

But here was the thing that was driving me absolutely insane. She wouldn't let me touch her.

At. All.

Every time I reached for her or tried to walk next to her, she skirted around me and shook her head at me. Right now, she was sitting at the bar, flanked by Nikki and Cora, while Pipe and I sat at a table behind them.

"Everything all right in paradise?" Pipe asked me.

I glanced over at him and scowled. "I'm being punished for some reason." I knew the reason why, but she was taking this way too far.

"Ah, the wonderful workings of woman's mind," he chuckled.

"Yeah, you laugh now. Just wait 'til you finally find a woman who will put up with your bullshit for more than one night."

Pipe shook his head. "Not going to happen, because I can't find a chick worth putting up with."

"I'm sure there's a chick out there that is right for you, but you probably told her to get lost before she ever had a chance."

"You're probably right." Pipe didn't seem too affected by this fact. "So, what are you going to do about your woman?"

I sipped my beer and watched as she peeked over her shoulder at me. Did I mention her hair was flowing around her shoulders? My hand was itching to run my fingers through it, and my lips were dying to kiss her lips and smear the lipstick that was framing her mouth. She was going to pay for this when we got back to the clubhouse. Hell, if she kept teasing me the way she was, the dark alley at the side of the bar.

"I'll let her have her fun," I mumbled.

The bar had started to get busy, and people were crowding the bar trying to get a drink. Cora got up to go to the bathroom, and I tipped my chin to Pipe. "You wanna keep an eye on her? I'll stay here with Karmen and Nikki."

Pipe grumbled under his breath about keeping track of a woman that wasn't even his, but I didn't care. Karmen was my main concern, but Cora still needed someone watching her because if anything happened to her, Jenkins would more than likely kill the whole club.

The crowd to the bar crushed around Karmen and Nikki, but I was still able to see them. I didn't want to crowd Karmen too much. She had been complaining about not being able to leave the clubhouse whenever she felt like it the past couple of weeks. I was only ten feet away from her, but I wanted her to feel like she was just hanging out with her girls at a bar, not with her man watching over her.

Nikki tossed her head back, laughing like she always was. Nikki and Karmen were complete opposites. Where Nikki was loud, Karmen was her quiet. I was glad Karmen at least had Nikki the last few years. Now she had Cora to add to her group of friends.

Two towering guys stood in front of me, completely blocking my view of Karmen. "Yo, you two think you can move?" There wasn't any reason for them to be standing so close to me. They both ignored and moved even closer to each other. What the fuck were these two asswipes thinking?

I stood up, ready to knock their heads together, when I heard a shrill scream and pushed past the two idiots to see Nikki pulling on Karmen's arm while a guy in a black hooded sweatshirt pulled on her other arm. Karmen's back was to me, but I knew she had to be terrified.

Nikki frantically looked in my direction. "Nickel!" she called

The guy who was trying to take Karmen jumped at Nikki's shout and turned to look at me.

Fucking Morski.

He dropped Karmen's arm, jumped over the bar, and ducked into the back.

Karmen fell to floor when Morski released her, and she took Nikki down with her. They were both laying on the floor shocked and afraid. I knelt down next to them and gathered Karmen in my arms. "Karmen." She wrapped her arms around me and buried her face in my neck.

"I'm so sorry, Nickel. That guy came over and took Cora's chair, and then the next thing we knew, he grabbed Karmen. I didn't know what to do other than hold onto her," I glanced at Nikki who was sitting on her knees on the dirty floor. Her face was flushed, and she was frantically looking around. "Do you think he is coming back?" she asked.

Morski was long gone. He hadn't expected me to get to Karmen as quickly as I had or that Nikki would put up a fight. "He's gone," I told her. "You did a damn good job of helping Karmen."

She wrinkled her nose. "She's my best friend. I would have done anything to keep her safe."

"What the hell happened?" Pipe was looming over us with Cora standing next to him.

"Morski tried to take Karmen." I managed to stand up with Karmen in my arms. "He took off back behind the bar. I didn't go after him."

Pipe nodded.

I looked behind him and saw the two guys who had blocked me maneuvering for the door. "The two tall fuckers headed toward the door. Get them. They tried to keep me away from Karmen."

Pipe took off out the door before I even finished my sentence.

Karmen slid down my body, and her feet touched the floor. This wasn't what I had planned for when she let me touch her. "You okay?"

She tilted her head back, and her eyes were squinty, and she was pissed the hell off. "That prick tried to take me like I was a package and he was the damn UPS guy. What an ass!" Well, that wasn't the reaction at all that I had expected.

Nikki helped brush the dirt off of Karmen's black dress. "I'm so sorry I couldn't help anymore," she rambled.

"I'm pretty sure you're the only reason that I'm standing here and not in asswipe's creepy ass van that I'm sure he drives."

Nikki stepped back with a sad smile on her face. "I was so terrified that he was going to take you," she whispered. A lone tear streaked down her cheek, and her shoulders shook as a sob racked her body.

Karmen stepped out of my arms and flung herself at Nikki. "Why are you crying?" Karmen asked as she started crying, too.

I glanced at Cora who shrugged her shoulders. "I don't do crying, man. You got me why they're crying." She held her hands up and looked about as uncomfortable as I felt.

"It's like they completely changed personalities," I mumbled.

Karmen and Nikki pulled apart and looked at Cora and me like we were heartless bastards. "I just almost got kidnapped, Nickel."

Uh. Yeah. "I know that, baby girl. I watched it."

"I do care. I'm ready to rip the fucking guy's balls off, not cry."

Nikki looked at Karmen. "His reaction is probably much better than ours."

No shit.

"You two need a little more time to hug it out?" Cora asked.

I was beginning to like Cora more and more. She was going to be good for Karmen. "We need to head back to the clubhouse, but first I need to see if Pipe was able to grab those two guys." I grasped Karmen's hand and pulled her out the front door with Nikki and Cora following close behind.

My eyes scanned the parking lot looking for Pipe, and I heard him in the alley where I had planned on taking Karmen. "We'll be by the car," I called to him. I wanted to talk to the guys too, but I didn't want to have Karmen by my side while I did. There was no way in hell I was going to leave her by herself right now, either.

"Did he say anything to you?" I asked Karmen.

She leaned against the side of her car and shook her head. "No. It was really weird. He had sat down next to me, and I figured it was just someone wanting to order a drink."

"I probably shouldn't have leaned around Karmen and told him the seat was taken," Nikki cringed and ducked her head.

"Yeah, probably not the best idea, but there was no way you could have known that it was Morski," I explained.

"Nikki talked to him, and then he just turned to look at me and then he grabbed my arm. I had no idea what to do. I tried to hook my heels on the barstool, but he managed to sweep my legs out, but thankfully Nikki had a hold of me, too."

I looked down at her arms and saw that the one Morski had been pulling on was going to be bruised in the morning. The one Nikki had been yanking on was red, but it didn't look as bad. My fingers grazed over the emerging purple on her arm, and I pulled her to me. "I'm so sorry I wasn't there, baby girl." She had gotten hurt when I was only feet away.

"Nickel," she mumbled into my chest.

I pressed her close and buried my face in her hair. Nikki and Cora moved to the other side of the car and turned their backs to us.

"Nickel," Karmen protested as she pushed against my chest. My arms loosened, and she leaned back and looked up at me. "I'm okay."

"Some asswipe almost took you away from me right under my nose."

She rolled her eyes and rested her arms on my shoulders. "I'm the one who is supposed to be freaking out right now, not you."

"Karmen, I'm not going to take your safety lightly. I should have been right next to you, but I was trying to give you space so you wouldn't feel suffocated."

She quirked her eyebrow and shook her head. "I don't feel suffocated. Do I wish I could run to the grocery store on my own? Yes, but I understand why I can't right now. I was just playing with you by not touching you. It was stupid of me to try and put distance between us just because I was mad at you."

I leaned in and pressed my forehead against hers. "Do you have any idea how calm you sound right now? Nikki is more shook up than you are, and she wasn't even the one he was after."

She lifted her shoulders. "I guess I'm good under pressure?"

Damn right, she was. "Yeah, I guess you could say that."

"Yo," Pipe called.

Karmen tried to move away, but I held her close. "What did you find out?" I asked.

"They don't know shit. They said Morski approached them in the bathroom, gave 'em each a hundred, and told them to keep you and me busy."

Son of a bitch. Again, Morski was getting people to help him but only giving them the bare facts. "You let them know they almost became accessories in a fucking kidnapping?"

"They were both half in the bag and said they had no idea what Morski was going to do. I told 'em next time a guy approaches them to do some shady shit, they should say no even if it's for a hundred bucks."

"Jesus," I scoffed.

"So, what are we going to do about Morski?" Karmen asked. This was the reason why I didn't want her around when I talked about Morski with the club. I didn't want her to have to take this upon herself and worry about it.

"You don't do anything," Pipe said to her. "This shit is way above what you can do, Captain."

Karmen growled. "But this is happening because of me, I should be involved in fixing it."

"And if it was something you could handle, we would all step back and let you handle it. This involves this guy hitting the dirt and not fucking coming up." I was glad that Pipe was on the same page as me when it came to Karmen helping, but he didn't need to lay it out to her like that.

"Pipe, chill out, brother."

He shook his head and pointed at me. "I'm not letting you bring your woman into this. That shit never ends well."

"I never even thought of doing that shit."

"Yeah, until she talks you into doing it." He ran his fingers through his hair and paced back and forth.

I had never seen Pipe like this before. He was normally laid back and kept his cool. Apparently, what had just happened was affecting him something bad. He pulled a cigarette out and stuck it in the side of his mouth. He fumbled with his lighter as he lit the end and blew a cloud of smoke into the air.

"You good enough to head back to the clubhouse?" I asked.

He shook his head. "No. I'm gonna take your girl home, and then I got some shit to take care of."

"Nikki?" Karmen asked. "I thought she was coming back with us."

"Yeah, and then I was going to take her home. Don't make sense for her to go back to the clubhouse just for me to take her home as soon as she gets there. I'll take her home now," Pipe informed her.

"But I thou—" Karmen started to protest.

"Pipe is right. I think it's best if we just head back to the clubhouse and lay low. If Nikki comes back to the clubhouse, then she might get caught up in this even more. You'll see her at work tomorrow." Karmen opened her mouth to object, but I squeezed her gently and shook my head.

She clamped her mouth shut, but I knew she wasn't happy.

Karmen and Nikki hugged after we told Nikki what was going on. She looked like she wanted to protest just like Karmen had, but she was smart enough not to. She managed to get on the back of Pipe's bike without flashing the whole parking lot and roared off in the direction of her house.

"I hope you know that I don't agree at all with what just happened." Her hands were propped on her hips, and she was staring me down. "There is no reason why Nikki couldn't have come back to the clubhouse. It's only nine o'clock."

"Yeah, but you also have to work tomorrow, and I'm pretty sure you're running on an adrenaline high that you're going to crash off of really quick, baby girl. Just trust me that Nikki going back to her house was a good idea, okay?"

Karmen looked at Cora who nodded her head. "I hate to agree with him, but he's right. What happened tonight was scary as hell, and you need to listen to Nickel."

Cora popped Karmen's bubble when she realized she wasn't going to have Cora in her corner about this. "Fine, but remember that I don't like this at all." She opened the passenger door and slipped into the car, the whole while glaring daggers at me.

And she was back to being pissed off.

"You just can't catch a break with her tonight," Cora laughed. "At least she got in the front seat and not the back. If she had gotten in the back, I would have said you were really screwed."

"You're right about that," I mumbled.

I rounded the car, moving to the driver's side while Cora slid into the backseat.

Karmen didn't talk the whole way back to the clubhouse, and Cora did like she always did and blended into the background.

I had expected Karmen to have a fun night out with her girls and then take her back to the clubhouse to have my way with her, but instead, she was pissed off at me, and I didn't know how to get out of this one.

What a fucking night.

****

Karmen

I was in bed. Alone.

When we got back to the clubhouse, Cora had gone straight to her room, and Nickel had taken me to his and locked the door on the way out. He had spoken two words to me, and neither of them were words of endearment.

"Stay here," he had grunted.

Stay. Here.

That was all I got from him after I had been almost kidnapped.

Granted, I hadn't really acted like I needed anything more than that. I seriously was pissed off that Morski had even tried anything tonight because I had so many plans for Nickel after we got home, and now they were all ruined.

I had turned on the TV before I had fallen into bed and had Legally Blonde playing quietly while I plotted Morski's demise. I knew neither Nickel, and certainly not Pipe, were going to let me help, but I could always daydream of Morski disappearing or being eaten by a bear. Nickel and the Fallen Lords taking care of him was high up on my list of things to happen to him. I liked Nickel and his friends on this side of the prison bars.

Nickel was surprised that I hadn't freaked out, and honestly, I was surprised as hell too that I hadn't broken down like Nikki. When Morski had let me go, all I wanted to do was go after him and demand to know why he thought I had to pay for something my dad had done. My life was finally something more than just existing, and now some douchebag was trying to take it away from me.

The door opened, and Nickel slipped into the room. "You're still up?" he asked, surprised to see me sitting up in bed. I had turned off the overhead light, but I had the lamp on the nightstand on.

"Can't sleep."

"Adrenaline," Nickel mumbled.

Not really. At least, I didn't think it was. "Where were you?"

Nickel walked into the bathroom, ignoring my question, and I heard the water in the shower turn on. "You tired at all?" he called.

Obviously not all since I was still up. "No."

"Come keep me company in the shower."

I tossed back the covers I had pulled over my lap and shuffled into the bathroom. I was just in time to watch the show of Nickel undressing. I leaned against the doorframe and crossed my arms over my chest. "Are you mad at me?" I really wasn't sure what Nickel was feeling.

He shook his head and pulled his shirt off. "No. I figured you were the one who was pissed at me."

I had been for a few minutes, but then my anger had shifted to Morski because he was the one who had caused the night to turn to crap. "Not at you."

He discarded his boots, kicking them next to the toilet, then his pants hit the floor. "Who you mad at?"

"Morski."

"Not me for siding with Pipe about taking Nikki home?"

Was it annoying that Nikki couldn't come back to hang out with me? Yeah, but I understood why she went home too. "Not really. I'll just see her at work tomorrow."

"You gonna get in with me?"

"I already showered." After Nickel had dumped me in his room, I had been a caged animal for a bit and had tried to shower to calm my nerves. It hadn't really helped.

"Then help me shower." He turned to look at me, and his fatigue was written all over his face. While I had been pissed at Morski for ruining my girls' night, Nickel had been meeting with the club figuring out how to actually take care of the problem and not just daydream of him getting eaten by a bear.

"Need someone to wash your back?" I joked.

"I just need you."

And that's where it happened.

Nickel standing in his bathroom, the weight of the world weighing down on his shoulders, and all he wanted was me.

I was completely and totally in love with this man.

"Okay," I whispered. I quickly shimmied out of my pajamas while Nickel took off his boxers and slipped into the shower.

The water was pouring over his head when I stepped into the shower. I grabbed the loofah I had left in the shower and squirted some of the manly body wash I had bought him. He had fought me on it at first, saying that men didn't use body wash, but he still used it because I had bought it for him. I lathered the soap into the loofah then scooted closer to him.

"I almost lost you tonight, and I've barely had any time with you," he confessed as I ran my hand and loofah over his back.

"I'm still here," I whispered.

He bowed his head, and let the water run down his neck. He was stuck on the fact that he felt he hadn't kept me safe, even though I was standing there with him in the shower.

I tossed the loofah on the floor and wrapped my arms around him. "I'm not going anywhere."

He turned around, his arms circling me. "I love you, Karmen. I'm not going to wait any longer to tell you. I didn't want to scare you by telling you, but honestly, I know I can't go another day without telling you. I love you, baby girl."

I stopped breathing.

He loved me.

I had the sense of panic, but I didn't run. I couldn't run from this man anymore. I licked my lips, trying to think of the right words to say. There weren't any words more right than the ones that were on the tip of my tongue. "I love you, too. I've loved you since you called me baby girl." I closed my eyes, afraid that I gave away too much. The last wall around my heart fell, and Nickel was the one who stood inside the rubble. I was his.

He crashed his lips down on mine. There wasn't anything more to say or do than to just feel everything he was giving me.

His fingers delved into my hair, tugging my head back, and his lips traveled down my neck, scorching a trail of kisses. My hands traveled over his back, wanting to touch him everywhere but not knowing where to start.

"Goddamn, I love you so much," he mumbled.

He pressed me against the wall and whispered in my ear, "Say it again."

"I love you," I gasped.

He growled low and nipped my earlobe. "How the hell did I get so lucky?"

I was the lucky one, but Nickel's roaming hands robbed me of all thought.

His tongue touched my lips, and my mouth instantly opened, welcoming him. He kissed me deep and hard as I went up on my toes and pressed into his body.

Everything was different. It was like I was kissing him for the first time. Touching his bare skin for the first time. It was different because I was finally giving him all of me, and I was drowning in the fact that he loved me.

His mouth broke from mine, but he didn't move far away. Our heavy breathing mingled, and I stared into his eyes. He dropped a kiss to my shoulder and stepped back. "You got two seconds to get out of here before I fuck you against the wall."

It was a warning I could tell he thought I should heed, but that wasn't how I took it. Goosebumps sprung up on my skin, and I knew there wasn't a chance in hell I was going to get out of this shower without Nickel.

I wrapped my arms around his neck and threaded my fingers through his hair. "You can't get rid of me. Not with the threat of having your way with me. That's a guaranteed way to make sure I'll stay."

His hands went to my ass, and he lifted me up. "You were fucking made for me."

My legs wrapped around his waist, and my head snapped back as he pressed me against the wall and sunk into me. A shiver ran up my spine as he thrust deep and hard.

My moans mixed with his low grunts every time he slammed into me. I was in a slippery, slick fog with Nickel giving me exactly what I needed.

I arched my back, pressing against the wall. "Yes, please," I pleaded, needing more. Nickel pounded into me, his eyes connected with mine. His bottom lip was clenched between his teeth, and this moment would forever be etched into my mind. Nickel Cunningham was mine, and nothing was going to take him away from me.

My orgasm slammed into me, and my legs instinctively tightened around Nickel. He groaned loud, my name ripped from his lips as he pumped his hips feverishly. He sealed his lips to mine, his tongue mimicking the thrust of his hips. I moaned into his mouth as he thrust one last time, and he filled my pussy with his cum.

He buried his face in my neck, his breathing heavy and labored. "Son of bitch," he gasped. He lifted me from the wall, my arms wrapped around his neck, and he managed to turn the water off with his foot and step from the shower.

I shakily stood, a shiver running through my body. Nickel grabbed one of the new fluffy towels I had bought and wrapped it around my shoulders. "Dry off, do whatever you need to with your hair, then meet me in bed. No clothes," he ordered.

Nickel grabbed another towel, dried my hair, then quickly toweled himself off. "Two minutes," he warned as he walked out of the bathroom.

I stood there, not knowing what to do next. What does one do when their life finally lines up the way it should and everything feels right even if you have some crazy guy after you trying to kill you?

You dry your hair and crawl into bed with the man who was going to make everything right.

Sans clothes.

****

Nickel

Two weeks.

It had been two fucking weeks, and Morski had ghosted again. Once he had left that bar, we couldn't even figure out which way he went down the damn street.

The whole club was on guard not knowing when or where he would appear again. Handel was still in solitary, but Wrecker had been able to get word to him that Karmen was being taken care of by the club. I'm sure Handel was scratching his head trying to figure out how his sweet, straight-laced daughter had gotten tangled up with the Fallen Lords.

Karmen had stopped complaining about not being able to leave the club alone, but I knew she just wanted this to be over.

"Hey, what are you doing up?"

I looked over at the bed and saw Karmen up on one elbow, rubbing her eye with the back of her hand. "Can't sleep."

She fell back into the pillows and laughed. "You can't sleep, and I can't seem to keep my eyes open anymore."

"Just go back to sleep. I'll be here when you wake up."

She lifted her arm in the air and pointed down at the bed. "But I'd rather you be right here. I can't sleep when you aren't in bed with me."

I glanced at the clock next to her. "I've been out of bed for two hours, baby girl."

She grumbled and sat up. Her arm covered her bare chest, and her hair was all over the place. "Well, it took me a bit to realize you weren't in bed, but when I did, I woke up."

"Can't argue with that logic," I laughed.

"Are you coming back to bed or not? Because if you aren't, then I'm going to have to stay awake, and then I'm just going to be grumpy all day because I don't deal well without sleep and then Nikki is going to call you to yell at you for not letting me get enough sleep because you weren't sleeping with me."

"That was a mouthful."

She blew her hair out of her face. "You have no idea. I'm surprised that even made sense coming out of my mouth."

This was the only good thing that had come out of the whole Morski situation. Karmen finally felt comfortable to be herself, and that included telling me whatever she was thinking, whether it was crazy or even didn't make sense. "Tell me you love me." This is what she had done to me. While she was more free and open, I craved to hear her say three little words that calmed me and righted my world.

"Only if you get back into bed with me."

"I can't sleep."

She pouted out her bottom lip. "I'll tell you a bedtime story. I promise it'll be a good one." She patted the bed next to her, and my body instantly moved toward her. I couldn't say no to this woman.

****

Karmen

Nickel climbed into bed next to me and pulled me into his arms. "This better be a good story with either sex or fighting in it," he rumbled.

Ha, there wasn't any fighting in it, but it had to do with sex, kind of. "I'll try my best to make it entertaining for you." I smothered a yawn and rested my head on his shoulder.

"Why don't you sleep, and we'll continue story time in the morning."

I shook my head and looked up at him. This was one story he was going to want to hear. I was nervous as hell, but I had been trying to find the right time to tell him what I suspected, and I wasn't going to let this chance pass me by. "I'm good. At least for a few minutes."

He grabbed my abandoned pillow and shoved it under his head. "Hit me with it, woman."

I cleared my throat and plowed forward. "Once upon a time, there lived a prince who drove a magical steed with a powerful engine and super loud pipes."

Nickel's smirk and rumble came out. "Sounds like my kind of dude."

I smiled and rested my hand on his chest. "He was the best kind of dude. He knew what he wanted and wouldn't let anyone stand in his way. One day, he met the woman who was taking care of his grandmother while she was sick. The prince was instantly taken with the woman, but he was too afraid to talk to her because he felt the nurse was much too gorgeous for him." Hey, this was my story to tell.

Nickel chuckled. "I can't believe you're actually doing this," he mumbled.

I patted him on the chest. "Shh, you are going to love the ending," I promised. His shoulder shook beneath me as he smiled down at me. "So, anyway, this badass prince finally got the nerve up to talk to the nurse after months of watching her. The prince finds out there is a bad man after the nurse and decides he's going to do everything he can to keep her safe. So, he whisks her off to his fortress to hide her away 'til he can capture the bad guy."

"Probably be better if he kills the guy," Nickel interrupted.

"Hey, this is my story. If you think you can do better, you can try after I'm done. So, all the while the prince has the nurse locked in his room, he falls in love with her and has wild monkey sex with her all the time." I wiggled my eyebrows, and Nickel busted out laughing. "So, while the prince was waiting for the bad man to show his face and having wild monkey sex, something magical was happening that he didn't even know."

Nickel looked down at me a quirked his eyebrow. "Is this where the twist comes in that all stories need?"

I nodded my head yes. "So, while the nurse worked during the day and kept the prince company at night, she grew more and more tired and started to feel sick." Nickel's body tensed underneath me. "The nurse snuck into the bathroom one night and found out after peeing on a magical stick and her hand—totally gross by the way—she found out she was growing her own little prince or princess."

Nickel lurched up, taking me with him. He spun me around until I was straddling his lap and placed his hands on my stomach. "What the hell?" he muttered.

Not exactly the response I had expected, but he at least didn't tell me to get out. "Wait until I tell our kid when they grow up that the first words out of your mouth when you found out I was pregnant were, 'what the hell.'"

He looked up at me and shook his head. "Fuck."

"Even better," I laugh.

"What? No. Woman, I have no idea what to say. You're having my baby?" His voice cracked, and my eyes watered.

I tried to swallow around the lump in my throat. "I haven't gone to the doctor yet, but yes."

"I'm coming with you to the doctors. We need to make sure he's okay. We should go right now. We can't be too careful." Nickel lifted me into his arms and rolled us off the bed.

I glanced over his shoulder and saw that it was only half past four. "Outlaw, it's only four thirty, and I'm not that far along. I should be okay until I make a doctor's appointment in the morning."

He stopped walking and looked down at my stomach between us. "How far along are you? How long have you known? You had wine the other night."

I giggled and hooked my fingers under his chin to tilt his head back. "I'm not sure exactly how far along I am, but it's probably around a month."

"Shit, Karmen. You've been drinking. Hell, you had that night out with the girls where you were drinking." Nickel looked around panicked. "We need to get you to the doctor right now."

"What? Are you crazy? Put me down and get a grip, Nickel."

He stalked toward the door and shook his head. "No, not happening. Not until I know that you and the baby are okay."

"Ah!" I cried.

Nickel instantly set me down on the ground and got down on his knees in front of me. "Are you okay?" he asked my stomach.

Jesus. If this was any indication on how Nickel was going to be the next nine months, he was going to drive me insane. I put my hands on his shoulders. "I'm fine, the baby is fine, we're all fine. I think you need to take a breath for a second." I needed to take one, too.

"You shouldn't be on your feet right now. Get back into bed and get some sleep. You look tired," he kept rambling.

I pressed a finger to his lips and shook my head. "Stop right there. Don't ever tell me I look tired even if I look like I've been run over by a Mack truck. Get a grip. I'm pregnant with your baby. There are millions of other people in the world who are pregnant also, and I can guarantee, they are not running off to the doctor at five o'clock in the morning. I'm going to go lay down, and I'm going to give you a second to get a grip." I leaned down, pressed a kiss to his lips, and shuffled back to bed. The man was crazy, but his concern for the baby and me was endearing.

After I burrowed under the covers and grabbed two of the pillows Nickel had on his side of the bed, I curled up on my side and watched Nickel.

His head was bowed, and his back was to me. He hadn't moved from the spot I had left him in, and I let him be. I had all day to let it sink in that I was pregnant. Don't get me wrong, I still hadn't completely wrapped my head around it, but I had a better grasp on it than Nickel did at the moment.

I was afraid, but I wasn't terrified. I knew that as long as I had Nickel next to me, we would figure out being parents. I kept reminding myself people became parents every day.

"Can you come to bed with me?" I asked quietly. Being alone in bed when Nickel was feet away was not how I wanted to fall asleep. "I don't know what you're thinking right now."

He slowly rose off of the floor and pulled his shirt off over his head. "My mom died when I was seventeen, and I never knew who my dad was." He turned off the lamp on the table next to the chair and moved to the side of the bed. He looked down at me and brushed his fingertips across my cheek. "My mother loved me with everything she had. She always talked about getting me out of the house and then having grandchildren taking over the house. I just realized how happy she would have been to know you were having my baby."

I grabbed his hand, lifted the covers with the other, and pulled him into bed. "You've never talked about your mom before," I mumbled.

He scooted me over, stealing my two pillows back, and wrapped his arms around me. "I never talk about her."

"Why not?" I rested my head on his shoulder and draped my arm around his waist.

"It used to hurt too much to talk about her. Still does."

"What happened to her?"

Nickel cleared his throat and pulled me closer. His hand rested on my belly, slowly rubbing circles. "She just died. Her heart stopped working. The doctor said she was dead before she even hit the floor. I was in my room, sneaking a smoke, when I heard a loud crash in the kitchen. I called her name, thinking she had just dropped a pan while making dinner, but she didn't answer me. She was on the floor, dead, by the time I made it to her."

My heart broke for Nickel knowing that he had loved his mother so much and he had to lose her like that. "I'm so sorry," I whispered.

"Thank you, baby girl."

I wrapped my arms around his shoulders and buried my face in his neck. "I wish she could have been here. I would have loved to have met the woman who raised you and made you who you are."

"She would have loved you. She would have loved having a little baby around, too."

I held on tight to him, silently giving him the strength that he needed. "I love you, Nickel."

He sighed and pressed a kiss to the side of my head. "I love you, too, baby girl. Now get some sleep."

"Are you going to leave me?" I whispered. I meant to leave the bed, but my heart clenched waiting for his reply.

"I'll never leave you, Karmen. As long as there is air in my lungs and blood pumping through my veins, I'll never leave you. And that also includes right now in bed."

I smiled and snuggled in. "Best answer ever."

He rumbled beneath me, and I was sure he had a smirk on his lips.

"I love you, Karmen, now sleep."

I closed my eyes and slept.

****

Nickel

"They put some goop on your stomach and then we'll see the baby, right?"

Karmen shook her head and adjusted the gown she was wearing. Her ass was hanging out, and she was doing everything she could to wrap the damn thing completely around her. "They do a vaginal ultrasound. The baby is too small to see with the one you are talking about."

I sat forward on my hard-ass chair and braced my elbows on my knees. "Hold the hell up. You mean to tell me they're going to shove something up your pussy, and then we see the baby?"

Karmen laughed. "In very basic terms, yes."

Holy hell. What in the hell had I signed up for? I knew I was going to see a baby pushed out of her vagina eventually, but I wasn't prepared for the good ol' doc to get so up close and personal today. "Is this normal?"

"I'm not an OB nurse, but from what I know, yes, this is normal. Every time I come to the doctor from now on, they'll do a vaginal exam to make sure everything is okay."

The door to our exam room opened, and a chick wearing fancy clothes and a white doctor coat walked into the room. "Hi. I'm Dr. Krane." She held her hand out first to Karmen and then to me. "So, we're pregnant," she sang out while she pulled out Karmen's file and sat down on the rolling chair next to the bed.

"The test results came back positive?" Karmen asked.

"Yup, you definitely have a baby on board. Congratulations!"

Have you ever felt like the floor was falling out from under you, but you floated away, not feeling anything? That was where I was. Floating around because I was going to be a dad. Karmen would forever be tied to me with the little baby she was growing in her belly.

I buried my face in my hands and tried to get a grip. It had been four days since Karmen told me she was pregnant. I thought that I had a grip on this shit, but the doctor had blown all of that away by cementing in the fact that I was going to be a dad.

"Um, is everything okay?" I heard the doctor ask.

"Oh yeah," Karmen laughed. "He's still getting over the shock of having a baby."

"Well, he'll have at least eight months to get used to it from what you said about missing your period for a few weeks. Plenty of time to get all of those nerves and jitters out."

I didn't have nerves and jitters.

I was happy as hell and kept wondering how in the hell I got so lucky.

"So, I'm going to do a little exam, make sure everything looks good, and then we can get down to the fun of seeing the little guy and hopefully hearing his heartbeat."

My headshot up. "We get to hear him?" Karmen hadn't mentioned anything about hearing him.

The doctor smiled, and she stood. "Yes, as long as he works with us and doesn't try to hide, you'll be able to hear his strong heartbeat." She told Karmen to lay back on the exam table and started checking her over.

The next thing I knew, she was yanking out these stirrup things on the table, telling Karmen to put her heels in them and to lay down. As soon as she laid down, the doc pulled over a small cart, whipped out a wand thingy, and then she was shoving the damn thing up Karmen's hoo-ha. I shifted uncomfortably in my chair, not really down with watching this.

"You can go up by her head if you want. That way, I can turn the screen so you both can see it."

I jumped up from my chair and stood at the head of the exam table. Thank God. Karmen grabbed my hand and groaned a little bit.

"You all right?"

She bit her bottom lip and grimaced. "Yeah, just weird."

"Just a little bit more pressure, and then we'll be there."

I didn't know we were on a journey through Karmen's vagina. "It's okay, baby girl." I brushed her hair off her forehead and pressed a kiss to her temple.

She looked up at me with a weak smile. "Bet you didn't expect this, did you?"

I chuckled and shook my head. "Not at all."

"Sorry," she whispered.

"I take it this is a first for you two?" We both nodded. "All right. Why don't you two have a look at your baby then." She turned the cart toward us, and we both eagerly looked at the small screen.

My head tilted to the left and then the right, trying to figure out where exactly the kid was. Thankfully, the doctor took pity on me and pointed out a blurb that was apparently the baby. I had to take her word for it because honestly, I didn't know what I was looking out.

"Now for the heartbeat." She flipped a couple of switches, and then there was a steady beat coming from the screen.

Karmen clapped her hand over her mouth and burst into tears. "That's him?" she gasped.

"Or her," the doctor beamed. "You won't be able to find out a for a bit if it's a boy or girl, but from everything I've seen today, I can say the baby is healthy and doing good. We'll have you go up to the third floor for some imaging so we can figure out exactly when your due date is."

I held my breath, memorizing the sound of the baby's heartbeat.

Karmen asked questions, but all I could do was stare at the screen and listen to the little life that Karmen and I had made.

The doc slowly took the wand out then packed up the cart. "I'll have you make an appointment to come back in next month just for a check-up and to go over any questions you have." She nodded to both of us, congratulated us again, and then she was gone.

Karmen slowly sat up and pushed down the paper gown. "Are you okay?"

I blinked slowly and delved my fingers into her hair. "You're having my baby," I said stupidly.

A huge smile spread across her lips. "I sure am."

****

Karmen

I held the tiny picture in my hand and couldn't stop looking at it.

After we finished up with the doctor, we went to make an appointment for an ultrasound and found out if we hurried to the third floor, they could fit us in right away.

So, after slipping into my second paper gown of the day and laying on a hard-ass exam table, I got to see our baby again.

"So how accurate is that due date?" Nickel asked as he pulled out of the hospital parking lot.

"I think it's pretty spot-on. The second week of January, you and I will be parents as long as this little bean doesn't decide to take up residence any longer."

Nickel laughed. "And if he does, are you going to serve him with eviction papers?"

I rubbed my belly and rested my head against the headrest. "He's good in there for now. Ask me again in seven months when I look like an elephant and am probably uncomfortable as hell."

"You make it sound so fun, baby girl."

I laughed and turned to look at him. "I really have no idea how this is going to go. Is it strange that I'm excited to get as big as a house?"

Nickel glanced over. "Probably not exactly what most women look forward to, but whatever makes ya happy."

And I was happy.

So damn happy that I was terrified something bad was coming.

****

Nickel

"Nikki is coming over after work, and I need to stop and get gas. I should have done it this morning, but someone decided fooling around was more important than putting gas in my car."

I chuckled low and held the phone to my ear with my shoulder. "Don't act like you didn't like it."

"I didn't say I didn't like it, I just said it messed up my plans a bit."

"Well, get gas and come on home. I should be back to the clubhouse in twenty minutes." Unfortunately, I had drawn the short straw and had to go on a run to do some dirty work for River Valley.

"Is there anything you need? I've been craving some Twizzlers all day, so I think I'll grab some when I'm at the gas station."

I knew exactly what that meant. "You mean you're going to buy every package they have, right?"

Her laugh rang through the phone, and I missed her like hell. It had only been eight hours since I had last seen her, but it had been eight hours too long. "You know me so well, Outlaw."

"Just keep Boink close by, okay?" It had been over three weeks since Morski had tried to grab Karmen, but we still knew that he was out there.

"Will do. I'll make him pump gas."

"You do that, baby girl. I love you."

Her voice softened. "I love you, too, handsome. See you soon."

I disconnected the call and shoved my phone in my pocket.

"Everything okay?" Pipe asked me.

"All good, brother. Karmen just has one stop, and then she'll be home. We'll probably be pulling into the parking lot the same time she does."

Pipe flicked the butt of his cigarette to the ground. He snuffed it out with the toe of his boot then swung his leg over his bike.

"Nikki is coming over tonight."

Pipe shrugged. "Good for her."

I twisted at the waist and looked at Pipe. "You wanna tell me why you get a stick up your ass whenever someone mentions Nikki or when she comes over?"

He cranked up his bike and shook his head. He revved the engine and shouted, "Don't know what the fuck you're talking about."

Yeah, right. He knew exactly what I was talking about, but he wasn't telling anyone what the hell was going on in his head. Pipe probably didn't even know what the hell was going on.

A shit-eating smile spread across his lips. "Let's get you home to Captain."

Fucking prick. Karmen was never going to live that shit down. If these guys had their way, they were probably going to teach our kid to call her Captain instead of Mommy.

I cranked the key on my bike and shook my head. "You know that drives her crazy," I called over the roar of my engine.

Pipe shrugged and didn't give a fuck. "Head it home." He merged onto the road from the shoulder, and I followed behind.

Pipe and the guys may act like I was a sucker and pussy-whipped, but I knew they were jealous of the fact that I had found my forever and they were still out there chasing around stray pussy.

I had found my home, and I wasn't going to let it go.

****

Karmen

"You want anything?"

Boink shook his head and stuck the nozzle into my gas tank. "Nah, Captain. Just wait for me to go in, though."

I scoffed and grabbed my purse out of the car. "It's twenty feet away, Boink, no one is in the gas station, and you'll be able to see me the whole time. I had told Nickel I would be home in twenty minutes, and that was eighteen minutes ago." There was no way in hell we were going to be home when I had said I would be.

"Captain, just damn well wait for me," he insisted.

"You know, I totally would have listened to you if you hadn't called me Captain. Now, I'm totally going to get

Twizzlers, and there isn't damn thing you can do to stop me," I called.

Boink called my name, but I didn't stop as I skipped into the gas station. Even when I didn't have Nickel with me, I still had some overbearing biker as a shadow who always needed to be in control. I swear, that was part of the criteria to be part of the Fallen Lords.

"Hey," I called to the clerk. He absently waved to me with his head bowed looking at a magazine.

I beelined to the candy aisle and had a hell of a time figuring out what to buy. I knew I had said that I wanted Twizzlers, but when I had a five-tiered candy display in front of me, I had to grab a little bit of variety on top of those delicious licorice whips.

The bell above the door dinged, and I figured it was Boink coming to check on me. I was mesmerized by all of the candy and already had five things in my hand when he came to stand next to me. My head was down as I tried to finally decide between Nerds and Sweet Tarts. "You decide, I can't." I grabbed both and held them up to him.

"Scream, and I will kill you."

The blood drained from my face, and my legs became Jell-O. I gulped around the lump in my throat and looked him directly in the eye. "Morski?" I whispered.

A sick, twisted grin spread across his lips. "I see my reputation precedes me. I bet your biker has been crazy looking for me."

I stood there, frozen.

Morski glanced out the window at the gas pumps. "Drop the fucking candy and move to the back of the store."

Out of the corner of my eye, I saw Boink hang up the gas hose and knew he would be in the store in thirty seconds.

The bell above the door jingled again, and another customer walked in. "Make one noise, and I kill you right here." Morski moved closer to me then something stabbed me in the side. I heard the click of gun and knew nothing was going to stop him this time.

The customer who had walked in moved two aisles over from us and grabbed two cases of beer out of the cooler. He looked at us, his eyes traveling over Morski and me.

The bell again rang over the door, and I knew that this was my only chance. Morski glanced at Boink who had walked through the front door, and I screamed at the top of my lungs. I chucked the candy in Morski's face and dove for cover. Gunfire whizzed all around me, and I covered my head with my arms. I managed to crawl to the other side of the aisle I was in and away from Morski.

"Stay down!" someone hollered.

Well, duh. I sure as hell wasn't going to stand up and stroll out to my car.

The gunfire stopped, and I peeked through my arms over my head to see the guy who had come in to buy beer now had a gun in his hand and had it pointed in the direction where Morski had been standing. Did everyone have a gun but me?

Beer guy turned toward the front of the store where Boink had been standing. "Lady, you with the biker guy, or do I need to shoot him, too?"

"Karmen, you good, Captain?" Boink called.

"Dammit, Boink. You call me Karmen and then Captain? You think you could drop the Captain in a shootout?" I hollered back.

"I'm going to assume she's with you and put my gun down," beer guy put in.

I watched as he slowly lowered his gun then moved past me over to where Morski had been. Now I had to figure out what to do. Morski had to be down, or he managed to escape again. I got on my feet but stayed low and scurried to the front door. I glanced to the back of the store where Morski had been and saw him sprawled out on the floor in a pool of blood.

Beer guy had his phone to his ear, and he was barking into it to get a shit ton of squad cars to the gas station. He threw a wink at me and turned the phone away from his mouth. "I'm a cop. You two get outside, and I'll check on the guy in the back."

Boink scooped me up in his arms and carried me out the front door.

"My store!" the clerk behind the counter exclaimed as Boink walked past him.

"Be glad you're alive, numb nuts," Boink barked at him.

He stalked across the parking lot straight to my car and set me down next to it. "Stay. Here. Listen for one time in your damn life, Karmen." His lips were downturned, and he ran a hand through his hair. "Nickel is going to fucking kill me." He pulled his phone out of his pocket and made his way back to the gas station.

"Boink," I called, "what about Morski?"

"He's dead, Karmen. No thanks to me, which is going to make Nickel kill me even more."

I grimaced and leaned against the car. "I'll, uh, just stay here," I mumbled.

Boink threw his hand in the air and mumbled under his breath, "Now she fucking listens."

I closed my eyes and bowed my head.

My hands shook.

Hell, my whole body was shaking.

Nothing like being part of a shootout to get the adrenaline going.

Boink was right. Nickel was going to kill him, and then I had no idea what he was going to do to me.

I lifted my head and opened my eyes. My lunch swam around in my stomach, and I got light-headed. My eyes slammed shut again, and I slouched down, leaning against the car.

Shit. Nickel was going to be so mad.

****

Nickel

"Where is she?"

"Sir, we're going to have to ask you to calm down."

I shook my head at the cop and pointed to the gas station. "Where the hell is my woman?" I demanded.

I was on edge. Hell, I was over the fucking edge, and all I wanted was to see Karmen and make sure she was okay. Boink had called me, calm as could fucking be, with the first words out of his mouth, "She's fine." Then he proceeded to tell me "she" had been in a fucking shootout at the gas station.

"Yo, Nickel." I spun around and saw Boink appear from behind the ambulance I had walked by.

Pipe caught up to me and patted me on the shoulder. "Go to your woman, brother. Send Boink over. I'm going to need him to give me a rundown on what the hell went down."

I nodded and watched Boink disappear behind the ambulance.

I jogged over to him and instantly demanded, "Where is she?"

Boink pointed to the ambulance. "She's in there. Nothing happened to her in the gas station. It was after when she was standing next to her car that she got light-headed and puked. She just got in the ambulance a couple of minutes ago."

My heart stopped in my chest, and my world tilted on its axis. I numbly walked around to the back of the ambulance where the doors were open. Karmen was laying on a stretcher, two paramedics over her body hooking up an IV while her eyes were closed, and she laid there listless.

"Karmen," I croaked.

Her eyes popped open, and she lifted her head to look at me. "Nickel," she sighed.

"Karmen, what are you doing?"

She looked up at the paramedic then down at me. "I didn't really feel like driving anymore, so I called these guys for a lift."

Boink laughed behind me, and I couldn't help but smile. "This doesn't really fit in with your whole shy and quiet act, Captain."

She sighed and laid her head down. "Yeah, but I figured shy and quiet doesn't really fit with the name Captain."

"Not really," I mumbled. I cleared my throat. "Baby girl," I called. She raised her head again and looked at me. "You need to tell me what the hell is going on right now before I lose my shit." I had a tight clamp on my control, but it was about to fucking explode if no one told me what was happening.

"I'm dehydrated. I puked, and it's all in my hair."

"You can ride along with us, sir. We're going to transport her just to make sure she and the baby are fine."

"Baby?"

I looked over my shoulder at Boink who looked surprised as hell. "Keep that shit to yourself."

"I ain't saying shit," he promised.

One of the paramedics moved to the driver's seat while the other sat on a bench next to Karmen. I moved into the ambulance and sat on the other side of her.

Boink slammed the doors shut and pounded on them. I hadn't told him to talk to Pipe, but I knew he would head over to him.

Karmen's eyes were closed again, and she was back to scaring the hell out of me. "Baby girl." I grabbed her hand, and her fingers tighten around mine.

"Puking is so exhausting," she mumbled. "I think I'm going to take a nap on the way."

I looked up at the paramedic who shrugged. "If I could take a nap right now too, I totally would," he mumbled.

"She's okay to do that?" I asked.

"No reason for her not to. We've got her hooked up to the monitors and everything looks fine. We're just taking her in for a checkup since she isn't very far along."

"But she's fine, right?" I insisted.

"I can't say anything for one hundred percent, but the fact we're not running lights and sirens should help calm you down."

I nodded, understanding that Karmen was going to be okay.

She lightly snored next to me, and I couldn't help but laugh at the fact that not only had she been in a shootout and now an ambulance ride, and she was sleeping like nothing had happened.

I grasped her hand with both of mine and bowed my head. She was going to be fine, and Morski was no longer a threat. Life was going to go back to normal. Well, at least as normal as it could be.

****

Karmen

I was going to kick him. Right in the balls. One shot. It would make me feel better, and he would probably shut up for a few minutes. Win, win.

"Lay back down."

I rolled my eyes and glared at Nickel. "I'm not going to lay down. If I lay down anymore, I'm going to scream."

It was over a week since I had taken my ambulance ride, and Nickel was driving me absolutely insane. "The doctor said you need to take it easy."

"No, Nickel. The doctor said I needed to take it easy for forty-eight hours, not nine freakin' days." I was beyond annoyed.

"I've never met someone before who fights relaxing and doing nothing," he grumbled under his breath.

I tossed off the blanket that he had draped across me and stood. "I'm fine, Nickel." I reached my arms above my head and jumped up and down. "The baby is also fine."

Nickel sprang up from the couch and put his hands on my shoulders to hold me down. "I know that, but I just want to make sure that you and the kid stay fine."

Oh Lord, have mercy. The first couple of days, I totally understood why he watched over me so much. He had been scared. Hell, I had been terrified when I had lost my lunch in the parking lot and almost fainted when Boink had tried to help me up. Absolutely terrified.

But now I was ready to get back to normal. "I want to move back to my place." As much as I liked being in Nickel's room at the clubhouse, I was ready to get back to my apartment where I could use the kitchen in my underwear and not worry about Boink or Pipe walking in. Not that I had actually tried to go in the kitchen in my underwear, but just knowing that it was an option to do that was something I needed.

"Why don't we wait 'til next week when you're back to one hundred percent."

I gritted my teeth and stomped my foot. "Nickel, it's freakin' Sunday! I'm going back to my apartment. If you want to come with, you can, but honestly, I really don't care if you do." I bent over to grab my shoes, and he hooked me around the waist and pulled me to him.

"Okay, we'll go back to your place. I know I'm driving you crazy, but I can't afford to have anything happen to you. I already almost lost you twice. When I say nothing is ever going to happen to you again, I fucking mean it."

I rested my hands on his shoulders. "Thank you for being so concerned, but you really need to bring it down a notch before I lose my shit." Seriously, I was so close to running away for a few days just to have a moment where Nickel wasn't hovering over me.

The rumble and smirk came out, and I sighed. It had been far too long since I had seen Nickel just let go and laugh. "Does that mean I get to move into your place now?"

I poked a finger into his chest. "Yes, but the first time you tell me I look tired or to go lay down, I'm kicking your ass, and I'm running away to raise this baby with the nuns in the mountains."

"Nuns in the mountains?" he chuckled. "Last I checked, there aren't any mountains around for miles."

"Well, whatever. I watched Sound of Music with Cora and Nikki yesterday, and it's stuck in my head." I flitted my hand in his face. "But you get the idea. You start freaking out, this baby and I are finding the nearest set of nuns and running away."

"Nuns come in sets?"

I smiled and slapped his chest. My Nickel was back. The one who was carefree and gave me shit all of the time. "Yes, at least, the good ones do."

"Well, I guess if you're going to try and run off, I would expect you to at least have the best nuns with you."

I busted out laughing and rested my head against his shoulder. "I love you so much, Nickel."

He sighed into my hair and pressed a kiss to the side of my head. "I'm pretty fond of you, Captain." He lifted me up and laid me back in his bed. He covered me with his body and slowly trailed kisses down my neck, over my chest, to my stomach. "I love you, too, little guy."

"Or girl," I reminded him. Nickel was hell-bent on the fact that we were having a boy, but I was keeping my mind open to the thought that it might be a girl.

He cradled my small baby bump and pressed a kiss square on my stomach. "I'm good with whatever, but it's a boy, Captain."

"I told Nikki yesterday," I whispered.

"What?" Nickel asked. "I thought we were going to wait a couple more weeks?"

"We were, but then Nikki told me she was quitting and moving away." My voice cracked, and I knew the tears I had been holding back were about to fall.

Nickel lifted his head and looked up at me. "What?" He was just as surprised as I was when she had told me.

I dipped my head and wiped the lone tear that was streaking down my cheek away. "She said she needs a change of pace. She's lived in Weston all of her life, and she needs a change." My best friend since we were fourteen was going to move hours away. I had been devastated when she had told me, but I understood why she needed to go.

While I was content in living in Weston for the rest of my life, I knew Nikki yearned for something more exciting than working in a nursing home and hanging out with me.

Nickel slid up my body and wrapped up in his arms. "Don't cry. Maybe you can talk to her, convince her to stay."

I shook my head and buried my face in his chest. I couldn't do that to her. I didn't have the right to beg her to stay when I knew she needed to leave. Although, I didn't understand why all of a sudden she needed to leave. "No, I can't. She said she'll come back to visit, and I can always bug her on the phone every day."

Nickel chuckled. "We're gonna have to make sure you have an unlimited phone plan."

"I already checked. I'm good," I giggled. That was one of the first things I had done after she told me. I leaned back and looked him in the eye. "But you do know what this means for us, right?"

"No, what's that?"

"I'm going to have way more time to spend with you, and I'm already worried about that because I was honestly two seconds away from kicking you in the balls before."

Nickel wrapped his arms around me and rolled us over, so I was laying on top of him. "Then I guess every time I start driving you crazy, I'm just going to have to kiss you until the feeling passes."

"You mean like when you used to kiss me when I thought too much?"

"Exactly like that. I haven't had to do that for a while, so I'll be more than happy to find another reason to kiss you all the time."

I pressed a light kiss on his lips and smiled. "Or, you could just kiss me all the time because you love me."

The rumble and smirk surfaced. "I can definitely do that."

"Does this mean my badass biker is back? The guy who takes whatever he wants but also gives me everything I need?"

He delved his fingers into my hair and pulled my lips to his. He kissed me hard and fast and, just like always, it was better than the last. "He's always been there, baby girl, you just managed to scare the hell out of him for a bit."

"Sorry," I whispered. "I'll try to keep the shootouts and ambulance rides to a minimum from now on."

"That would be much obliged."

"I love you, Nickel," I whispered against his lips.

"I love you, too, Karmen."

Life wasn't always going to be quiet and orderly anymore. I knew for a fact, with Nickel by my side, it was going to be wild and crazy, but he would always keep me safe.

My badass biker wasn't going anywhere.

****

Nikki

"Nikki! Open this fucking door and let me in."

I pressed my back against the door and slowly slid down. My arms wrapped around my knees, and I closed my eyes.

"Son of a bitch, Nikki. You need to let me in."

A lone tear slid down my cheek, and I choked back a sob. I wasn't going to let him in.

I was never going to let anyone in.

The end...

Coming Soon:

Black Belt in Love, book 3 in the Powerhouse M.A. series.
September 2017

Pipe, book 2 in the Fallen Lords MC series.
November 2017

About the Author

Winter Travers is a devoted wife, mother, and aunt turned author who was born and raised in Wisconsin. After a brief stint in South Carolina following her heart to chase the man who is now her hubby, they retreated back up North to the changing seasons, and to the place they now call home.

Winter spends her days writing happily ever after's, and her nights zipping around on her forklift at work. She also has an addiction to anything MC related, her dog Thunder, and Mexican food! (Tamales!)

Winter loves to stay connected with her readers. Don't hesitate to reach out and contact her.

www.facebook.com/wintertravers

Twitter: @WinterTravers

Instagram: @WinterTravers

http://500145315.wix.com/wintertravers

Check out the first chapter of Lie by Mayra Statham!

Lie

(Right Men, Book 1)

Box office sensation, Marcus Wright is ready to take on the role of director. Romance author and single mom, Grace Rivera, is shocked when the sexiest man alive knocks on her door with the intent to bring her book to life.

He is willing to do anything to get what he wants, even use his charms on the beautiful, curvy woman standing in his way. Only it doesn't take long for the shy woman to unknowingly embed herself under his skin.

In a world where one plays make believe and the other writes it, will they determine everything between them is a LIE? Or will they be able to LIE in one another's arms when the truth comes out?

Lie

Chapter One - One Month later

Marcus Wright

He closed his eyes and drew in a deep breath of air that smelled of fresh rain and dirt. He was sure he'd never smelled anything better. It's what he needed to clear his mind: the fresh air and this place. It reminded him life wasn't as complicated as he usually thought it was.

Marcus tried to go to his Montana home at least three times a year. Especially when it felt Hollywood and every pair of eyes were dead set on him and everything he did. It was only April, and he'd been there four separate weekends. That was how out of hand his life felt lately.

Every single wall felt like it'd been quickly closing in around him.

But here he could breathe. Exhaling, he watched the sun start to rise over the horizon. He sat on the Redwood deck of the main house of his sprawling property, his feet kicked up against the stark white railing. He sipped his coffee as he looked toward the majestic beauty of a new day rising and felt the stress of the tabloids and paparazzi running wild with his and Hollywood's 'Good Girl' Katie Wells' breakup as well as the mess with *'Russy'* start to wear off. The tension at his temples and shoulders loosened up.

Donald 'Donnie' Bosco, his childhood friend and manager, sat next to him, handing him a book. "What's this?" he asked without looking at his friend, his eyes still taking in the light of the new day painting the land.

"This, buddy, is *IT*." Marcus didn't know what the fuck he was talking about.

"What?"

"What we have been waiting on," Don clarified. Marcus scowled as he looked down at the cover of what seemed to be a romance novel.

"What the fuck are you talking about?" he asked, finally glancing at his friend.

"Your directorial debut for our new production company," Donnie explained, a cheesy fucking grin on his face, which caught Marcus' attention. Don knew how important this was to him. Shit, it was just as important to Don. Sitting up, he looked at the back of the book, the small blurb on the back catching his attention.

"How'd you find this?" he asked.

"Grandma." Marcus couldn't help shut his eyes tightly. What the fuck was Donnie's problem? Out of everyone in his life, Don was the only one who knew exactly how stressed out he'd been lately. Don should definitely know he was not in the mood to fuck around.

"Nicola?"

"Do we have another one?" Though they weren't blood, Donnie was his brother nonetheless, having grown up in the Wright family fold. "I know it sounds crazy, but listen to me, okay?"

"Okay." Marcus fought from rolling his eyes. He was supposed to be relaxing and winding down, not listening to a story about their crazy-ass grandma. He loved Nicola, but she was a character and a half.

"She overheard us talking the other day and then made me read this. I thought she was nuts," Don chuckled, "but this time she was not wrong. No joke, Marc, she's on the money with this."

"I don't know, man…A romance novel? I mean, who even published this?"

"That's the best part, Marc, it's independently published, which means…"

"Less red tape," he murmured, taking in the bright colors of the paperback.

"Exactly." Donnie smiled and pointed at the book in Marc's hands. "This story… Marc, this is it! This is the movie we are going to start our production company with. This is what's going to give you an Oscar nod for directing at the very least." Donnie's overconfidence could have been annoying if Marc hadn't known him as well as he did.

Don had always been a man of few words, making each one count, and his excitement and confidence on this made something in Marc start to perk up. "Read it," Donnie pushed again, pointing at the book.

"Right now?" he asked, suddenly feeling all the weight of the last couple of weeks right back on his shoulders. All he wanted was a couple of days alone at his ranch in peace.

"Right-freaking-now, man," he said enthusiastically, snapping him out of his thoughts, and he sighed.

"Fine." He opened the book then felt Donnie move and turned, "What? Are you going to watch me read?"

"Yes, asshole. Just fucking read it!" Don shook his head, a sly grin on his face. "Trust me. Shit."

Marcus opened it and read the dedication.

Lexi-bell: everything I do, I do for you.

He scowled, and his expectations dropped incredibly.

They had talked extensively about the type of movie Marc and Don wanted to be their first. They had been buying time and saving money, all so that they could one day do something more. He knew he had to trust his best friend. Don knew what was at stake.

Diving into the book, he had no clue, none whatsoever, not even an inkling, that this moment would be the catalyst that would change the course of the rest of his life.

Check out the first chapter to Down in Flames by Samantha Conley!

Down in Flames

(Silver Tongued Devils, Book 1)

Samantha Conley

Just when you think you have your life together, a spark ignites with the potential to take everything down in flames.

Kristen Daniels worked hard for her career, and when her dream job came to fruition, a sexy rock star won her heart. But one night changed everything, shattering the perfect life she thought she had, and she begins to doubt everything.

Brett Ingles is on top of the world. His band, the Silver Tongued Devils, is quickly rising to the top, playing sold out shows and topping the charts, and he has a beautiful, smart fiancée to share it all with. Until he makes the mistake that rocks his world.

Derek Calloway is a loyal friend—the one you can depend on. He's following his dream of playing in a rock band with his best friend, but what happens when he falls in love with the girl who should be off limits? Battling his emotions day in and day out is like a two-ton weight on his shoulders, but is giving in to them worth losing everything—is she worth losing everything?

Down In Flames

Chapter 1

Kristen

Something startles me awake. Maybe the plane hit some turbulence. I never thought I would fall asleep on a plane, but I've been working my ass off lately to be able to get a four-day weekend to fly up to Minneapolis to see Brett and the guys. I haven't seen Brett in six months, and Skype and texts just aren't cutting it anymore. I haven't even gotten to talk to him in the past four days, with the band on tour, and me working 12-hour shifts at the hospital. If I ever decide to work five straight, 12-hour days again, someone needs to shoot me for stupidity. At least I'm not stuck in economy class and have a little room in my seat to stretch out, all thanks to the band's manager, Brian. I'm glad that he's helping me surprise Brett. The only thing that sucks is that my flight was delayed due to mechanical difficulties, so we took off nearly two hours late. That means I won't get to see Brett before the concert, and I'll more than likely miss the concert altogether. I'd texted Brian about the delay, and he said he would have a car at the airport to pick me up to take me to the venue or the hotel the band is staying at. We'll get to stay in Minneapolis for three days before the band must leave for the next leg of their tour.

I sit here and think back to the beginning, when I met Brett and the guys for the first time. Brett and I dating, spending as much time together as we could between our schedules. I was always working at the hospital, while he worked construction for Derek's uncle at Calloway Construction. But I wouldn't trade it for the world. It's been a roller coaster five years. It all fell into place when Brian Jefferies walked into the bar one weekend. Brian had only listened to the band play a couple of songs before he decided he wanted to represent them. Brian got them on satellite radio, and they became the hottest thing on the radio overnight. They started playing at different bars, opening for other bands, and gathered a huge following. Now they were on their second headlining tour with the release of their second album. Brian had them traveling all over the place promoting the new album. After Minneapolis, the guys are heading to Europe for the last leg of the tour. Man, I wish I could go with them, but with work and school, there's no way. Maybe after I finish my current semester I could fly over for a week or two. Lord knows I have enough vacation time.

Sometimes, I wonder what the hell I was thinking, going back to school for my master's degree, but a girl's gotta do what a girl's gotta do. My dream is to be a pediatric nurse practitioner. I love working with kids, and I love my job at the children's hospital.

I glance down and stare at the big rock sitting on my left ring finger, as the glow of the overhead light makes it sparkle. Brett proposed to me at Jake's Bar before this tour started four months ago. I'm just so excited, thinking about our future together. I can't wait to see him tonight.

I'm pulled from my thoughts as the pilot announces our landing, so I gather my stuff and get ready to get off this tin can. I'm glad I only packed my carry-on, so I won't have to wait at the baggage claim. I shoot off a quick text to Brian to let him know I landed, and he suggests I go to the hotel and wait for Brett. He's given the driver the key to the room, which is great for me. It'll give me time to freshen up before Brett arrives.

I don't have to wait long before the driver pulls up and whisks me away to the hotel. Pulling up, I feel out of place. I dress for comfort when I fly, so I'm in a T-shirt, jeans, and flip-flops. I can see the doorman giving me a weird look as I get the key from the driver and he gives my carry-on to the bellhop that comes to the car, then off we go to the elevator. We get to the room and the bellhop puts my bag inside the door as I look around the room. *Holy moly, this place is nice.* Way too rich for my blood. The bellhop clears his throat and I realize he's waiting for a tip. I dig in my pocket, but only pull out a couple of ones. "I'm so sorry," I tell him. "It's all the cash I have on me."

"Thank you," he says formally and leaves the room.

Great. He probably thinks I'm cheap, but I never carry cash. Maybe I need to start.

Brian texts me to let me know that Brett should be at the hotel within the hour. I head to the bathroom to freshen up and change clothes. I brought one of the slinky dresses that Brett likes to surprise him, then I sit and wait.

I'm sitting in the chair when I hear someone outside the door, so I turn off the TV, ready to surprise him. I can hear him say something, then some female giggles. I pause. Maybe it's not him. I mean, why would there be a girl with him? I hear fumbling with the door, like the key won't work, but finally, the door opens and Brett walks in with his lips attached to some barely dressed blonde. Following them through the door is an even less dressed brunette with her hands all over his ass. I can hear her talking about all the things she wants to do to him. I'm completely frozen from shock.

The brunette starts to pull his shirt off and he only detaches his lips from the blonde so the shirt can go over his head. He looks at the brunette and says, "Strip and get on the bed." She eagerly complies. He turns back to the blonde and says, "Take my dick out and suck it like a good girl." The blonde can't get her hands on his belt fast enough.

How long am I going to sit here and watch this? They're so caught up in what they're doing, they don't even see me. I feel like I'm in a nightmare. I watch as the blonde takes his dick into her mouth. Brett groans and sways on his feet. He just keeps staring at the ceiling and moaning. I glance at the brunette and she's buck naked with one hand on her tit and one on her pussy. Brett pulls the blonde off his dick and tells her to get on the bed too.

"Daddy," the brunette moans. "I've got some more blow for us. I want you to snort it off my pussy." She has a dreamy look on her face and it dawns on me that they're all high as kites.

I can't watch anymore. I spy my carry-on by the door, so I stand and make my way toward it. As I open the door, I hear one of the girls ask "Who's that?" I glance back to see Brett look at me—look *through* me.

"That's nobody," he says.

Nobody. My heart shatters into a million pieces. I never knew my heart could hurt so badly.

I think I'm in shock. I don't even notice my surroundings. I head out the door and quickly throw on some clothes from my bag in the hallway. Once I'm dressed, I take the elevator down and make my way through the lobby to the sidewalk. The doorman asks if I need anything.

"A cab," I say, and he waves one down.

"Where to, Miss?"

"The airport."

I feel like I'm moving in slow motion and I can't think. Before I know it, I'm at the airport. Thank God, I can use my debit card to pay for the cab fare. I move to the ticket agent, and I'm so out of it, I don't even hear her speaking to me, not until she reaches over the counter and touches my shoulder.

"Oh, I'm sorry. I need to get back to Dallas as soon as possible." I know she can see that something's wrong and takes pity on me. I hand her my ticket and she starts working on her computer. Luckily, there's a flight leaving in an hour and they have a few open seats in economy. I take it and head to the gate.

Finally, I'm on the plane and headed home. But what is home anymore?

DIVE INTO THE FIRST CHAPTER OF LOVING LO

LOVING LO

DEVIL'S KNIGHTS SERIES

BOOK 1

WINTER TRAVERS

Chapter 1

Meg

How did just stopping quickly to get dog food and shampoo turn into an overflowing basket and a surplus pack of paper towels?

"Put the paper towels down and back away slowly," I mumbled to myself as I walked past a display of air fresheners and wondered if I needed any.

"Oh dear. Oh, my. I... Ah... Oh, my."

I tore my thoughts away from air fresheners and looked down the aisle to an elderly woman who was leaning against the shelf, fanning herself. "Are you ok, ma'am?"

"Oh dear. I just... I just got a little... dizzy." I looked at the woman and saw her hands shaking as she brushed her white hair out of her face. The woman had on denim capris and a white button down short sleeve shirt and surprisingly three-inch wedge heels.

"Ok, well, why don't we try to find you a place to sit down until you get your bearings?" I shifted the basket and paper towels under one arm to help her to the bench that I had seen by the shoe rack two aisles over. "Are you here with anyone?" I asked, as I guided her down the aisle.

"Oh no. I'm here by myself. I just needed a few things."

"I only needed two things, and now my basket is overflowing, and I still haven't gotten the things I came in for."

The woman plopped down on the bench chuckling, shaking her head. "Tell me about it. Happens to me every time too."

"Is there something I can do for you? Has this happened to you before?" She was looking rather pale.

"Unfortunately, yes. I ran out of the house today without eating breakfast. I'm diabetic. I should know by now that I can't do that." My mom was also diabetic, so I knew exactly what the woman was talking about. Luckily, I also knew what to do to help.

"Just sit right here, and I'll be right back. Is there someone you want to call to give you a ride home? Driving right now probably isn't the best idea." I set the basket and towels on the floor, keeping my wallet in my hand.

"I suppose I should call my son. He should be able to give me a ride," the woman said as she dug her phone out of her purse.

I left the woman to her phone call and headed to the candy aisle that I had been trying to ignore. I grabbed a bag of licorice, chips, and a diet soda and went to the checkout. The dollar store didn't offer a healthy selection, but this would do in a pinch. The woman just needed to get her blood sugars back up.

I grabbed my things after paying and headed back to the bench. I ripped open the bag and handed it to the woman. "Oh dear, you didn't have to buy that. I could have given you money."

"Don't worry about it. I hope if this happened to my mom there would be someone to help her if I wasn't around."

"Well, that's awfully sweet of you. My names Ethel Birch by the way."

"It's nice to meet you, Ethel. I'm Meg Grain. I also got you some chips and soda." I popped opened the soda and handed it to Ethel.

"Oh, thank you, honey. My son is on the way here, should be only five minutes. You can get going if you want to, you don't need to sit with an old woman," Ethel said as she ate a piece of candy and took a slug of soda.

"No problem. The only plans I had today was to take a nap before work tonight. Delaying my plans by ten minutes won't be a problem."

"Well, in that case, you can help me eat this licorice. It's my favorite, but I shouldn't eat this all by myself. Where do you work at?" Ethel asked as she offered the bag to me.

"The factory right outside of town. I work in the warehouse, second shift." I grabbed a piece and sat down on the floor. If I was going to wait for Ethel's son to show up, might as well be comfortable while I waited for him.

"Really? Never would have thought that. Figured you would have said a nurse or something like that. Seems like you would have to be tough to work in a warehouse, sounds like a man's job."

I laughed. "Honestly, Ethel that is not the first time I have heard that, and it probably won't be the last. You need a certain attitude to deal with those truckers walking through the door. I have an awesome co-worker, so he helps out when truckers have a problem with a woman loading their truck."

"Sounds like you give them hell. My Tim was a trucker before he passed. I know exactly what you are talking about." Ethel took another drink of her soda and set it on the bench next to her.

"Feeling better?"

"Surprisingly, yes. It's a wonder what a little candy can do. How much do I owe you?" Ethel asked as she reached for her purse by her feet.

"Don't worry about it. I'm just glad that I was here to help."

"Mom! Where are you?" Someone yelled from the front of the store.

"Oh good, Lo's here. You'll have to meet him." Ethel cupped her hands around her mouth and yelled to him she was in the back.

I started getting up off the floor and remembered I wasn't exactly as flexible as I use to be while struggling to get up.

"Ma, you ok?" I was halfway to standing with my butt in the air when his voice made me pause.

It sounded like the man was gurgling broken glass when he spoke. Raspy and *so* sexy. Those three words he spoke sent shocks to my core. Lord knows the last time I felt anything in my core.

"Yes, I'm fine. I forgot to eat breakfast this morning and started to get dizzy when Meg here was nice enough to help me out until you could get here." Ethel turned to me. "Lo, this is Meg, Meg this is Lo."

Oh, lord.

I couldn't talk. The man standing in front of me was... oh, lord. I couldn't even think of a word to describe him.

I looked him up and down, and I'm sure my mouth was hanging wide open. I took in his scuffed up motorcycle boots and faded, stained ripped jeans that hugged his thighs and made me want to ask the man to spin so I could see what those jeans were doing for his ass. I moved my eyes up to his t-shirt that was tight around his shoulders and chest and showed he worked out.

I couldn't remember the last time I worked out. Did walking to the mailbox count as exercise? Of course, I only remembered to get the mail about twice a week, so that probably didn't count.

His arms were covered in tattoos. I could see them peeking out from the collar of his shirt and could only imagine what he looked like with his shirt off. Tattoos were my ultimate addiction on a man. Even one tattoo added at least 10 points to a man's hotness. This guy was off the fucking charts.

My eyes locked with his after my fantastic voyage up his body, and I stopped breathing.

"Hey, Meg. See something you like, darlin'?" Lo rumbled at me with a smirk on his face.

Busted. I sucked air back into my lungs and tried to remember how to breathe.

Lo's eyes were the color of fresh cut grass, bright green. His hair was jet black and cut close to his head with a pair of kick ass aviators sitting on top of his head. He was golden tan and gorgeous. The man was sex on a stick. Plain and simple.

"Uh, hey," I choked out.

Lo's lips curved up into a grin, and I looked down to see if my panties fell off. The man had a panty-dropping smile, and he wasn't even smiling that big. I would have to take cover or risk fainting if he smiled any bigger.

"Thanks for looking after my ma for me. I'm glad I was in town today and not out on a run," Lo said.

Ok. Get it together Meg. You are a 36-year-old woman, and this man has rendered you speechless like a sixteen-year-old girl. I needed to say something.

"Say something," I blurted out. Good Lord did I just say that. Lo quirked his eyebrow, and his smirk returned.

"Ugh, I mean no problem. I didn't do that much. No problem." I looked at Ethel while Lo was smirking at me; Ethel had a full-blown smile on her face and was beaming at me.

"You were a life saver, Meg! I don't know what I would have done if you weren't here." Ethel looked at Lo and grinned even bigger. "You should have seen her, Lo. She knew just what to do to help me. I could have sworn she was a nurse the way she took charge. She's not, though, just has a good head on her shoulders and decided to help this old lady out."

"That's good, Ma. You got all your shit you need so we can get going? I got some stuff going on at the garage that I dropped to get over here fast."

I took that as my cue to leave and ripped my eyes off Lo and bent over to get my basket and paper towels.

"Yes son, that's my stuff right here. I just want to get Meg's number before she leaves."

"Why do you need my number?" I asked, as I juggled my basket and towels.

Ethel grabbed her purse off the ground and started digging through it again. "Well, you won't let me pay you back for the snacks you got for me so I figured I could pay you back by inviting you over for dinner sometime. So, what's your number, sweetheart?"

"I don't eat dinner," I blurted out. I was going to have to have a talk with my brain and mouth when I got home. They needed to get their shit together and start working in unison so I wouldn't sound like such an idiot.

"You don't eat dinner? Please don't tell me you're on a diet." Lo said as he looked me up and down.

"No," I said. Lord knew I should be.

Lo and Ethel just stared at me.

"So, no, you don't eat dinner?" Lo asked again.

"Yes. I mean no, I'm not on a diet. Yes, I eat dinner. I just work at night, so I meant that I wouldn't be able to come to dinner." I looked at Lo and blushed about ten shades of red. "Why is this so hard?"

"What's hard, sweetheart? Can't remember your phone number? I can barely remember mine too. Don't worry about not being able to make it to dinner; I can have you over for lunch. You eat lunch right?" Ethel asked with a smirk on her face. Lo had a full-blown smile on his face, even his eyes were smiling at me. That smile ought to be illegal.

I could see where Lo got his looks from. With Lo and Ethel standing next to each other, I could totally see the resemblance. Especially when they were both smirking.

I had to get out of here. I'm normally the one with the one-liners and making everyone laugh, now I couldn't even put two words together.

"Lunch would be good." I rattled off my number, and Ethel jotted it down.

"Ok, sweetheart, I'll let you get your nap. I'll give you a call later, and we can figure out a day we can get together." Ethel shoved the pen and paper back in her bag and leaned into me for a hug.

I awkwardly hugged her back and patted her on the shoulder. "Sounds good. Have a good day, Ethel. Uh, it was nice meeting you, Lo," I mumbled, as my gaze wandered over Lo again.

"You too Meg. See you around," Lo replied.

I gave them both a jaunty wave and booked it to the checkout. Thankfully there wasn't a line, and I quickly made my escape to my car. I threw my things in the trunk and hopped in. I grabbed my phone out of my pocket and plugged it into the radio and turned on my chill playlist, as the soothing sounds of Fleetwood Mac filled the car.

Music was the one thing in my life that had gotten me through so much shit. Good or bad, there was always a song that I could play, and it would make everything better. Right now, I just needed to unscramble my brain and get my bearings. Fleetwood Mac singing "Landslide" was helping.

I pulled out of the parking lot and headed home. All I needed was to forget about today. If Ethel called for lunch, I would say yes because she did remind me so much of mom, but I wasn't going to let Lo enter my thoughts anymore. A woman like me did not register on his radar, he was better just forgotten.

When I was halfway home, I realized I forgot dog food and shampoo.

Shit.

======

Lo

I helped mom finish her shopping and loaded all her crap into the truck. I looked around the parking lot for Meg, hoping she hadn't left yet so I could get another look at her. As soon as I saw her ass waving in the air as she struggled to stand up, I knew I had to be inside her.

It took all my willpower to not get a hard-on as her eyes ran over my body. Fucking chick was smoking' hot and didn't even know it.

"Thanks for coming to get me, Lo," Ma said as she interrupted my thoughts about Meg.

"No problem, Ma. I'll get one of the guys to bring your car to you later. Make sure it's locked." Ma dug her keys out of her huge ass purse and beeped the locks. We both got into the shop truck, and I started it up.

"Sure was nice of that Meg to help out. I don't know what I would have done without her."

"Yup, definitely nice of her." I shifted the truck into drive, keeping my foot on the brake, knowing exactly where mom was headed with this.

"You should ask her out." All I could do was shake my head and laugh.

"Straight to the point huh, Ma?"

"I'm old, I can say what I want. Meg is just the thing you need."

"I didn't know I needed anything." I pulled out of the parking lot and headed to Ma's house.

"You need someone in your life besides that club." My mom grabbed her phone out of her purse and started fiddling with it.

"We'll see, ma. Meg didn't seem too thrilled with me." She liked what she saw, but it was like she couldn't get away from me quick enough when she saw that Ma was going to be ok.

"Well, you are pretty intimidating, Lo. Thank goodness you didn't wear your cut."

My leather vest with my club rockers and patches was a part of me. "What the hell is wrong with my cut? If some bitch can't handle me in my cut, she sure as shit doesn't belong with me," I growled.

"Not what I meant Lo. That girl has been hurt, you can see it in her eyes. You'll have to be gentle with her."

My phone dinged. I dug it out of my pocket and saw my mom had texted me. "You texted me her number, ma?"

"Use it, Logan, fix her," she insisted.

I sighed and pulled into mom's driveway. "Maybe she doesn't want to be fixed, ma. Maybe she has a boyfriend."

"She doesn't. Call her, or I'll do it for you," she ordered.

I knew my mom's threat wasn't idle. She totally would call Meg and ask her out for me. Fuck. "I'll help you get your shit inside, ma."

"I'll make you lunch, and then you can call Meg," Ma said, as she jumped out of the truck and grabbed some bags.

I watched her walk into her house and looked at the message she had sent me. I saved Meg's number to my phone and grabbed the rest of Ma's shit and headed into the house.

Looked like I was calling Meg.

========

Take a ride with the Jensen Boys.

Meet Violet and Luke in the first chapter of DownShift!

DOWNSHIFT
SKID ROW KINGS
BOOK 1

WINTER TRAVERS

Chapter 1

Violet

It was half past seven, and I should be on my way home already, but I wasn't.

I watched the lone girl who was sitting at the far table and sighed. She came in every day after school like clockwork, stayed till five forty-five then left. Except today, she didn't. The only way for me to get the heck out of here was to tell her the library was closing, but I didn't have the heart to.

She appeared to be well taken care of, nice clothes, good tennis shoes and well groomed. But she was never with anyone when she came in. Even when other kids would come in to work on homework or such, she stayed by herself at the far table.

I glanced at the watch on my wrist one last time and knew I had to go talk to her. All I wanted to do was go home, eat dinner, and take a nice long bath with my latest book boyfriend. Was that too much to ask?

After I skirted around the desk, I hesitantly made my way over to her, not wanting to tell someone they had to leave. I wasn't one for confrontation. "Um, excuse me."

The girl looked up at me and smiled. She couldn't have been more than thirteen, fourteen tops. Shiny braces encased her teeth, and black-rimmed glasses sat perched on her nose. "Yes?"

"The library closes at seven."

She glanced at the watch on her wrist and hit her hand on the table. "Crud. Luke was supposed to pick me up over an hour ago. I'm really sorry," she said, gathering her books and shoving them into her bag.

"Did you need to call him?"

"No, he probably won't answer the phone. He's only managed to pick me up once this week. He's busy getting ready for Street Wars. He's probably stuck under the hood of a car right now." She zipped her book bag shut and slung it over her shoulder. "I'm really sorry for keeping you here so late. I know the library closes at seven, but I was so into my book I didn't even notice the time."

"It's OK." I had totally been there before. That was the whole reason I worked at the library, I got to be surrounded by the things I loved all day.

"I'll see ya," she waved and headed out the door.

I quickly flipped off all the lights, making sure everything was ready for tomorrow and walked out the door. "Shit," I muttered as I got pelted with rain as I locked the door. I ran to my car, looking for the girl but didn't see her. Was she really going to walk home in the rain? I glanced up and down the street and saw her two blocks up, huddled under a tree.

Whoever this Luke was who was supposed to pick her up was a complete douche monkey for making this poor girl walk. I assumed it was her father, but it was strange that she called him Luke.

I ducked into my car, tossing my purse in the back and stuck the key in the ignition. I cranked it up and reversed out of my spot. As I pulled up to the girl, all I could do was shake my head. What did she think she was doing? Standing under a tree during a thunderstorm was not a bright idea.

"Get in the car," I hollered over the wind and rain. That was one of the drawbacks of the library, there weren't many windows so I never knew what the weather was like until I went outside. "I'll give you a ride."

She shook her head no and huddled under her jacket. What was she thinking? It didn't look like the rain was going to let up anytime soon. "I'm not supposed to ride with strangers."

Well, that was all fine and dandy except for the fact me being a stranger looked a lot better than standing in the rain. "You've been coming into the library for months. I'd hardly call us strangers."

"I don't even know your name," she said, her teeth chattering.

"It's Violet. Now get in the car."

She looked up and down the street, and it finally sunk in that I was her only chance of getting home not sopping wet. As she sprinted across the street, I reached across the center console and pushed open the passenger door.

"Oh my God, it's cold out there," she shivered as she slid in and closed the door.

"Well, it's only April. Plus, being soaking wet doesn't help."

She tossed her bag on the floor and rubbed her arms, trying to warm up. I switched the heat on full blast and pointed all the vents at her. She was dripping all over, and I knew the next person who sat there was going to get a wet ass. "Which way?"

"I live over on Thompson, on top of SRK Motors," she chattered.

I shifted the car into drive and headed down the street. "How come your dad didn't come and pick you up?" I asked, turning down Willow Street.

"Probably because he's dead."

Oh, crap. Whoopsie. "I'm sorry," I mumbled, feeling like an idiot. She seemed too young to have lost her dad.

"You can rule my mom out, too. They're both dead." She pulled a dry sweatshirt out of her bag and wrapped it around her hair, wringing it out.

OK. Well, things seemed to have taken a turn for the worse. "So, um, who's Luke? Your uncle?"

"No, he's my oldest brother. I've got three of them. They all work at the garage together that Luke owns, he's in charge."

"So, your brothers take care of you?"

"Ha, more like I take care of them. If it weren't for me, they'd spend all their time under the hood of a car."

"What's your name?" Here I was giving this girl a ride home, and I had no idea what her name was.

"Frankie."

"I'm Violet, by the way, if you didn't hear me before," I glanced at her, smiling.

"Neat name. Never heard it before." That would be because my mother was an old soul who thought to name me Violet would be retro. It wasn't. It was a color.

"Eh, it's OK."

I pulled up in front of the body shop and shut the car off. It was raining even harder now, the rain pelting against my windows. "I'll come in with you to make sure someone is home."

"I'm fourteen years old. I can be left alone.'

"Whatever. Let's go." She was right, but I didn't care. I was pretty pissed off that her brother had left her all alone to walk home in the rain.

We dashed to the door, my coat pulled over my head, and I stumbled into the door Frankie held open. "Oh my God, it's really coming down," I mumbled, shaking my coat off. My hair was matted to my forehead, and I'm sure I looked like a drowned rat.

"I think Luke is in the shop, I'll go get him." Frankie slipped through another door that I assumed lead to the shop, and I looked around.

Apparently, I was in the office of the body shop. There was a cluttered counter in front of me and stacks of wheels and tires all around. Four chairs are set off to the side, which I assume is the waiting area, and a vending machine on the far wall.

The phone rang a shrilling ring, making me jump. I looked around, trying to figure out what to do when the door to the shop was thrown open, and a bald, scowling man came walking through. He didn't even glance at me, just picked up the phone and started barking into it.

"Skid Row Kings," he grunted.

I couldn't hear what was being said on the other end, but I could tell Baldy was not happy. I looked down at my hands, noticing my cute plaid skirt I had put on that morning was now drenched and clinging to my legs. Thankfully I had worn flats today, or I probably would have fallen on my ass in the rain.

"What can I help you with?"

My head shot up, baldy staring at me. "Um, I brought Frankie home."

He looked me up and down, his eyes scanning me over. "Aren't you a little too old to be hanging out with a fourteen-year-old? You're what, sixteen, seventeen?"

"Try twenty-seven." This guy was a piece of work. He was looking me over like I was on display and he thought I was a teenager.

His eyes snapped to mine, and his jaw dropped. Yeah, jackass, I'm older than you are probably. "What the hell are you doing with Frankie?"

"She works at the library. You know, the place you promised to pick me up from today?" Frankie said, walking back into the shop. She had managed to find a towel and was drying herself off. I would kill for a towel right now.

"Fuck," Baldy twisted around and looked at the clock behind him. "Sorry, Frankie. Mitch and I were tearing apart the tranny on the Charger."

She waved her hand at him and tossed the towel to me. Oh, thank you sweet baby Jesus. I wiped the water that was dripping down my face and squeezed all the water out of my hair into it.

"How the hell did you get so wet if she gave you a ride home?"

"Because I started walking home, Luke, until Violet was kind enough to stop and give me a lift."

He watched me dry my hair, confusion on his face. "Violet?" he muttered.

"That's me," I said, sticking my hand out for him to shake. "I didn't want Frankie to get sick walking home. Plus, it's getting dark and someone her age shouldn't be out then."

"She's fourteen years old," he sneered. "I was out on the streets when I was twelve."

"Oh, well. If that's how you want to raise her." Luke was a gearhead that was also an ass. I didn't have time for this. My bath was definitely calling my name now that I was soaking wet. I tossed the towel back to Frankie and pulled my jacket over my head again. "You're welcome for bringing your sister home."

"I didn't ask you to."

"I know," I turned to Frankie and smiled. "I'll see ya tomorrow." She nodded her head at me, smiling, and I turned to walk out the door. I twisted the handle, and the door blew into me, rain pouring in. I glance back at Luke one time, a scowl on his face, and figured the pouring rain was better company than he was.

I pulled the door shut behind me and sprinted to my car, dodging puddles.

Once I was safely in my car, I looked up at the two-story building and sighed. I wish I could say this was a hole in the wall garage, but it was far from that. The building itself was a dark blue aluminum siding with huge neon letters that boasted, Skid Row Kings Garage, also known as SRK Garage. There were five bay doors that I'm assuming is where they pulled the cars into and over the office part is where I believe they lived. It was monstrous. Everyone in town took their cars here, especially the street racing crowd.

I had never been here before, mainly because I have never really needed repairs done on my car. I always went to the big chain stores to get my oil changed and thankfully hadn't needed any major repairs.

I started my car, thankful to be headed home. I turned around, the big looming building in my review as I headed down the street.

Hopefully, that was the last time I would ever step foot in Skid Row Kings garage and never see Luke again. He seemed like a total ass.

= = = = = = = = = = = =

Get a taste of the #NinjaHotties!

Dropkick My Heart

Powerhouse M.A.

Book 1

Kellan

"Left, Ryan." I shook my head and watched Ryan punch to the right. "Your other left, Ryan." In my fifteen years of teaching martial arts, I discovered left and right was a concept that was hard learned by anyone under the age of ten, especially when they were just excited to be punching and kicking the shit out of stuff.

"Okay! Lock it up." I stood in front of my class of twenty-five under belts and watched them all fall to the floor, eagerly looking up at me. I waited for all eyes to fall on me. "Good job today, guys. We need to work a bit longer on delta, but for only working on it one day, you guys are killing it." Clinton raised his hand eagerly, and I tipped my chin at him. "Go ahead, Clinton."

"Mr. Wright, when are we going to get to put all of the combos together?" he asked meekly.

"As soon as we learn them all," I assured him. Clinton asked the same question every class. The kid was the most eager to learn, but he had the attention span of a squirrel. I surveyed the class, then looked over the crowd of parents waiting to pick up their kids. "Now, remember that belt graduation is in three weeks, and you need to have your homework turned in before. Otherwise, you don't graduate."

Everyone groaned at the word *homework*, and I couldn't help but smirk. They didn't have any clue how much homework I had done to reach sixth-degree black belt. "Everyone up," I said, motioning up with my hands. "And bow," I ordered, placing my hands at my sides and bowing.

All the kids started running up to me, giving me high fives and then scurrying off to their parents.

"Is Mr. Roman going to be here next time?" Carrie asked me as she high-fived me.

"He should be. He had a couple of things to do today and couldn't make it to class." Like sleeping until noon and screwing me over completely. Thankfully, it was the last class of the day, and I could hopefully find some time to sit down for five minutes.

Finally, the last parents left with their kids, and I locked the door behind them. I loved classes on Saturday, but they were exhausting when I was the only instructor.

The phone rang on the desk, and I knew it was Roman with some lame-ass excuse for why he didn't make it in today. Roman and I were business partners with Dante and Tate, but most of the time, it was all on me to make the school a success.

Roman's name flashed on the caller ID, and I picked up the phone. "So, what's your excuse this time?"

"Ugh, I'm fucking sick, man."

I shook my head and sat down behind the front counter. "That's called a hangover, Roman. Drink some fucking coffee, and get out of bed."

"Nah, man. This is worse than a hangover. I think I got food poisoning from the burger I ate last night at Tig's." Roman moaned into the phone, and I sighed.

Food poisoning from Tig's was a definite possibility. "I guess you should stop eating nasty shit while you're getting shit-faced every night."

"It's not every night," Roman grumbled.

"Sure, keep fucking telling yourself that."

Roman sighed. "Look, I was just calling to tell you sorry about not coming in today. If you wanna take off next Saturday, you can. I'll take care of the monsters all by myself."

"Nah, don't worry about." I made the mistake once of trying to take off a Saturday. Roman had called me halfway through the day, and I could barely hear him over yelling parents and screaming kids. I ended up coming in and spending most of the day putting out fires he had started between yelling at the kids and telling the parents to shut it while he was teaching. "Just get better, and I'll see you Monday night."

"What time do classes start?"

I closed my eyes and counted to ten. "Four. Same as every Monday," I reminded him.

"Got it. I'll be there."

I hung up the phone and sighed. Roman was one of the most talented guys I knew when it came to karate, but his adulting skills were severely lacking. At the age of twenty-eight, he should have his shit figured out.

When Roman, Tate, Dante, and I opened Powerhouse, we expected to help kids the way we were taught when we were young and just starting karate. Roman, Tate, and I began karate at the same time and worked our way through the belts together. Dante was a red belt when we were white belts, but he took us under his wing, and we all became close friends.

While Dante was almost ten years older than most of us, I was the highest black belt. Dante was a second-degree black belt, while Roman and Tate were fourth-degree. I was going for my sixth degree this year.

We all came together to start the school, because we all had our own specialties that, when put together, created a karate studio unlike any around. Dante was an international sparring champion six times over, while Roman and Tate were geniuses when it came to kamas and bo staff. I rounded us out with my expertise in forms and people skills the three others lacked at times.

The school had only been open for six months, but Dante and Tate already thought we needed to open another location. Not only had Roman bailed on me today, but so had Tate and Dante to go look at a space two towns over for a new studio.

I was in the minority when I said we should just focus on the Falls City school. Dante and Tate had decided between themselves that if we were doing so well here, another studio would be a goldmine. I didn't think they were wrong, I just wanted them to slow down, and wait for all of us to agree.

I threw my phone on top of a pile of new student paperwork and propped my arms on my head. I pushed off on the floor and spun around in the chair. Most days, it was hard to believe this was my life, and today was another one of those days. Dante, Tate, and Roman were my closest friends, but sometimes it felt like everything rested on my shoulders, while they were off somewhere enjoying life, and spending all the money we were making.

The days we didn't have classes, I was giving private lessons, or working on lesson plans for each class. Most of the time, the Kinder-kicker class was like herding a pack of cats that were all hyped up on catnip, and the Little Ninja class wasn't much better. Although, I still tried to teach them forms and basic karate to help them get to white belt. Once the kids hit white belt, things became more serious, and I buckled down on the curriculum.

The highest belt level we had right now was an orange belt, but in the stack of paper on the desk, there were three kids wanting to transfer over to Powerhouse. One of them was a purple belt, and the other two were red belts. I was rather shocked the two red belts wanted to transfer schools when they were close to being black belts, but I knew it was because in the short time we had been open, we already had a reputation of being the best.

If you were even a little bit into karate, you would have at least heard of one of us. We were the best, and we had the trophies and medals to prove it. That reputation was bringing in students left and right, but I couldn't keep doing this on my own anymore.

But, I wasn't going to stress about that right now, because a knock on the front door made me jump, and I turned to see my next private lesson through the glass.

My five-minute break was up, and it was back to the grind.

Someone had to make Powerhouse a success, and that someone was going to be me.

****